DANCE ON THE WATER

Laura Lynn Leffers

Blue Star Productions
A Division of Book World, Inc.
9666 E. Riggs Rd. #194
Sun Lakes AZ 85248

DANCE ON THE WATER
A Blue Star Productions Publication
February 1996

No part of this book may be reproduced or transmitted without written permission from the publisher.

This is a work of fiction. The characters, names, incidents, dialogue and plot are a product of the author's imagination or are used fictitiously.

ISBN 1-881542-10-6

Published by Blue Star Productions
A Division of Book World, Inc.
9666 E. Riggs Rd. #194, Sun Lakes AZ 85248
Ph/Fax: 602.895.7995
E-Mail: BDebolt@aol.com

Acknowledgements:

The author would like to thank Chief Eldress Lora Siders and Carol Mongosa, of the Miami Nation, for their generous support and encouragement, and Nick Clark, Executive Director of the Prophetstown Foundation, for his guidance in the significance of dream messaging. The vision, wisdom and tolerance of these three give honor and strength to our Great Lakes Indian People.

Jack Elam, of the Turkey Creek/Syracuse Historical Museum, in Syracuse, Indiana, provided significant historic data to this work of fiction. Arleen Corson, of Lake Papakeechie, read for accuracy and neither they nor any of the many who helped bring this tale into print are responsible for misinformation which might have survived, nonetheless, all of the attempts to perfect this novel.

The Leffers and McCoy family genealogies were responsible for many of the anecdotes contained herein, including the recipe for squirrel soup, which was given to the author by her grandmother, Helen Marcella McCoy Leffers, whose great-grandmother was Polly George. The genealogies, in fact, started a character named Belle MacKay on her path of learning . . .

Dedicated to:

The future of the People of the Great Lakes

The future lives within the past and the present,
to honor one is to honor all.

Foreword

For at least 15,000 years, the People of the Great Lakes have been accumulating layer upon layer of tradition making a life-fabric both strong and colorful. That fabric has been tested over the past five hundred years, as a new and dominant civilization brought cultural change, devastating disease, environmental upheaval, horrible divisiveness and in many cases, their forced removal on foot from precious homelands. Yet, the cultural fabric of the Great Lakes People is as strong and dynamic today as ever and is being shared and preserved for this and future generations.

As European and American forces advanced into the Great Lakes at the turn of the nineteenth century, Tenskwatawa, the Shawnee Prophet, had a vision that if Great Lakes Indian People united to establish a new settlement where they honored their teachings and traditions, they could hold back European intruders and preserve their homelands and way of life. Thousands answered the call and, knowing they faced overwhelming odds, bravely offered their best to realize that dream. It was not to be — at that time.

Just as the past emerges into the present for Belle MacKay, one of the subjects of this novel, Great Lakes People are being joined by the descendants of those who won the Battle of Tippecanoe, in preserving and interpreting the rich legacy of Woodland People. On the very site of Tenskwatawa's Prophetstown, a new cultural center will be constructed in order that the past, present and future of

Great Lakes Indian people may be preserved and shared with all who visit and participate. The Prophet and the nearly 600 warriors who fought so valiantly at the Battle of Tippecanoe in 1811, lost a military victory. But the descendants of ALL those who fought there now build a new Prophetstown, where the accomplishments and hopes and dreams of this and future generations will be realized. What could better illustrate the Woodland belief that life is a circle, and if that circle is reality, all dreams eventually come true.

Nicholas L. Clark
Executive Director
Prophetstown State Park Foundation, Inc.
First Floor, 22 N. Second St.
Lafayette, IN 47901

Dance on the Water

A Novel of Fiction/
Native American Mysticism

~ ONE ~

"Hey babe!"

Then there was a series of grunting sounds, like hogs in fresh mud. I kept jogging. What did I know about hogs?

"Yo, sweetness! I be talkin' to you, babe!"

I ducked my head. Mud, yes.

"Baby, baby, you a ripe one, baby."

These boys seemed to think I was just another female prey for their hormonal ineptitude. I watched the cracks in the sidewalk come up with an odd regularity.

"Come on, sweetness."

Something happened to me, then. Something in that cocky, crappy attitude made me turn around and start running at them. Syllables came flying out of my mouth strident, rushing from a vast open hole crammed full of anger.

"Who are you? What's your name?" I was yelling.

I remember that shrill screeching now, like a rusty gate swinging, protesting, slamming shut. Too much anger, too many tears had corroded the hinges of control.

These guys didn't know how to pick their victims.

There was another noise, a different sort of squealing: tires on a hot pavement. And a shout from the driver's side of a minivan. I wanted a fight, I know that. I know I kept yelling, kept running. I must have freaked the hell out of those boys.

It was as if I needed to place accountability for everything, all the trivial injustice, every snide, cruel comment. And the big things too — the rapes, the wars, every foolish murder of faith.

Those boys saw a wild screaming woman, and they scattered.

I was ready to follow them home, talk to their mothers. I must have looked like I'd kill them.

Maybe trying to pin names on them pricked their manhood, let the air out of their puffed-up egos.

I remember the man in the blue van. He took up the chase too, must have circled the block while I followed the slowest kid around an old shopfront and into the alley. When I came out the other end, the man in the van was waiting. He asked if the boys had stolen my purse.

"No," I said. I stood there shaking, sweat dripping into my eyes, fury and frustration trickling the taste of bile into my throat. My hands were clenching, just as if I'd ripped the balls off those pubescent kids, and I was maniacally squeezing, clawing, drawing blood.

No, they hadn't stolen my purse. They'd taken the last of my faith. But I didn't say that, then. I didn't know it yet.

So the man in the minivan just shook his head, said, "That's okay then," and drove off.

I walked home wondering at my own savagery. John liked to say that I was the princess of propriety, that together we held the kingdom of control.

But my hands ached for a hank of hair, at least, to dangle from my belt. I needed a trophy, something to mark this day.

I did know, already, that I was grateful to those boys. My long and passive career as a victim was over.

It cooled me off, the long walk home. Not enough to change my mind, but enough to keep me from grating my teeth, from dripping sweat onto the dun-colored carpet of the apartment complex office.

Mrs. Simmons looked up from her neat module, took her pink-tinted fingernails off the keyboard and placed them, dainty, in her lap.

"Been for a jog then, dear?" she asked.

"Yes," I said, and stared at her. She looked and smelled like a sweet old granny with her hair pearl-white and slightly waved, a faint flowery scent, a dusting of rouge.

She looked back, patient, puzzled.

"I'd like to give notice."

"Sorry to hear that. I'll pull your file. Your unit, please?"

"Number one twenty-two."

"And your name, dear?"

Of course she didn't know me. "Belle MacKay," I said, and waited. This was a large complex, sprawling over what had once been a rocky pasture complete with cows. I'd always used the night deposit for the rent, on my way to work, at seven forty-five in the morning, just as John liked it.

Mrs. Simmons rolled over her carpet protector, propelled by a practiced foot in an elegant little pump. She selected a file from the drawer and glided back to her computer, keyed in my number.

"Unit One Twenty-two. Your lease won't be up until June, Ms. MacKay." She frowned.

"I've lived here eight years, Mrs. Simmons. My lease was up long ago."

She opened the file and drew out the contract, flipped the pages and held it up for my inspection.

I reached for it, but she had an iron grip on the sheaf. Her frown intensified subtly, etching deeper lines through those downy, rouged cheeks. The penciled-on arch, where her eyebrows once sprouted, drew together over fierce eyes.

I gave up.

Victory made her more gracious. She smiled, and the withered facade of her face relaxed and plumped like a polyester pillow.

"You have an excellent payment record, Ms. MacKay, but rules are rules. Renewal of contract is implied, you know, when the conditions of the contract have not been breached by said tenant. It saves a great deal of paperwork dear, not to mention the landfill."

"Well, I'm breaching, Mrs. Simmons."

She heaved a disappointed sigh, put down the file, and tapped away at the keyboard. "Unit one twenty-two," she said to herself, "forfeits deposit of," she squinted at the screen, "seven hundred dollars."

She transferred her gaze to me, and her eyebrows peaked. "You do understand, dear, that you retain responsibility for the rental payment until such time as the apartment is reoccupied, or the term of lease has expired? Whichever comes first."

And what's your expiration date, I wondered.

"I understand," I said, and smiled sweetly at her. "I'm certain that management will expedite the, rental process."

"Of course, dear." Mrs. Simmons squinted at her computer again. "You do understand, however, that Unit One Twenty-two has not been painted in quite some time. Over ten years. And the cleaning — "

"It's clean. And I had it painted when I moved in. There were crayon marks all over the walls." My words were coming through my teeth somehow, so I forced another smile.

"Oh, but we would have done that for you, dear."

"As I recall, he said he'd get to it by Christmas."

She raised her eyebrows at me, rolled her eyes slightly and tapped away, chatting to herself: "Paint work eight years old. Needs complete renovation . . . "

I gave up. "Where do I sign, Mrs. Simmons?"

She smiled, made a sweep with her mouse and clicked once, twice more, then a final time, and placed her hands neatly on her lap, nodded at the suddenly whirring printer.

We both stared at the stuttering eruption of white. It reminded me of John, methodical, buzzing away at our lives like a mechanical bulldozer in a carnival booth, searching out just the right goal, the only prize. The paper spit itself onto a tray.

Time's up, I thought. Pay up or make way for the next guy in line. But there was nobody behind John, waiting for me. John was the only one I'd ever wanted.

I looked at the form stupidly, suddenly unsure. Mrs. Simmons, with all the answers at her fingertips, placed a pen on the counter of her white module, placed her hands back onto her lap, and waited.

I signed. And I walked out clutching my copy with damp hands and damper eyes. Burning all my bridges was new to me.

~ *TWO* ~

"I've made up my mind."

He leaned back in the swivel chair and gave me that frown, distracted, annoyed. It usually worked like a conductor's baton, guiding me through his holy requirements in harmony.

I heard myself giggling off-key. How strange.

"What now, Belle?" He frowned again, firm.

"I'm going to Papakeechie," I said. "I'm going to do it."

"Oh come on, Belle. We've been over all that." He shifted his weight, slammed his elbows onto the desk and rubbed the tips of his fingers over his temples.

This was my cue to walk behind him, rub his forehead and his tense shoulders, see the error of my ways.

For a moment, I was tempted. I saw myself capitulating. I could feel the curling hair at the nape of his neck, the melting inside begin. His hands would reach behind, my lips would soften for the tasting, the suckling. I loved him. I knew I loved him.

But I'd packed my boxes, my pots and pans, my mother's dishes. All weekend long I'd washed windows, cleaned the stove, vacuumed the standard-issue couch and chairs, even rented a machine for the wall-to-wall, industrial strength 'woven' synthetic carpeting.

He looked up, puzzled.

"Belle? We've gone over it all. You know how I feel."

"Hmm," I said, ashamed at my weakness, my wanting to go on loving, go on being loved.

"For God's sake Belle, you make sixty thousand a year here." His eyes narrowed. "And I can't give you any more."

A strange sound came out discordant, like the giggle had, from my dry throat. He didn't believe me, didn't really know me.

"It isn't about money, John."

"I never thought it was," he said, smirking.

"It's about family." I heard the pleading in my voice, but rushed on anyway. "It's about all the years of never having relatives, nowhere to go at Thanksgiving, at Christmas."

"Sure." His eyebrows lifted, mocking. "I've always known you wanted the proverbial white pickets, nice little babies arranged in a neat little stair-stepped row. Give me a break, Belle."

"I am not trying to manipulate you, John. I'm leaving."

"Shit."

All the years of trying to convince him that I believed in loving, believed that you couldn't own it, or form it, or restrict the giving of it; the countless times I'd prayed he'd know it too, they came to this.

Those boys, with their taunting, raping voices — they'd stolen only an empty faith, a blind faith.

"It's only six months, John," I said.

"So go, Belle. Go on out and live on an island."

"Only two-and-a-half hours away. An easy drive."

"Give it up, Belle. I've told you how I feel about this. It's a stupid move. If you want to do it, fine." He shrugged. "But don't expect me to come chasing after you. Don't expect your job back, either."

"So that's all? After eight years, that's all you can say?"

"Hey. I told you how I felt." He smiled, leaned back in the soft padded leather of the chair, and let his eyes grow soft. "I like it the way it is. But that was always the deal, Belle. You always knew you could walk."

"You think you're calling my bluff, don't you John?"

He grinned. "That's why it's so good between us. We can't take each other for granted."

I had never taken him for granted, not for a moment. I'd been dazzled by him, dazed with love, from the first. I'd spent eight years on his terms, always simply grateful for his love, needy. Now, somehow, I wanted more.

"It's not enough, John. And you know, I think it never was."

I watched his grin fade downward.

"Don't be a fool," he said.

"No. No, I won't be a fool." I turned my back to him and picked my purse off the corner of his desk.

His chair was gliding back over the hardwood floor, slamming against the bulwark of the file cabinets. I could feel him staring, feel his disbelief.

"I do love you Belle," he said softly.

The warmth of his voice attacked, locked me in. I wanted to believe, how I wanted to believe, even now, especially now.

Then my skin prickled and the scroop of my office silks sent a subtle warning of chill, fluttered this one last dress, kept out of the suitcase for this one last day. It billowed out as if it could not contain me.

I forced my legs stiff and let myself cherish his face. His irises were almost golden and his mouth was tight, unyielding despite the sweetness of the words.

He saw the hesitation, the fragility of my nerve. I know, because his eyes lit up for the kill, and he laughed.

"It won't work," he said. "Don't leave like this. I won't be coming to size your ring finger, Belle."

"I know," I said. And I did. My mind was clear, but my body had a whole other outlook. Fury, or fear, loosened my knees again, rattled my nerve, insisted on revenge or at least a primal rage. It was that savage side of me again, in another sudden visit.

My eyes slid away from his face, fixed themselves smoothly onto objects in the course around to the door, found the way out. On the wall behind me, facing the windows and John's massive desk, was a collection of masks he and I had artfully arranged; they were souvenirs of our vacations. Every trip had seemed a honeymoon. As I tracked across them now, I saw the masks as facets of denial, my own, and his.

I chose one. It didn't matter which. It seemed a good symbol, so I simply reached out and flung one to the floor. I bent down and rummaged through the shards for a slice of the wreckage, a hefty, pointed, colorful piece. My trophy.

"Why Belle, I never thought you could be so primitive, so ordinary," John drawled.

"This wasn't a trap," I said, and the words seemed calm. "I'm sorry you thought so."

That was it then. I heard the sound of my heels on the polished floor. I kept going, past my desk in the cramped outer room. Down the hall. Out the door.

And I shut it, shut it on a whole large piece of my life, with some small remnant of control.

~ *THREE* ~

I must have been living a prefab sort of life. It had all been so easy — the packing up, the leaving. Two months ago, when I got that letter from the lawyer who had the unlikely name of Ben Beanblossom, Benjamin Barrow Beanblossom to give the man his due, John and I had laughed and laughed. It had seemed ludicrous, to go up into the lake country and spend six months writing a family genealogy. On an island. Impossible.

For one thing, I was in love with John, and I wouldn't dream of leaving him, not for any reason. Certainly not for Reason MacKay, the grandfather I'd never even met.

Grandmother had always called him 'Unable Reason,' after all.

These people's names were incredible, made it seem that a whole segment of the state was full of buffoons. The fact that I was related to some of them made it even more mythical. I was a city girl, cosmopolitan, composed.

Or I had been, until I developed an allergy to composure. More precisely, until the savage emerged out from under the carefully fabricated layers of my ordinary, civilized life.

So now I was driving between rolling fields of ripening winter wheat, remembering how we'd laughed at Mr. Beanblossom's letter. John had snickered first, while I was still trying to understand exactly what was wanted of me. I wondered if John had laughed so hard because the security of his noncommittal lifestyle seemed threatened.

He'd positively howled at the names. I spoke them aloud now, over the muted hum of my old Volvo, on this lonely stretch of highway. Reason and Isabelle MacKay. I'd been named for her, had grown up with her, after my father was killed in Viet Nam and my mother ran off to Reno, trying to better her luck, no doubt. I hadn't thought of her in years, couldn't remember her face, even.

Maybe my psychiatrist was right. Maybe John was right. They both thought I had a fixation on my lack of relatives.

At least Doctor Limano never laughed at it.

Funny how those names sounded normal, out here on the road, in the country. Reasonable.

Reason MacKay was dead. I hadn't even known him, and now he was dead. Grandmother left him long ago, left him behind in the lake country and never looked back. She'd almost never spoken of him. Her own father, her mother . . . I knew all about them. Too much, in fact. They were all dead, too. Mother was alive, of course. I suppose she was alive, somewhere.

Mr. Beanblossom's account of Reason MacKay's life, and his death, was a revelation to me. He'd been the great-grandson of a chief, the chief that the lake had been named for Papakeechie.

So that made me, what? One-thirty-second Miami Indian? One-sixteenth? It had intrigued me. I'd stopped in the library a few weeks ago, to find out more about Chief Papakeechie. His name translated into "Flat Belly," of all things. One account said his name meant "Bedbug." Yet another illustrious name to add to those John and I had chuckled over. Only it didn't seem so funny now, now that I was about to take over Reason MacKay's passion, his island, his ancestral duty.

I slowed for an intersection, and waited for the light to change. It seemed odd, obeying a dangling box of lights, when there were no cars, not a soul to see or care.

I stepped on the gas and tiptoed across the rural road.

No accountability. John had trained me well. The stoplight didn't care. I had no cats, no dogs, no ties. Not even a philodendron to care if I came or went. Mrs. Simmons referred to me as a "unit," ready to go, needing a change in wall color. The closest thing I had to a friend was John. Easier that way, John said. Easy for him.

I smiled. Maybe he'd have trouble training a new recruit.

I glanced into the back seat, checking the meager heap of boxes, belongings. The office had been my real home, anywhere I was, in fact, with John Schaffer. And all I had left of him was a pointed piece of mask, like an arrowhead.

Ordinary. Primitive, John had called me. And now I was migrating, all my worldly goods bundled along behind me.

Yes, I was bitter. There was an eagerness though too, for escape and for what lay ahead, unknown. Doctor Limano had insisted that my relationship with John was feeding a tendency to distance myself. That I really wanted, needed commitment.

But John was all I had, the only love I'd known.

The doctor, at least, had been thrilled to hear of the incident with the boys. He called my savage reaction a breakthrough, said I'd made contact with reality. I told him violence was destructive. Then I told him that I had left John, that I was completely alone now.

He said, "You have your person. Go on, go live on your island, write this history of your family. You will put the ground under your feet."

Doctor Limano often spoke as if he still thought in Italian.

"But everybody's dead, they're all dead," I wailed.

"That is not true. You are not."

I'd thought about that, and then I'd grinned at him.

"It's times like this, *Dottore*, that make me think you missed a course. An American psychiatrist would never send a paying patient away."

"Oh, but *cara* Bella, you are not a real patient," he'd said. "You do not pay so good. No American doctor would accept your *casseruola* for what you call the currency."

He was right, although the casserole had been a gift. My cooking was rudimentary, at best.

"And when your wife leaves town again, I'll be too far away to save you."

"Ah yes," he'd said, "salvation."

He'd rolled his eyes, I remembered now, and I laughed out loud. And then I realized I was acting crazier than ever, lately, wondered if it wasn't time anyway, for me to leave polite society, time to wriggle free of civilization. Somehow, suddenly, I'd become incapable of passivity.

Another highway intersection was coming up, and I checked the route number with the directions I'd sketched out for the trip. Highway Thirteen, my final stretch. I turned onto it and headed up the last eighteen miles to the lake.

Huge clouds puffed on the horizon, but the sun had broken through an earlier patchy fog, and its gray gleam lit a mix of farmhouses and winter-ravaged fields. Every crest of the road brought a new gloomy view to the same grim aspect.

Not the time of year to come to live at the lake, I thought. Yet Reason MacKay had lived year-round in his cottage, and the lawyer had promised that the house had plumbing and heat, its own well, a telephone.

I drove through a couple of self-important little towns, spruced up and quaint, sprouting antique shops on every other corner. Very few people were scattered about, bundled up, walking dogs. It must be very different in summer. There was a tattered banner that read "Onion Festival." Alien images floated free in my mind; a parade, an onion queen and her court. Rural America.

Then a highway to cross, more miles of deserted, rolling fields, sprinkled about with all sorts of vintage homes. Sign posts began prefixing the word "Lake" in front of their placenames. Soon I was driving through an actual city, big enough to hold warehouses full of pleasure boats, in cold storage like so many furs. There was a grocery store, a school. There were people about, cars in the parking lots, a forlorn empty carnival complete with a rusty mountainous slide and miniature concrete fairways dotted with dirty plastic palm trees.

And in a flash there was countryside again, a couple of miles of it before the road curved into Syracuse. I checked my directions again and looked for a road opposite the entrance to a golf course. It would wind me around a section of Lake Wawasee's shoreline, according to Mr. Beanblossom.

Chief Wawasee was Chief Papakeechie's brother I knew, from my visit to the library, and the lake that bore his name was a great bloated splotch on the map. Lake Papakeechie was barely a connected dot.

The unmistakable snipped, winter-gold grasslands of the golf course blinked over a fencerow, and I found the road off to the right. I turned into it, was immediately driving past a lakeside fringe of summer homes, tennis courts, guesthouses, plots of landscaped, weeded wilderness.

Mr. Beanblossom's number came up and I turned onto his drive, drove a hundred yards through pruned woods before I saw even a glint of the lake. I pulled up in the circle of asphalt behind the house, and turned off the car to stare at the contrived comfort, this ideal of lake country living. It wasn't a grand house, exactly. But it reeked of opulence from every lace-lined, shining clean window, from the squat yellow stone facade and a slate, blue-gray tier of overhanging roof.

I walked up a cobbled path and stone steps that meandered through shrubbery and flower beds. I'd called the lawyer last Friday after I'd breached my rental contract, to tell him I'd changed my mind and to ask if he'd turned the property over to the Papakeechie Preservatory yet, as had been stipulated by Reason MacKay's will. I learned, then, that Mr. Beanblossom was retired and handled just a few things for old friends. He hadn't gotten to the quit claim deed, and he was delighted to have put it off. I knocked, wondering if he'd really just planned to give me a little extra time.

He answered the door, one hand propped on a knobby cane.

"You Miss MacKay, then?"

I nodded. "Mr. Beanblossom?"

"Call me Ben, and come along out to the sunporch." Over his shoulder, he yelled, "Honey!" A woman appeared behind him, smiling, her hand out to reach for mine.

"Here's old Reason's granddaughter at last, Maude."

Maude pulled me ahead of Ben down the hall to the front of the house, settled me at one of the picture windows. It framed views of the sloping yard and the lake, which I studied while she went off to get me a cup of tea. Ben clumped in and creaked his body into another of the old rattan wing chairs.

He hooked the crook of his cane over his thigh and stared, nodding as he ticked off a series of nonverbal assessments. "You'll do," he finally said.

It was a compliment, I decided, and nodded back at him.

"I wanted to thank you, Mr. Bean — er — Ben . . . "

He laughed out loud. "Mr. Beannerben, yes, I like it," he said.

"People used to call him 'Beannie-boy'," Maude said from behind me, and handed over a cup and saucer. "Mint. I grow it myself, dry it, store it for the winter."

I thanked her, and she walked over to a massive old

desk in the corner, and rummaged through a drawer. She came back with a large brown grocery bag and dumped it at Ben's feet, pulled a basket chair close and sat down, smiling at us both.

"Now what were you saying, Belle, as I was bringing in your tea?"

"I just wanted to thank Ben for holding up the quit claim deed. You see, I'd let go of my apartment before I even thought to call and cancel, let you know I wanted to come after all. I'm not normally so . . . so incompetent."

"I don't think you're incompetent," Ben said. "Quite the opposite. Didn't you tell me you're a paralegal?"

"Well, I was. I guess I'm a genealogist, now."

"Plenty of research, still." Ben cleared his throat. "Only all the perpetrators have passed."

"It'll be very interesting, I would think," said Maude, and glanced at Ben.

They looked at each other with smiles that only softened the edges of their eyelids, an efficiency earned by years of affection, I supposed.

Ben's eyes narrowed at me, though. "In your ... er, former capacity, you surely encountered many cases of inheritance?"

"None with conditions like these."

"They're odd, I'll admit. Let's go over them now, so they're perfectly clear. After all, my dear, the Preservatory is aware of the terms, and would benefit by your failure to comply."

"I understand."

Ben reached into the grocery bag and pulled out an old piece of freezer wrap. The room began to smell faintly of fish.

"I drew up the legal document, which Reason signed, naturally. I have retained it, along with the title to the property, in my vault. I sent you copies, if you recall. But I would like to read aloud his original intentions, in his own words.''

I nodded, and sipped at Maude's mint tea.

Ben leaned back and smiled. ''I should tell you perhaps, that when he wrote this he was putting me on, dragging out every legal cliché he could think of. Told me he was doing my job for me. But he wasn't kidding about the stipulations regarding your acquisition of the bequest. I thought you might like to hear them, the stipulations, as he set them down.''

He adjusted the half-moons of his wire-rimmed lenses, and began:

> ''I, Reason Able MacKay, being of sound mind and fair ability and reason, hereby place, upon my death, all of my worldly goods and property into the keeping of Belle Regina MacKay, my grand-daughter and closest kin, subject to her satisfaction of the terms and conditions outlined herein.''

I choked, and Ben looked up. ''His name was Reason Able?'' I asked.

Ben nodded solemnly. He cleared his throat, and continued.

> ''The terms withhold her inheritance for six months, and instruct my agents, Benjamin and/or Maude Ellen Beanblossom, not to deliver said property unto her until such time as she has compiled a complete and extensive genealogy of her paternal blood-line. Further, she must satisfy the following condition in order to attain her right to inherit: she must have as her primary place of residence the island known as *Peelaazau,* for said period of withholding.''

''Excuse me,'' I said. ''Pee-lay-zoo?''

"Pee-lay-zah. 'Little Turkey'."

I looked at him.

"Miami, you see." He smiled, and added kindly, "Lake Wawasee, this larger lake, was known by Reason's Native American ancestors as 'Turkey Gobbler'.

"Oh," I said.

He cleared his throat again, turned his attention back to the piece of unfolded fish wrap.

"If, upon completion of this period of residency, she can and does present to my agents or their representatives proof of her compliance of these terms and this condition, to their satisfaction, she is to be surrendered the deed to my property, and title to all that I posthumously own.

"If, however, the terms and the condition stated are not met, she will relinquish all claim to my estate, and it will be turned over to the Papakeechie Preservatory for sale to benefit, or for further development within the guidelines of their chartered association.

"Additionally, the signatures below attest to the fact that all legal fees are paid in full."

Ben leaned back, closed his eyes, and snorted.

Maude smiled. "His little joke, Belle," she said.

"You mean he didn't pay you?"

"Hell, no, he didn't pay me." Ben said. "Damn fool said he'd already paid plenty."

."Ben handled Reason's divorce proceedings," Maude said.

"But that would have been," I stopped, added up the years,

"Thirty-nine, almost forty years ago."

"Isabelle, your grandmother, managed to relieve Reason of his property on Lake Wawasee," said Maude. "She sold it for quite a sum, and that's when Reason went to live in his fishing house on the island. He was always bitter about that. It was family land."

"Oh," I said.

"It wasn't so bad, Belle." Ben's eyes were on the lake, and he sighed. "He had a good life, just rather solitary."

He deposited Reason's hand-written will back into the ragged grocery bag, and pushed it across the floor to me with his cane.

"What's this?"

"This? Why it's your research material, Belle. Dates, deaths, burials. Every family has this stuff. Most folks don't use old fish wrappings, receipts, brown paper bags to keep it all in, that's all."

"Oh," I said. I seemed to have been reduced to simple words.

"I'm curious Belle," Maude said. "I remember telling Reason there was no way in the world that a girl today, with a good job, would go for this deal of his."

"Oh?"

"After all, the cottage isn't worth much, the island — well, it's as near inaccessible as possible. Why did you come, Belle? Why on earth would you agree to this?"

Why? Because there was nothing else. This was all I had.

I shrugged. "Family," I said.

Maude shook her head slowly back and forth. "That's what he said. That by now you would have seen a need for family."

"I wish I'd known him."

"You will, Belle, you will," Ben said.

~ *FOUR* ~

When I first set eyes on the island, it occurred to me that Reason MacKay would not have been an easy man to know.

His mailbox hung drunken from its perch, at the head of an overgrown gravel drive. There was no name on it, no number, nothing but rust to define its sagging bulk. Ben had told me to look for the lot markers, numbers thirty-eight through fifty-two, and even they were camouflaged, refugees of order ignored in a foreign, confident culture.

A game preserve was on my left, and trees merged over the winding road. The day had turned colder, grayer, dismal. Leafless, thick undergrowth managed to hide most of the markers and many of the high, curving views of Lake Papakeechie.

The last marker I'd seen was number twenty-two, so I was unprepared and drove past to number fifty-six, had to back up. I turned into the drive and was immediately swallowed whole by the brush and the scrub trees, the dropping grade of the drive. That's when I saw it. Stunned, I braked, skidded on whatever meager stone wasn't knit up with weeds.

The sun had dipped, but a weak, wintry glimmer surrounded the island in a halo, traced dappled waves of light across open water, through a neck of land and beyond, in an endless shimmering line over the larger, far portion of the lake. There, like a belt cinched tight around a slim waist, was a band of earth and roadway. Then the line of the sun stretched onward, buttoning the bosom of Lake Wawasee. It was blinding.

After I'd swallowed enough of the view, I let the car roll downhill around hairpin, sloping curves. The drive hissed through terraces of staked, withered plants. A shrunken tomato dangled from a petrified twig, a splash of blood on a brown corpse. When the drive dead-ended into a shed, my shoulders heaved in relief.

I got out of the car and looked back uphill over the tops of the shriveled vegetables. Only this central section seemed to have been tended, terraced for gardens. I looked sideways, through a fringe of thick trees — oak, maple, poplar maybe, then down over the shoreline. It was under-cut by water, hung over with bare, branch-dripping stalactites. It seemed a relief to let my eyes sweep into the clear and race over the water to the island.

Here at the bottom of the hill the halo had vanished. The house was backlit by the setting sun and dark, hidden by a thick green juniper hedge and shuttered windows.

Chimney stones rose squat and smug over the bulk of roof, and walls barely hovered over the hedge, blended into the dark water and darker hillside of the far shore. The place was full of a ragged conceit, complete.

Maybe I was beginning to know Reason MacKay.

To the left of his island there was another, a nub of land with a sparse hank of brush, a naked tree or two. It was like a scrawny backbone, humped up out of the water.

I followed black power lines from Reason's island back to the shore, where they connected to a pole and tethered themselves to the world. Electricity, telephone wires. They were the first hint of dependence.

Below those lines was another, a cable that faded into a listing pier over on Reason's island. There was an old pontoon boat here on the shore, which connected to the cable by a pair of poles which must form a sort of running leash. It had to be the boat Maude had told me would ferry me across.

I eyed it warily. She'd explained that no motors were allowed on Lake Papakeechie, that to reach the island I would have to haul myself across, yanking on an overhead cable.

I sighed, and glanced at the sun. It was sinking fast into its path across the vast double puddles. There was no more time to assess, to explore. I'd have to make the best of it, whether the cottage was ready to sustain life, or whether it was not. I shouldn't have taken the time to stop at the market after I'd left Ben's house.

A dozen trips to and from the car later, the boat was loaded, the car locked — out of habit, mostly. I stepped aboard and reached for the cable, tugged hard.

Nothing happened. I looked the boat over, slipped its loops of line off the pilings. I tried again, and the boat moved under my feet, dumped me in a heap into my suitcases.

A long, hearty laugh swirled over the quiet dusk of water, and I scrambled onto my knees and peered over my boxes, found a man in a canoe grinning at me from the shallows, not thirty feet away.

"There now, pick yourself up. Try it again," he called.

It had been so quiet. I'd been busy loading the boat, and I sure thought there'd be no one in this god-forsaken place, but me. All the houses scattered over the arc of shoreline had looked deserted, closed up for the season.

I did pick myself up, but I stood and stared at him. In the dim light he looked young, trim in a dark sweater and jeans. He was lounging back in the boat, legs long and hooked over the crossbar, rod and reel propped on a knee and a can of beer in his hand. He seemed more interested in watching me than in fishing, and I wondered how long he'd been at it. His eyes glinted, and I could see the flash of his teeth.

I hadn't realized I'd stood up until the boat bumped the pier.

"Hang onto the wire," he yelled.

I'd already grabbed for the cable, had steadied myself.

His boat lurched as he put down his beer, settled his rod, unhooked the length of his legs and reached for a paddle.

"It's all right," I yelled back. "I can do it."

I panicked when I realized he was coming anyway, and jerked on the overhead wire. It jerked back, and threw me off my feet again. I was upright at least, gripping the cable, feet treading air.

He was laughing again, bent over, chest heaving.

I ignored him. I got my feet firm on the pontoon and tried again. The boat rushed out from under me and suddenly I was scrambling over boxes. My computer — in its padded case, thank God — tipped over into the canvas grocery bags with a rattle of cans.

He was spluttering through some very obnoxious cackling sounds by now, choking out, "Walk it, walk with it!"

Yes. Well, that worked. I suppose he really was trying to be helpful. But I was tired, sweating under my heavy coat, after loading the boat. And now I was bruised. So I'm afraid I didn't thank him.

He controlled himself, except for an occasional gargling noise, and paddled across the lake beside me. I could hear him over the sound of the rusty pulleys. But I concentrated on plodding along like a mule at a grindstone, literally walking across the water to the island.

He got there ahead of me, jumped out to tie off for me. Then he started in again, yelling, "Not so fast! Whoa!" in between bursts of fresh laughter and shoves at the pontoon, to slow it down.

And it did take both of us to get the pontoon stopped, keep it from ramming into the stone breakwater, toppling all of my worldly possessions into the lake. When that was done I stepped onto the listing dock and glared at him.

Up close now, I could see he was working hard at clamping off a grin. He grabbed for his glasses and made a big deal out of setting them straight.

"Thanks, I guess," I said.

He bent over, and his teeth glinted pink in the sunset while he finished tying off. Then he straightened up and matched my stance; his arms were folded over his sweater, legs spread and one knee bent to accommodate the tilting dock.

"You're welcome, I guess," he said.

I stood my ground in lopsided dignity. Besides, he was between me and the island.

"Need any help with all this?"

"No," I said. "I can handle it."

He cocked his head sideways. "You have got to be related to the old codger," he drawled. "You've got the same good manners."

"And you might find people a bit more receptive if you weren't so busy laughing at them."

He grinned.

"What old codger?"

"Old man MacKay, of course. This was his island."

"Not that it's any of your business, but I am related. He was my grandfather."

He looked again at the loaded boat. "You're not moving in?"

"Why shouldn't I?"

He was serious, finally. He stared at me, at the boat, at the water.

"Why shouldn't I?" I said again.

"No reason."

He turned away, stepped off the dock and slipped into his canoe. Then he dug his paddle in through the lily pads and stared up at me.

"Good luck," he said, and shoved off.

I watched him dip several strokes in the water, and then he turned and yelled, "By the way, I'm Juda Kinzie."

And then, quickly, he was out of sight, around the curve of the other island, and I turned to take my first close look at the house. I shivered. The sweat had chilled on my neck and on my forearms, where I'd shoved up the cuffs of my down jacket to pull the boat along.

I got my purse and searched for the keys Ben had given me. There was an outdoor light overhead, so I decided to go in first and find the switch. There'd be time later to wonder about Juda Kinzie, time to explore.

I followed a dirt path to a small uneven rock patio, found the lock and tried the key. The door opened into a thick dark waiting sensation, and I felt around the door jamb for a light switch, found it.

And then I regretted my rudeness, wished Juda Kinzie was here with me. The house was a shambles, everything in it unrecognizable, papers scattered, cushions tumbled, slashed open . . .

Reason MacKay had been robbed.

All my years of big city living, the awareness of crime, the precautions — they were worthless to me now. I suppose there is something about the pristine nature of the country that makes it particularly vulnerable, when it's violated. This felt sacrilegious, like grave-robbing, or the rape of an innocent. I shut the door behind me and locked it, closed my eyes, waited for the scream inside my blood to fade away.

Finally it did, and I wandered through the rooms, trying to see the house rather than the havoc. It was impossible to do more than get the lay of the mess. The front room was huge and had a large stone open hearth, a kitchen area in one corner, a nineteen-forties' style chrome table and ghastly yellow vinyl chairs, set in front of one of the big shuttered windows. More windows were set around the walls generously, mullioned with metal spacers. It might be cheerful in daylight, with the shutters open.

Beyond, down a tiny hall, a bathroom was tucked in behind the kitchen. There was a big bedroom on the other side of the fireplace. Another room across the hall from it, behind the bathroom, was full of junk — all of which had been dumped, knocked over, bulldozed by the vandals.

I went back to the front room and began clearing a space to bring in my things. Mostly, I shoved stuff into a corner; things like a broken lamp, a clutter of newspapers and magazines, pictures with their backs ripped out. I returned cushions to the overstuffed chair, the musty old davenport.

And then, resolutely, I found the switch to the outdoor lights, carried in my own junk, dumped it all in the center of the room. I had the sense to put the few perishables I'd bought into the refrigerator.

Finally, with the door locked and all the lights left on, I rolled up in a comforter and fell soundly asleep on the one, unmade bed.

I was struggling uphill. Someone beside me was banging away on a drum. I couldn't understand why he wouldn't stop whacking away with what couldn't even be called a musical beat, and help me clear the trail. *Wham. Bamm, bamm.* I lifted my arms over my head and fought away the twigs and slippery, mossy, dank-smelling leaves. But they turned into a sliding mass of puffy stuff, and I woke up.

Bamm, bamm.

Someone was at the door. I threw off the comforter and untwisted and pulled at my sweat shirt, stumbled through the unfamiliar rooms.

"Who is it?" I thought to ask.

"Juda Kinzie. Open up."

"What do you want?"

"For God's sake, woman, I want to speak to you." I

shook my head, realized he couldn't hear that, and ran
my fingers through my hair.

"What do you think I want?" he demanded.

I pulled the door open a few inches and wedged my foot
behind it. When I looked out, his face was already too
close, his hand reaching for the door jamb.

"Hey!" I yelled, and he stepped back.

He looked at me oddly, and said, "Oh. Guess I woke
you up. Sorry."

"What do you want?"

"Your lights were on."

"And?"

"Well, I thought you were up, moving in or something." He took a breath. "Look, have you seen a kid
around?"

"I was asleep, as you so astutely noticed," I said. "It
being what, one in the morning, or something?" I turned
around, searching for a clock somewhere on the walls.

"Yeah. Well, like I said, your lights were on."

I turned back to him and realized that he was looking
past me, into the house. His mouth formed a whistling
shape, but no sound came out.

"What happened here?" he asked.

"I wish I knew."

"You've been robbed?"

"Maybe. Maybe someone just did it out of meanness."

"That's some meanness. You should call the police."

"Yes . . ."

"I will, if you want. Got a phone?"

He reached for the door, smiling, and it reminded me of
all that cocky chuckling he'd done earlier, at my expense.
My foot held the door steady, and I smiled back.

"Don't bother," I said nicely. "You have your own
problems. You're looking for a child? Here?"

"My son." He stepped back again, and his eyes
dropped, his lips made a straight white line in the light fall-

ing through the door.

"Why did you think he'd be here?"

"He used to come a lot." He shrugged, added, "To see Reason."

"Oh?"

"And — and since then, too. Since Reason died, I mean." He looked horrified, suddenly. "David wouldn't do this, though! He helped Reason look after the place, it's not in him to wreck things."

"I see," I said.

"Really," Juda Kinzie said.

"Okay."

We looked at each other for a moment. His hair stood up in a wedge of black and as I watched, his hand rushed through it, calmed it down. He gave me another quick smile, denting the bristling edges of a neat mustache, cutting a deep groove in each of his cheeks, sending a flash off his glasses.

"Well," he said. "I'll go look for David."

"Might be a good idea. Want me to call the police for you?"

"No. No, he'll be around the lake somewhere."

He was backing off, glancing nervously right, left, back at me. I wondered if he was searching for David, or for the best escape route.

"Okay," I called out. "If you're sure . . . Good luck."

I closed the door, thinking; he'd said those same words to me, just a few hours ago. And I locked the door again.

It didn't occur to me till morning that the door had been locked when I got there, and it hadn't made a difference.

Everything was different, though, when I stumbled outside in my wrinkled clothes, into the fogs swirling, dancing in wisps, waiting their turn to be wafted away in the first rays of sunshine. I unlatched the shutters and swung them open all around the house, went back inside and put on my jacket, rinsed out a bowl and spoon, and poured cereal and milk.

And I refused to look at the mess, just yet.

Then I went out to wander the little island. I found another dock, a sturdy small pier on the opposite side of the house. I sat on it and spooned breakfast into my mouth, felt the sun rising at my back, watched as it burnt holes in the restless mist.

It made a lot of difference in my attitude, gave me the idea that the days ahead, the work that waited inside would pass. And, perhaps, bring pleasure, like the promise of spring in this glittering glimpse of morning on the lake.

~ *FIVE* ~

Musty. That was it, the peculiar smell. I stood in the middle of the big front room and decided that the first thing I'd do was air the house. Then I shivered. No, the first thing I'd do was warm it. But I couldn't get to the fireplace. The burglar, or whoever it was who'd ransacked the place, had dumped what looked like the collections of a lifetime in front of it. And my stuff was still mounded up, blocking the mess. Between the smell and the junk, it was all too big a chore.

The first thing was to set up my coffee maker, wash my face, reconsider the decision to live on an island.

And call the police.

I picked up the phone and stood there thinking about Juda Kinzie and about his son, who'd apparently helped my grandfather to keep the place up. I thought about Juda Kinzie's face, when he realized I might suspect his son of wrecking Reason's cottage, instead of keeping an eye on it.

Funny, how sometimes you'd never think a thing, till someone thinks you'll think it.

How old would David Kinzie be? Old enough to be out

on a boat in the middle of the night. Young enough, for his father to call him a "kid" and worry.

I listened to the silence on the phone, and slowly put the receiver back in its cradle.

That did it — the very thought of setting the police on the trail of a child. I didn't need them here anyway, asking me what was missing among Reason's swap shop-reject possessions. Besides, the phone was dead.

A closet in the hall turned out to contain a small propane gas furnace. I turned it on and took another look around.

Gradually, I began seeing pieces of Reason's life. His clothes were strewn all over the bedroom floor, his blankets dumped in a corner and the mattress slightly askew on its springs. Did David, or whoever, think he'd kept money in his mattress? I picked up the blankets and folded them, spotted a furnace vent behind them.

I forgot about making coffee and started methodically around the house, finding the muffled surges of hot air in each room, stacking old bills, magazines and statements against the walls, clearing the floors. By noon my grandfather's things were piled up like pilasters, his lamps and tables and file cabinets were upright, his drawers empty, back in the big old dressers.

In a final surge of energy I moved his personal things into the little back room, trying to organize as I went along — clothes in one corner, bedding next to those, bills and papers against the empty file cabinets. Everything went in that room, even the photos and prints with their backs ripped out. Everything but the furniture and two old portraits, which I hung back on the wall.

Finally I made my coffee, fixed a sandwich and went outside again. My own things were still heaped in the middle of the floor. I guess I hoped that when I came back in, I would feel I'd just arrived, that no one had ever been there and violated my new space.

I was always good at pretending.

The sun was warm and there was a stillness to the water, a peaceful quiet all around the verges of the island. Nothing but a *lap, lap, lap* of contented, rhythmic waves. I found an old deck chair under the eaves of the house and carried it out to the good pier, and sat there in the sun, eating my lunch.

There was no movement at all on the lake, no fishermen, not even birds. Too early in the spring, maybe. I stared at the shorelines, picturing summer; I could imagine the children crying, laughing, swinging out over the lake on ropes that dangled here and there, from trees. The cottages were set high into the woods on the south side, on a steep ridge. On my right the slope was gentler, trees sparser, rooted into patchy chunks of lawn. But on both sides the cottages had an air of desertion. I was the sole proprietor.

Then I remembered Juda Kinzie, who had disappeared, yesterday behind the scrubby little island. His cottage must lie on the southeast shore, where the ridge swooped around to the back of the lake, where Reason's terraced garden made its ravaged trek uphill.

I wondered about him, and about the others I'd met.

My quick stop at the lake market had given me the feeling that I'd stepped back in time. The ma and pa owners gossiped with customers between the soaring, ancient shelves, under a soaring, ancient ceiling. The meat and cheese case was almost a period piece, the scales a hulking monster of white porcelain. The customers were an eclectic mix of age and appearance, but all of them seemed a bit shabby, all carried the same look of, well, of not being comfortable in a suit.

Juda Kinzie was different. He was too good-looking, too cosmopolitan. He didn't fit in. I wondered what the old couple who ran the store knew about him. I wondered what they thought of me — I didn't fit in either.

"Staying long?" the man had asked, eying me, wiping

his hands on his canvas apron.

"A few months," I'd said.

"Which lake?"

"Papakeechie."

"Want the local paper?"

"Not just yet," I said. "I'll get settled first. But I'm glad to know I can get a newspaper."

"My boy runs the route around Papakeechie." He looked me up and down. "You'll maybe want an account here."

"You do that?" I'd said, astonished.

"Do it for some." He'd given me another visual pat-down.

I giggled to myself, remembering. I hadn't wanted to offend him after being judged worthy, so I'd agreed. After he'd studied the form I filled out, he'd stared even harder.

"Thought you might be kin to old Reason."

"Really?"

"Yep. Been expecting you to come along in." He shoved a long-fingered, bony hand at me. "Name's Uriah Sopwell. Over there's my wife . . . Zillah!" he yelled.

I remembered stifling a laugh. More of these names, so odd, so right for a culture this alien to my own. My culture now, though. Now that was funny, and I broke the stillness of today's drowsy lake, by laughing out loud.

I folded up the chair and went back inside, and found that the magic had worked. Or maybe it was the laughter. Either way, it was as though I'd just arrived, and all my own things lay piled, waiting to be put away. The house was warm and comfortable, the sun poured in, the smell of coffee welcomed.

I wandered about enjoying the look of the house, the way it should have met me last night.

Everything was nineteen-forties, or thereabouts. The lamp on the end table made me laugh aloud again. That base was just too sweet: a young girl snuggling a deer in her lap, the lamp shade stitched up with black lacing. The couch was an old-time davenport, with an arched back and nubby deep-green upholstery. There was a matching, over-stuffed chair, an overhanging brass floor lamp with a green glass knob weighting its base.

The kitchen/dining table was that peculiar chrome and mottled Formica that used to grace kitchens all across America. There were padded yellow, vinyl and chrome chairs to match.

The whole front room was like a movie set from the forties, complete with drapes of a blowzy, feathery pattern: maroon and forest green fronds, giant yellow lilies on a background of heavy, blue-gray cotton. Incredible. . I'd wandered into a home for retired sit-coms.

That, too, made me laugh. I could accept this. I'd had a lot of practice; I'd always lived with other people's taste. And this was homier than my apartment's modern, generic-issue furnishings.

When Grandmother Isabelle left Reason she must have taken most of the furniture. He'd been left with his fishing cabin, and this was how he'd fixed it up. Maybe she let him keep the davenport and matching chair, or maybe he'd bought them used. The four-poster in the bedroom, and the solid old cherry dresser — they must have been family heirlooms. It gave me a start to realize that now they were *my* family heirlooms.

I went in and had a closer look, decided I'd start with the bedroom, clean it, get myself settled.

The sheets were already off, thanks to the person who thought there was money in the mattress. All I had to do was unpack my own bedding, vacuum the mattress, make the bed.

I took the empty drawers back out of the cherry chest and mixed a solution of bleach and water to get rid of the smell of mildew. When I was done with the drawers, I tackled the bowels of the cobwebby chest, laid waste to the resident spider, turned the chest on its side to vacuum underneath.

I sucked up the dust inside the chest, butting the nozzle against hidden old struts. It seemed to want to suck them up, kept hissing-out mechanical frustration. I bent over to see, and the struts turned out to be black notebooks taped to the underside of the dresser top. There were two, one tucked into each of the cavities.

The masking tape was new, and peeled away easily. But the pages inside the books were all shades of yellow, with fragile, ragged edges. I sat in the middle of upturned drawers and opened one of the books. Several types of paper had the same neat holes punched, all were carefully reinforced with little stick-on tabs. The notebook covers were stiff and held the papers with a faded grosgrain ribbon — the old-fashioned kind, thick and sturdy.

"Dear Brother," I read aloud from the hand-written first page, dated "Twelve November, Year of Our Lord, Eighteen Forty-two." I gaped at it and lifted the page. Pieces of its corner sprinkled specks of paper dust. "I am well. Father is well, but Mother is Ailing still. I Regret to tell you, they are both in Distress, having received Poorly the notice of your Marriage."

I skipped to the bottom of the page.

"Brother, I will write to you if I am Able, when Father allows that I go to the Post. Henry will accept rec't of your own, and carry them to me when he goes upon his rounds. Your Loving Sister, Clara."

Apparently, Clara was able. There were a dozen letters or more from her. And there were more letters behind hers, different dates, different hands writing in varying styles of cursive.

The other book appeared to be a journal. It started badly, the letters were crudely formed at first and large, becoming slowly more consistent in size and shape as the pages progressed. I went back to the first page and read what appeared to be the hand of a child, practicing his first letters: ''Hiram, 1871, 12 Juli.   I staret Frum a Goodebooke.''

Along with several scrawled passages written by Hiram, there were other attempts at copying from the Bible and a rough practice on the numerals. I flipped back through the notebook, marveling at how the hand had changed, how the lettering had matured into a fluid script.

Perhaps this was the child of that scorned marriage . . . The marriage which had brought the MacKay line to a stumbling halt, in producing me.

But why had Reason hidden them? Who would want old accounts of pioneer days? The person or persons who'd broken into the house, searched it, robbed it?

It didn't seem the sort of treasure a child would want.

A shiver crawled silently up into my shoulders.   I decided to put the notebooks back for now, into their hiding places, and went to find some new tape. And while I was at it, I locked the front door.

Sunshine was pouring in through the windows, reflecting off the water. Crime, and thieves in the night, seemed far away, as remote as this island. No one had any reason to harm me after all, and there was nothing here that would be easy to carry off on a boat.

I put away my clothes, cleaned the cupboards in the kitchen, washed all the dishes and put them back sparkling. My pile of worldly goods diminished, vanished into closets, cupboards and drawers. I was able to vacuum the cleared floors of the cottage, all except for the little spare room. I got a fire laid and lit, wrestled with the draft, ended up opening windows to clear the air, then closing them at last onto cozy comfort. When the sun set over the lake, it washed into the bedroom and the large front room through polished windows, cast a scattering of light like rose-colored glasses.

The mouse dirt on the toilet paper, the droppings in the utensil drawers were just a dim memory.

I scrambled eggs, made toast for dinner, and laid my plans for the pantry as I ate. Reason had left very few provisions: a few rusty cans of stew, some molding cheese and a limp and fuzzy bag of carrots in the refrigerator. On the other hand, the liquor cabinet was well-stocked, the woodshed was full. Life could be sustained, even comfortable, after a trip into town for groceries.

Maybe I could find a card table too, or a small desk for the computer. I'd be able to begin this chore he'd left me, stake my claim to earn the island.

Did I want to? Did I have a choice? Really, the grim truth was simply that I needed something to do, anyway.

The television stood on an old typewriter stand I'd found in the spare room. I shrugged and turned it on, remembering that John had given it to me one Christmas.

I shook myself. No John. I would not even think of him. I would simply stay busy, fill my days with work. This is contentment for now, I thought, and added "telephone hooked up" to my list.

And so began my life on an island. Routine was an easy thing to establish, once I'd filled the pantry. Really, I was self-sufficient here, thanks to the well and the woodshed. All I needed was electricity for the pump, the refrigerator, the hot water heater. And the computer. I watched the news on television at night, weeded through Reason's brown paper bag by day. I cooked my own meals, all of them, for the first time in my life. I even made a loaf of bread now and then. I managed quite well, really.

Until the first time the howling came at night, out over the water, shattering right through the bedroom window. It boiled through my sleep and rose my blood like a war cry, tingling at the roots of my hair.

~ *SIX* ~

It was late April. The warm days had come and gone again. The blue gleam on the lake had dissolved into a gray sulk.

That first week, I remember, I'd begun to believe that life on my island was washed in sunshine. I wasn't even lonely. Then the cold, moody days set in, and the blustery wind kept me from crossing water whipped like meringue. I was forced to stay indoors.

Worse, I had to search through Reason's old clothes for anything clean enough and small enough to wear, since a trip to the laundromat was impossible.

So it seemed to me those random midnight howlings tipped both my life and the weather into the bowels of fate.

It was a thin wailing and piteous, as if it came from a young, trapped animal. The first time I heard it, I lurched out of bed and stood confused and shivering, listening as if it was a foreign language. But the only sense it made ran for the heart, and yanked.

I couldn't see anything from the bedroom window. Whatever was making the noise was out over the water, in the lea of the other island. That first night there was no way I'd go outside for a better view.

It came again the first weekend in May, and the second. I began to recognize an adolescent tone. Something young was out there, howling at whatever slip of moon appeared. But only on weekends.

When the other voice started its howling I knew right away; this was a performance, like one of those copy-cat murders I'd read about. For one thing, it made its appearance during the week. For another, it was far more chilling and not at all pitiful. This person wanted to scare someone. Maybe the someone was me.

That realization put my back up, and in a strange way made me more courageous. I remembered walking in, the night I'd arrived at the island and finding Reason's house ransacked. I figured that whoever was doing this imitation war cry wanted me out so he could get back into the house, to continue searching for — whatever.

Which meant he hadn't found it.

It also meant he wasn't the type to attack face-to-face.

So, I dealt with the cries in two different ways. When they came during the week, woke me up and set me peering out of windows, I stayed indoors. But when they came on the weekend, I went out and hid in the bushes, for all the world like a mother hovering over her child's sickbed.

I had a regular post there, a niche in the juniper hedge where late, shaded daffodils were poking through the earth.

Finally, about the fourth time I heard the weekend howler, I saw him. The wind had been up that day, blowing the surface of the lake, confusing the currents. A full moon peeked around a jagged corner of cumulus in the midnight sky, and there was the boy, standing against the sudden light on the water. He raised his hands to enhance his howling and did a little shuffle. The canoe rocked but he didn't seem to mind; he kept dancing, kept up the keening noise.

My heart lurched right along, keeping time to the tune.

When he fell overboard I wasn't even shocked, wasn't surprised by the chill when I threw off Reason's sweater, kicked my shoes away, gasped at the incredible cold of the water. The shallows were choked with weeds, and I had to kick them too, fight them off, shrug aside the sensation of slime and wormy, tangled strands, get myself clear.

A pounding fright transferred from my heart to my head, took away the cold, put power in my strokes.

His head bobbed for a moment and I could hear a wailing, forlorn, without hope of any kind. He went under right away and must have tried to live, wanted to live, because he came back up. There were no cries this time, and he didn't see me. He just laid his head back in the water and looked into the moonlit clouds, as if he was saying good-bye. And then he was gone.

It seemed ages before I was close enough to dive for him. I tried over and over, down centuries of time. I kept going under, grabbing at the slippery growth in the muck of the bottom. At last I felt a different texture drifting in the weeds, and yanked him up, heard a blessed gasp. At first I thought it was my own.

I couldn't believe it — he started fighting me, throwing actual punches, shoving and squirming in the water. "Stop it!" I yelled, and gobbled air.

"Let me go! Let me go!" he shouted back, thrashing, heavy in his water-logged jacket, in his shoes that had already found my shins, my kneecaps.

"Stupid little shit!" I shouted, hanging on, bucking his feet, treading water, gulping more air. "Kick me again and I'll kill you myself!"

And he stopped fighting. We looked at each other, both of us aware suddenly.

That had been his intention.

"Stupid shit," I said again, in a whisper. His face shone wet in reflected moonlight, and his hair dripped over his eyes, like black tears. I grabbed him then, turned him over, gripped his neck in the classic method of saving fools like him. I started for the shore of the bony, humped island, and he dangled behind, limp, weightless and white.

I got him up onto the little island, by shoving, and went back for his listing canoe. It had to be dragged up through the muck and slime, dumped out.

It made a muddy mess of the slope and I fell on my butt, slid down till my toes stubbed an algae-slick rock.

Behind me the kid was moaning, and I turned to look. Pale hands were up in the air, his head tilted back on his neck, and weird sounds were coming from the black hole of his mouth.

"*Al-ka-ha-ma-nee,*" he wailed. "*Alkahamanee . . .*"

Or something like that. Good Lord. I flung myself back into the water, grappled with the canoe in the seaweedy shallows, manhandled it onto more of the land.

Then he started shrieking, over and over, what sounded like *kah-twah-when-jee,* so I managed not to yell at him again, just got him into the boat and paddled fast for home.

We were both shaking by the time I jerked him onto the pier, tied up the boat, marched him dripping into the dark cottage.

I pulled his jacket off, then his shirt, and threw one of Reason's blankets over his shoulders and head, muffling the sobs that were heaving his bony chest. I pushed him into a chair and left him, went to change my own clothes with my lips clamped blue and tight over the fierce fresh surge of anger, the furious question: why? Stupid kid.

We both needed the moment alone, I guess. When I came back, warm at last and with a selection of Reason's old clothes for him, he was quieter. I managed somehow to muster up some of the concern I'd felt, listening to this boy howling over the water in the dead of night.

I handed him the clothes and stirred up the ashes in the fireplace, added a log, went to fix cocoa. He got out of the chair and walked directly to the bathroom, shut the door. He didn't come out until the hot chocolate was bubbling, the fire flaring up.

"You must have known my grandfather," I said, and handed him a cup.

He sat down in the yellow kitchen chair and leaned his face into the steaming mug.

I stared at him. He'd rolled the sleeves of the old flannel shirt up, cuffed the jeans and belted them with what must have been his own belt, because it fit. Funny, he didn't look all that odd, though the clothes were miles too big. He sniffed at the cup, and carefully tasted its contents.

I laughed. He looked at me, puzzled.

"You're awfully careful with liquids, for someone who just tried to drink the lake."

"It's hot."

I sat down at the table across from him and we stared at one another.

"So you're the girl," he said.

"I'm the girl?"

"Reason's girl. He said you'd come."

"I came." I smiled at him, and when one corner of his mouth twitched vaguely back, I realized my fury was melting fast. He seemed so young to have found life unbearable.

"Can you tell me what you were doing out there?"

"Why should I?" he shot back.

"Because," I said slowly, "you nearly got us both drowned."

"Would have been your own fault."

"What!"

"Nobody asked you to jump in."

I leaned back in my chair, stunned. Of all the ungrateful . . .

"I suppose you want me to apologize to you, for ruining your plans."

"I didn't plan nothing. But it happened, just like it happened to the Chief." He sniffed, and sipped his cocoa.

"Who? What chief?"

"Papakeechie."

"You mean he drowned out there, in the lake?"

He rolled his eyes at me, got up and started doing some kind of Indian dance, shuffling in the rolled up jeans, his bare feet swallowed whole. His fingers tapped at his mouth as he started chanting. It was the same noise, but unshredded by the breezes over the lake. Then he tripped on the bunched-up fabric at his ankles and fell, sprawling, on the floor.

"See?" he said.

I was horrified. All the anger came back, all the fear.

"What were you doing?" I yelled. "You're out there, in the middle of the night, playing Indians?"

He pulled himself to his feet, took up a stance in the middle of the room, raised his fists to the ceiling.

"I am the great Pahedketeha," he said, his voice faking a low and menacing growl. "I am Flat Belly, with two hundred and fifty brave warriors. *Alkahamanee,* I have failed, but my brothers will eat the hearts of the pale-skinned peoples who steal our lives."

He paused, and shook his hands in the air, shouting *"Kah-twah-when-jee!"* His eyes were closed, and he raised and lowered his head, hopped from one foot to another, in time with some imaginary beat. The firelight flickered over his strange jigging figure.

In a moment I would scream. I searched wildly for something to say, and found myself clapping instead. "Very nice," I heard myself saying. "What do you do for an encore?"

He stopped, annoyed, and looked at me.

"Kah-twah-when-jee? What on earth does that mean?"

"Katwaawendgee," he said, as if correcting me. "It means 'why'."

I looked at the clock, and yawned. "I'll tell you what. You should be in bed. Your mom and dad are crazy to let you out alone this time of night."

"Pahedketeha will not sleep in the bed the white man gives him," he droned. "He will not sleep in the brick tepee they have given to make him feel he is brother, to make him think he is one of them. Pahedketeha is Miami.

He does not sleep."

"Well, I do." I stood up.

He glared at me.

"Come on, Pehed — Flat Belly, whatever. I'm taking you home."

"No!"

He was a little boy, suddenly. His hair was drying, and it sprung up from a high forehead, thatching over ears ever-so-slightly jugged. One of his hands reached and swiped his hair back, reminding me of someone, somebody who'd made that same nervous gesture. Yes. Juda — Juda Kinzie.

"Why not?" I said softly. "And what's your name, Flat Belly, your real name? Who's your mom and dad?"

He hung his head.

I walked over and put my hands on his shoulders. "Don't you think we should tell them what you've been doing? We have to tell them."

His eyes were just inches lower, and gazed innocently up at me. "You can't," he said, and grinned.

"Oh, but I can. I'll wake them up. They'll want to know."

"She can't hear you."

"Who? Your mom?"

"Not her. She's dead."

I swallowed. "So your dad then. We'll go and tell him."

"He's not here."

"Where the hell is he?"

"Warsaw. He's home."

"You're here at the lake alone?"

"Nope," he said smugly.

I shook his bony shoulders. "So tell me! Who do we talk to?"

He laughed, right into my face. "Told you," he said. "You can't tell anyone. Only one there's Mrs. Koher, and she's got her hearing aid out. Takes it out every night."

He snickered.

I turned my back on him. He thought he had all the answers. He had to be Juda Kinzie's son. I was tempted to smack him, for all the nights he'd woken me, for the unwelcome midnight swim, for this. I whirled around and glared at him.

"Tell me your name."

"Pahedketeha."

"In English."

"Papakeechie."

"Right. What's your name, kid, or I'll drag you home, rip Mrs. Koher out of her bed . . . "

"David Kinzie," he said.

"Well, David Kinzie, so you have another name. And you have a place to live, and a what — a housekeeper?"

He nodded.

"All right. What if this housekeeper wakes up in the middle of the night and finds you gone?"

"She won't. I lock my door." He grinned again.

I had to admit, he had quite a few answers.

"So you'll sleep here, on the couch," I said. "We'll talk to her in the morning." I went down the hall to the spare room, and grabbed another of Reason's old blankets, came back and threw it on the davenport.

He was still standing where I'd left him, and his face was crafty in the firelight. He was working his mouth, gnawing on his lips. Good. I went over and switched out the light over the kitchen table.

"Make you a deal," he said.

"No deals. We're telling her."

"Hell, she don't care. But she'll tell my dad."

"Good."

"How about *you* tell my dad?"

"I'd love to, David. I'd truly love to."

He brightened. "See, I'll go home in the morning. She'll just think I was out fishing, if she sees me. Then she won't tell my dad, and he won't stop bringing me to the lake."

"What happens when I tell your dad?"

"Oh. Well, how about you don't?" He looked up, hopeful.

I collapsed into the chair, suddenly feeling a chill from my still-damp hair, feeling the exhaustion of that terrified swim, the struggle in the water.

"I'll come over and work, for free, like I did for Reason."

"What did you do for Reason?"

"Everything. I can weed the gardens this summer, I can row over to the store on the other side of the lake, and get food for you. Please?"

I hadn't even thought about the gardens. All those terraced plots, facing west, stepping up the hill.

"No, David. I've got to tell your father," I said. "If I want you to work for me, I'll pay you."

"You will? Really?"

"Yes. But we've got to let him know what you did. It was very dangerous. You nearly got yourself killed."

He shrugged. "Okay. But I'll tell him first."

"Sure you will."

"I will. I promise."

How could anyone so hell-bent on suicide look so innocent?

But I was too tired to argue.

"Right. I'm going to bed. But I want you to promise me something now. There'll be no more dancing on the water, David, not in the middle of the night, not any time. Promise me." I pulled myself up and stood over him, put all the force I could manage into being fierce.

His Adam's apple bumped. "I won't. I don't want to do it again."

"You're not Papakeechie, David." I kept up the glare, getting the energy from somewhere.

"Course not. He's dead. That was his last war dance, and now he's dead."

I sighed. "Go to sleep, David."

"The white man won," he said.

~ *SEVEN* ~

I watched him go off in his canoe after a scant five hours of sleep. He waved when he started around the curve of the little island, and threw me a grin. The boat reappeared in a moment, making straight for shore, bobbing in the calm of a sleepy dawn current.

He tied up across on the south shore, and jogged up a manicured lawn to a modern ranch-style house. I could barely see his baggy pants wriggling in an open window, but I could picture him changing clothes, unlocking his door, going blithely in for breakfast.

Two men so far, had breached my isolation. Just two visitors in five weeks. I wasn't used to such seclusion.

I hadn't seen Juda Kinzie again. I might not see David again, might never have an opportunity to talk to his father, about his son's delusions. I lived on an island. It wasn't as if I met the neighbors, chatted over coffee.

But that morning, as I hung out the wet blanket and the clothes, still dripping from my midnight dip in the lake, I saw the first hint of sociability.

Two paddle boats ambled together, circumnavigating the shoreline, and the occupants were sipping from those funny, wide-bottomed dashboard mugs, holding an in-depth conversation as if they were on a morning stroll. They inched closer and one of them waved, called out a cheery, "Good morning."

I flapped a wet shirt meekly at them, and they bent their heads together, dropped their voices. "Reason's girl," I could imagine them saying, just as David had.

The first sign of spring, I thought. The birds have flown north. People are on the lake, and perhaps the season has begun.

I went inside and started work. Reason's family, my family, were all charted into the computer, but I was still weeding through that brown grocery bag. I'd organized its contents the first week, had put all the death certificates, the newspaper obituaries together with paper clips. The marriage certificates and the births were in another bundle.

I was methodically adding dates and names by now, locations of deaths and burials.

I'd decided to get them in order first, then write the history. I'd read only a little in the notebooks before getting confused about who was who. There were so many of them, for someone used to being the only one in a final generation. Someone who'd never even heard their names.

But I couldn't concentrate. I kept glancing out the windows, as if I expected David to try his Indian act in broad daylight. I'd given him twenty-four hours to tell his dad, threatened to get their Warsaw phone number, call his father at home. David had promised. But I was still uneasy, still felt I should not have trusted him.

His voice, this morning, had been so clear. His eyes true, unwavering when I'd asked if he had a key to Reason's cottage.

"Sure I do," he'd said.

"Hand it over," I'd said.

"Hell, no."

We'd glared at each other. His chin jutted out, and he shoved fists into the pockets of Reason's drooping jeans.

"Why not?" I said. "I'm here now."

"Reason gave it to me. Told me you might not stay. Told me all about it."

"But I'm here, and I intend to stay." I blinked. Well, perhaps I did intend to stay.

"Yeah. You got six months."

"How do you know?"

"I know lots of things. Reason, he told me things, all kinds of things."

I straightened up, stopped trying to stare him down. And I let him go, figuring that anyone who admitted up front that he had a key to the house, would probably not have been the one to wreck it.

But all day long I wondered who might have broken in, if not David. The house had been locked, after all. I'd made a mistake, not going into town and dragging the police out to take fingerprints and see the carnage before I cleaned it up.

So I didn't get much accomplished, waded through the day practically in my sleep, stared out the windows, a lot.

Midway through the afternoon, I heard something and opened the door, scanned the southeast section of the lake where the little island poked its bony back out of the water. A man was kneeling in a rowboat, bending over. His elbows were stuck out like scarecrow arms, and he was singing. The lyrics of the Counting Crows band wafted back at me disjointed, badly sung.

He obviously thought himself alone.

He leaned back into the boat then, and I could see he was adjusting a camera lens. I hoped that whatever he was shooting wouldn't be frightened off by his singing.

He wasn't concerned, but he surely had no idea how awful he sounded. His voice retreated into occasional hmm-hmming sounds, he bent over again, and I heard the click of his camera.

Then he was singing again, tucking his equipment away in a padded case, picking up the oars. Looking over the water at me.

"Yo, doll!" he shouted.

I gulped, caught, and made a little movement of my hand, a partial wave.

He grinned, and headed straight for my island. It took

him less than two minutes, pulling hard on the oars, to swing the boat around to the good dock, throw the line over the piling, hop up and take the earplugs out.

I swallowed this third breach of my island with as decent a cheer as I could muster, and walked down the path to meet him. He had on a skin-tight, long-sleeved shirt that showed muscle anywhere you looked, and shorts. His calves were covered in blond, curly hair, and a crop of medium brown, matching curls dribbled over blue-blue eyes.

He hooked the earphones onto the box dangling from his belt, tapped the button that turned his music off, and reached out a hand all in the same fluid second.

"Adam Andrew," he said.

I took his hand, felt it barely grip and then slide smoothly over my own, more a caress than a handshake.

"Belle MacKay."

"No," he said.

"Yes."

"But you a fine lookin' towngirl, doll."

"Thanks, I guess."

"I can't believe that old dog Reason had anyone like you hiding out in his family. Full of surprises, old Reason."

"Apparently," I said, and filled out the rest of the description I'd managed, walking down the path. There were blond streaks in his curly hair — real or fabricated, and it didn't matter — and if he wore blue contact lenses, I couldn't tell.

"Take a picture?" he offered, and grinned again.

Caught once more, I thought.

"I see you have the equipment."

"Of course," he said, and looked smug.

"Camera equipment," I said, and pointed down into his boat, so he'd make no more mistakes.

"Naturally."

He still looked smug. He had this routine down, I could see.

"Well," I said, "nice meeting you." I backed up a step and smiled politely.

Adam Andrew looked disappointed. He smiled back, a weak imitation, and pointed at the neck of the lake.

"I've got the log cabin there on the peninsula. Come any time, if you need anything at all."

"That's very kind of you."

"Nope. Not kind. I like towngirls," he said. "Beats the hell out of the local attractions." He sighed, and stepped back into his boat. "Not," he added, "that they're totally, like, uninteresting."

"I'm glad to see that you're kept amused," I said.

"Why yes, doll. I am." He pushed off, yelled, "Be seeing you, towngirl. Take care, now!"

I watched him pull for his place. He never even looked back, though I watched him clear across this section of the lake. I could see the spot of color his red shirt made as he tied up, there where a spit of land thrust out and almost cut my part of the lake off from the rest of Papakeechie.

Adam must have a view of both the rising and the setting sun from his place. It sat like a smug toad at the humped edge of the promontory and reminded me of him: the way he never looked back, as if he was used to being out in the open, and expected to be looked at.

No, I didn't get much accomplished. But I'd met another neighbor, waved at the ladies on their ponderous way around the lake on paddle boats. And I'd fished David out of the muck and the seaweed, so I supposed I was making progress.

And I was beginning to enjoy the place. I ate a late dinner on my good dock, facing Adam's cabin, and watched the sun gather up its trailing, liquid gold skirt, and get itself ready to go to bed.

I went inside and poked at the fire, and the phone rang.
I nearly dropped a burning log. It was the first time it had
rung since the line was checked, weeks ago, after it was
hooked up. I stood at the fireplace staring at it, at the
strangeness of the once familiar sound.

Maybe John would call, I used to think. But weeks had
gone by, and he hadn't.

When I picked up the receiver I had to clear my throat,
and my "hello" came out gruff and funny.

"Belle MacKay?"

"Uh, yes," I said, stupidly.

"This is Juda Kinzie."

"Yes?"

"I'm calling about David."

"Oh. Oh, yes."

"I hear you've offered my son a job."

"Huh?"

"A job. I think it's a fine idea. He needs some
occupation, something to keep him from brooding."

"Brooding?" Suicide is a bit beyond brooding, I wanted
to say.

"Yes. You know his mother passed away. He said he
told you."

He seemed so matter-of-fact, impatient even. "Yes," I
said.

"Well, a weekend job might be just the thing, and that
market garden you're planning should keep him busy all
summer."

Market garden? I took a deep breath, and plunged in.
"Mr. Kinzie, I'm not sure what he's told you, but your son
needs more than a job."

"What do you mean, Ms. MacKay?"

Funny, he wasn't nearly so formal at midnight, when he
was banging on my door. And it wasn't Ms. MacKay, when
he was laughing his head off at me, the night we met.

"He needs professional help, Mr. Kinzie."

I could feel his antagonism, right through the wires.

"If you're referring to his despondence, due to his mother's death, I can assure you, Ms. MacKay, that he has received professional attention."

"Good. But is it adequate?"

He was seething now, I could tell by his frigid silence.

"Has he told you what happened last night?" I prodded.

"Yes, Ms. MacKay, he has. I suppose I should thank you."

Ingratitude must be carried through genes. The Kinzies' bloodline was saturated with it. "Don't bother," I said.

"Look. Are you offering him a job or not?"

I shrugged. "Sure. Why not?"

"I'd be happy to see him get the job. He wants it. But, Ms. MacKay, I hope you don't intend to indulge in any amateur psychology. I can assure you that he's seen the best therapists, and they feel his condition is entirely normal."

"Really?"

"Yes. Fragile perhaps, but normal."

"Fragile," I repeated.

"I'd appreciate it if you don't undermine all the work we've done with him."

"I see," I said.

"Yes. Well then, that's settled. I usually bring him to the lake on Saturday mornings, but I can come Friday night, if that would be more convenient."

The less time with you, the better off he'll be, I thought. "So I can expect him over here early Saturday morning?"

"Yes. He's anxious to start work. School's out at the end of May. Don't plan on more hours till then."

"I wouldn't think of it."

"Good." He paused. "Well, he was worried about getting the job. He said you might hire someone else, someone who could put more time in, this spring."

Wait till I get my hands on you, David. "Well yes," I drawled. "I had someone older in mind."

"David's strong, Ms. MacKay, and he knows the place. he helped your grandfather all last summer."

"Hmm."

"What will he be paid?"

I couldn't believe it. I had to pay for this? And good God, I'd have vegetables coming out my ears by July.

"Ms. MacKay? I asked, what are his wages?"

"Um. Do you happen to know what Grandfather paid him?"

"Not much, I know. A dollar an hour, a dollar and a half perhaps. He's only eleven. I'm sure he doesn't expect minimum wage." He laughed, and sounded suddenly like his son.

I managed an answering chuckle, more of a choke, really, but he didn't seem to notice. At least we weren't doing that rather muted form of yelling anymore.

"A dollar and a quarter?"

"That will be fine," he said. "Good-bye, then. David will be there Saturday morning, early."

I put down the phone and started laughing. That sly, manipulative brat. He'd got out of trouble by making it seem an accident, a simple fall from the boat, I'd bet. And then he'd hooked me into giving him a job, probably so his dad wouldn't stop taking him to the lake.

He was sick, though, a seriously disturbed little boy. I remembered those foreign sounds, the ones he'd said meant he was a failure, and I stopped laughing.

I was stuck with him for the whole summer, and for weekends throughout the spring.

I walked over to the window facing east, sat at the kitchen table and looked out at the slope of hill across the water. My market garden. The sun was still sinking, and its trail sprinkled final colors over the water, dribbled light on the tangle of old weeds and tomatoes that stepped so raggedly uphill.

There was a shed down low near the shore, and it held gardening equipment, I knew. There was a gas-powered tiller. There were shovels and rakes and hoes, none of which I'd ever had any sort of relationship with.

I sat there, groping about for some other means of putting David to work.

No, I wouldn't let him paint. I could see puddles spilled all over the carpet, just thinking about it. He was too young to fix the slanting pier where the pontoon was moored. There wasn't enough ground to keep him busy on the island. Damn. There was nothing to do with him, except allow him to plant the terraces.

I could call his father back, insist all this was a mistake. But I'd be calling David a liar. David was, apparently, a liar. And now I was, too. I'd gone along with the story.

I looked at the hillside, golden in the setting sun and bursting with green buds on the trees, on the bushes. I tried to imagine neat rows of corn and carrots, radishes. But I wasn't quite sure what it was supposed to look like. David had better know what he was doing.

In the morning I sat there again, staring at the hillside, desperately visualizing vegetables out of murky shadows. When the sun topped the hill I had to stop; light crawled down the rows and struck stars in every drop of dew. It would be another brilliant day.

Monday, and the coffee klatsch was out again, had added a third paddle boat to their procession around the lake. I stood and watched through the window as the center boat rounded the little island first, like a mother with her ducklings in tow. The woman kept turning to cluck at one or the other of her cronies, kept nodding in response. One of her hands clutched the steering rod and the other gripped her mug. Occasionally, she put the mug down and fiddled with her blue-gray curls. And all the while her feet were planted firmly on the pedals, humping one knee, then the other, up into the slow beat of her stroll.

The phone rang behind me and I went to answer, not nearly so startled as I'd been last night.

"Hello, Belle. Good morning."

"Mr. Beanblossom, how nice of you to call."

"Ben, Belle. Just Ben, remember? And I'm not being nice at all. I'm acting on instructions."

I laughed. "Okay," I said.

"I have a number of things to discuss with you, Belle. Will you be home, today?"

"You aren't thinking of coming out?"

"Certainly, Belle, if you'll have me."

"But . . . how?"

"It's an island, Belle, not a cloister. The judge and I used to visit Reason on occasion."

"The judge?"

"A neighbor of yours. He has one of those pedaling boats. He's on the bench this morning, though. Can't come. Maude's after me to bring her along. All right with you?"

"Of course, Ben. I'd love to see you both."

"We'll be along, then."

Company, I thought, as I hung up the phone. I was beginning to see the island as a hub of activity, a crossroads of cultures. I looked down at the clothes I'd put on and realized I was the high priestess of camp.

Two months ago, I'd worn tailored silks and tinted lips every single day of my life. Now one of Reason's rayon shirts was rolled and bunched around my wrists, his bulky Shetland sweater was shoved up, to under my elbows. I no longer even vaguely resembled my old self.

The jeans, the underwear were my own, and only by

rinsing those out in the sink had I avoided pilfering Reason's supply of boxer shorts. The jeans would have to visit a laundromat soon, or I'd be trying on Reason's pants.

I put on a silk blouse and straightened up the cottage, shuffled the stacks of papers next to the computer into neater piles, and went out to wait for Ben and Maude.

The judge must live near Adam Andrew, I realized, as I spotted the reedy thread of a cane, Ben's peculiar crab-like walk on a pier at the far end of this part of Papakeechie. He took his time settling into the boat, but once underway he and Maude came along at a good clip, arrived at my feet in under ten minutes.

Maude jumped out and helped Ben haul himself onto the dock while I tied off and held the paddle boat steady.

"Very good, Belle," Maude said. "I see you've gotten the hang of this boating thing, already."

"I've seen a lot of these, on the lake. They seem steady," I said. "But Ben, I thought your legs, I mean..."

His eyebrows went up. He stomped the tip of his cane on the pier like a foot, and headed for dry land. "Didn't work?" he said. "Well, I'll tell you Belle, we got us a new physical therapist, a year back." He laughed, and added, "Got all us older folks to pedaling, pedaling to nowhere, these days."

"Oh," I said, and followed Maude, who turned around to smile at me, dissolving my embarrassment. I wondered if the coffee klatsch ladies were getting their therapy over with, trading in stationery bikes for a bit of a view, with their exercise.

"So, dear," Maude said, "has the isolation been too much for you?"

"Not at all. I've met or seen all sorts of people, on the lake. Just this morning I watched several ladies do their morning rounds. They have foot-pedal floats, just like that one, and they've been out in force two mornings in a row. Nonstop gossip, right on my doorstep."

Ben let out a long-winded chuckle. "That's got to be Sally and old Jeannie DeVane," he said, his voice rattling into a belly laugh before he could continue. "They didn't always go down to your end of the lake. Getting plenty of exercise now you're here, are they?"

"They waved at me, yesterday."

"Don't encourage the old bats. They were after Reason for years. He used to bring his shotgun out and pretend to sight ducks on that other island. The gunshots finally wore 'em down, kept 'em on their own end of the lake."

I giggled, at the picture of Reason aiming over the heads of the coffee klatsch, the ladies scattering, clucking.

Ben and Maude moved on and I hurried after them, opened the door, watched them glance around and then go directly to the seats they must have chosen often, when Reason was alive.

Ben settled in the big green chair, began abruptly with his business. "Your grandfather asked me to check in with you at five weeks. Actually, he said that if you survived five weeks, I was to check in."

"We have to forgive him, Ben," Maude said. "He didn't know her."

"Ah, my dear, but he did." To me, he said, "He was sure of your stubborn stock. But he was always a cautious man."

"You need to check on the genealogy, right?"

"Yep."

"Then let me finish my charts. I'm almost done with the names and dates, everything in the grocery sack."

"Is that so, Belle? But it was jammed full of junk."

"You never went through it? It just needed organizing, really. There were certificates of births and deaths and marriages, that sort of thing. And there was a jumble of obituaries, news clippings, notes on scraps of paper about books in a number of different libraries."

"I told you, dear," Maude said. "She's a capable

girl.''

"Well," I said. "I'm still working on my cooking. And I can't offer you a cup of mint tea."

"I used to keep Reason stocked, dear. I'd be happy to do the same for you."

I thanked her, and realized she was stroking the fabric of the old davenport. She sniffed and seemed to concentrate on being cheerful, stood up and walked over to the fireplace.

"I'm anxious to get to the notebooks I found," I said to Ben. "That's why I hurried with the grocery sack. I need to be able to look at the charts so I'll know who's who, in the notebooks."

"Notebooks?"

"Yes. I found some very old, hand-written letters and a journal, here in the house."

"My, my," he said.

There was a moment of silence.

"My dear, I believe you've gotten to the ten-week point."

"The ten-week point?"

"Yes. I was to check in again at ten weeks, give you the location of certain other materials for the genealogy. Really, this was to become a history of the family, you know, not a simple chart."

"I gathered that."

"Not your ordinary 'conditions of inheritance' clause, Belle."

"No, I've never seen anything like this."

"Still, you've done well. Your grandfather wished to see your progress encouraged."

"Thank you, Ben. You should wait till you see the charts, though. I've never done this before, and they might not be right."

"Of course." He was all business again. "When will you be done, so you can bring them along with you, pay us a visit?'' He smiled before adding, ''And pick up your tea.''

''I'll try to finish by Thursday. Nine, Friday morning?''

''Fine. We'll look forward to seeing you.''

I'd get some shopping done then, too, I thought, and wondered what I had in the house, that I could offer them now. My last effort at home-made bread was edible, but not exactly attractive.

''What on earth?'' Maude was saying. ''Why Belle, you haven't found an arrowhead here, surely?''

Ben pushed himself out of the chair and followed me over to the fireplace. Maude was handling my broken piece of mask with one hand, getting her glasses out of the pocket of her windbreaker, with the other.

''Heavens no, honey,'' Ben said. ''At least I've never seen one that looked like that.''

''No, no it's not,'' I said. ''It's just a broken piece of pottery. I put it there to remind me of . . . of someone.''

''I see,'' said Maude. ''Forgive me, dear, for picking it up.'' She looked around and sighed, said, ''Come along now, Ben dear. If we stay too long, I'll be tempted to reminisce, and you do hate it when I get all soggy on you.''

Ben picked the piece of mask out of her hand and hefted it, as if testing its weight. ''Never mind, honey. Belle surely knows we've been here before.'' He glared at me, and added, ''Not that Reason was exactly cordial, the past ten years. But in the old days we'd come here to fish, you know. Caught some nice bluegill, too. The girls would cook 'em up, pan-fried, and then we'd play cards half the night, cozy as could be.''

He and Maude smiled at each other. I could almost see the ghosts of the past, in that look. It must have cheered Maude up, because she drifted down the path to the boat admiring everything, as if I'd been tending the patchy daffodils. As if I'd even planted them.

''Friday morning then,'' Ben reminded me, as I threw

the mooring line into his hand.

"I'll have your tea ready, dear," Maude said.

I started a list of groceries, seeds, fertilizer with a question mark butting against the word, and then I sighed. If I was shopping for fertilizer and seeds, David had won. I should have a look at the gardens, see if I could figure out what I had on hand and what might be needed.

I'd peeked into the lean-to tacked onto the back of the house, and I'd had a look into the one across the lake during my first week on the island, but the spider webs had run me off. Me, who chased grown boys, who could break off an eight-year love affair, who could run away to live on an island, alone. I was frightened. No, I was at the mercy of spiders.

And disturbed children.

I bravely shoved Reason's old sweater over my head, over my silk blouse, and went to check the storage sheds again. Behind the house, I gathered up my courage and unlatched the plank door of the lean-to. Just inside there were old boarded panels, probably used to secure the cottage for winter in the old days, before it was turned into a year-round home. I closed my eyes and grabbed the first spider-webby panel, then the next, and leaned them up against the house. When they were all out of the way, I peered into the gloom to see what the shed held.

An old four-poster, of the same vintage as the one in my room, covered with a moldy canvas tarpaulin. There was a chest of drawers too, and an old spinning wheel. Heirlooms, hidden under layers of dust and the stench of mildewed canvas.

I laughed out loud, realizing that the thieves who'd plundered Reason's house hadn't thought to look in this dilapidated old lean-to. It occurred to me, too, that I could furnish the spare room. I could give David a bed if he dared to dunk himself in the lake again, if I dared to dive in after him. That sobered me, and I wondered if I'd hear his howling again.

I put all the panels back in place, concentrating on keeping clear of spiders, hoping never again to hear my other midnight howler. To him, I said aloud, "I hope the ancestors swoop down on you, put you to work so you don't have time to play that game again." Then I slammed the door, and mentally added furniture refinishing supplies to my shopping list.

I dusted my hands on the seat of my jeans, and told myself the other howler wouldn't be back. It was just a prank, something a big kid thought up because he heard the little kid doing it. That was all. Besides, I hadn't heard him lately.

By now I was good at the pontoon-walking business, and I practically jogged the boat across the water. There weren't any heirlooms in the other shed, but it proved to hold every single gardening implement a novice might want. There was a box of envelopes on a shelf, all labeled neatly. Seeds. It was full of seeds, every kind, even flowers. And I looked closer at a heap of rotting vegetation behind the shed and thought it might actually be a compost pile. I'd read about them, had never thought I'd be using one. I walked the boat back across to the island with a surge of respect for Reason.

Not that I wanted to garden.

But David was right. There was plenty of work here, for a boy who knew the routine. And for a woman starting a new life. I looked at my hands, wondering, standing there on the tilting dock, and for the first time in my life planning to get them dirty, callused perhaps. I would need help. Yes, David was right.

I laughed aloud, and the sound echoed over the shallows between the shores, tap danced on the lily pads.

I smiled into the spring morning, listened to the lap of the water on the stones surrounding the island. I noticed the tips of the juniper fronds, lime green with new growth. I saw tulips beginning to follow the daffodils in niches of the shrubbery.

I had changed. I wasn't running away any more. I might just be home.

~ *EIGHT* ~

The noise that night was enough to wake the dead. It had turned warm on Monday afternoon, and I'd left the windows in my bedroom cracked open a bit when I went to bed. I lay there listening to a billion insects shrieking, expressing in a million different ways their reawakening.

All day Tuesday I worked in a sleepy daze, shuffling Reason's scraps of paper, dribbling bits of information into the computer.

On Wednesday I was still inching through the charts and my date with Ben was looming closer. I had to keep at it, which made it easy to ignore the ladies on their constitutional around Reason's island. I did notice, from the window, that their knee-humping stroll was straying nearer, and their eyes were drifting idly over the short lawn, sweeping the perimeters. But I followed Ben's advice and kept to myself.

I was minding my own business in fact, working on the charts as if a time clock ticked away somewhere. When the phone rang, I was actually annoyed.

"Hello, Belle."

John. It was as if my life flashed past and was pulling me back, drowning me in memory. Those golden eyes, the pale streaks in his hair that matched them, blown dry in tousled waves. The curls that lost themselves somewhere in the starched collar of his shirt, had to be rescued...

"Belle?"

I gulped, shoved at his chest as if he were there in the

room with me, dropped the phone, grabbed it back.
"Yes."

"You haven't called. I've been worried about you."

Reality crashed into my momentary lapse. "Of course I haven't called, John. Why would I?"

"Belle, darling. You know I care how you're getting on. Eight years, after all."

"That was my line, John. If I remember right, you told me that I always knew I could walk."

"And you did."

"I guess I did. Walk, I mean."

There was a pause, and I could see him considering, plotting his move, digesting my surly tone.

"I've found a temp, a real beauty. She might work out."

"Good."

"It's a good job, Belle. She likes it."

"Give it to her, then."

"Maybe you'll change your mind, when you've run through your savings."

"I thought you weren't going to hold the job for me, John. What's the matter, having second thoughts? Maybe your little beauty can't find your power point?"

"Don't be crude, Belle. It doesn't suit you."

"John," I said, "I don't think you'd know what suits me."

"Apparently not. I never suspected this penchant for grubby yokels. I hope you make them wash?"

"John." I made my voice drip sap. "It's not just the sex that makes this place attractive. It's real life. It suits me. I'm very happy."

"Well good, Belle. I hope you have lots of ugly babies."

"Thank you."

There was a moment before he slammed the phone down, and I had to bite my lip to keep from saying his name in the old way, the soft way. I had been lonely. This wasn't real life for me, this was completely alien, all of it. I wasn't happy. I was bitter, and rude, and I was turning mean. No wonder he'd hung up on me.

Self-pity, the sound of his voice, the remembered feel of his body next to me in bed, all of it was too much. I fell into the overstuffed, ancient green chair and closed my eyes, as if I could shut it all away.

Even here, hours away from him, I could feel the soft curls of his chest, the sliding hard warmth of him, hear the murmuring, welcome the sweetness of his words. I missed him. I wanted him, wanted desperately what I'd thrown away, thrown in his face. With my eyes closed he was so close, so turgid, strong. My lips swelled, my fingers tingled to touch him. I tasted the tears, opened my eyes to the empty room.

The day was cloudy, chilly with damp, and I reached my hands around to my shoulders, rubbing warmth, cradling.

The fire was dying. I got up finally, and gave it a brisk poke. At eye-level, facing me on the mantle, was the piece of mask I'd broken that last day of the old life: my trophy. Maude had squinted at it, questioned it, had thought it was an arrowhead. Near enough, I thought. It was sharp and jagged and its glaze, though fired in heat, had shattered all the same. Like John and me. I glared at the fire, shoved at the remnants of a log.

Then I added some wood and the fire took heart, threw spurts of flame, hopeful.

John had not been real. I simply missed the loving, the familiarity, the security I'd manufactured into that life. In a way I was doing that again with the computer, with the lists of names, the relationships.

No. They might all be dead, but they were real, they were family, they were my own.

I preferred spending time with them. I sat myself back

down in front of the computer, and got on with it.

The last pile from Reason's bag lay on the small desk, next to the computer. I'd filed away the other odds and ends as I worked through them, but this was a stack of receipts, the most rag-tag collection he'd had.

As if he'd toured the countryside in search of bits of information, stopped into a gas station and bought a snack, gone on to the local library, these items were all recorded on odd sales slips. They were like a travelogue of local towns: Albion, Syracuse, Warsaw, Columbia City, and more. On the back of each slip he'd written something.

"See John MacKay," I read aloud, "page 205, from the *History of Kosciusko County, Indiana.* Eighteen thirty-five, arrived from Fayette Co, Penn."

They were all like that. I'd have to save this bundle and go in search of all these books, as if the notes were signposts leading me along by the nose. I sighed. Most people would have slotted a coin into a Xerox and made a copy of the article they wanted, instead of leaving hints like rabbit pellets. Like these.

By the time I went to bed, the last bundle had been weeded through, tucked away in the briefcase I'd used long ago, to carry John's research.

The charts were nearly ready to print. David Reason MacKay had married Angennetta, who bore him John Hiram. John Hiram had married first to Minerva McFarren, who'd died in childbirth, and had then married a woman called Polly who, late in life, bore him Hiram. Reason, son of Hiram and of Anna Galway. I'd noted their forebears and found Clara, the sister left behind when John MacKay went into the wilderness. I had the dates of their beginnings, and the dates of their endings.

Their lives gave credence to the harshness of the time and of the frontier. I'd noted down the babies lost, and those few who'd managed maturity. Their burial sites were in the computer now, and all the places of their births from

Scotland to Pennsylvania, to Indiana. So many, many babies had been laid in the earth of the new country.

I was ready for the notebooks, armed by a logical procession of ancestors, ready to begin understanding. The books were still carefully taped under the top of the chest of drawers and they were, in a way, my reward.

Maude Beanblossom had been right when she said my legal training would help with this project. It was like taking over a mismanaged case, and John had gotten quite a few of those. I was used to outlining the participants, the claimants, organizing by precedence. I always had reviewed the previous research and noted down whatever merited further study. I did the grunt work first, laid bare the bones of the case. Tomorrow, when I printed out the charts, all the bones would be connected, a wired-up skeleton of the project to guide me through the flesh.

Those notebooks were the meat of the thing, I thought. They had tantalized me from the moment I'd found them. The last thing I did before going to bed was to take them out of hiding, put them in my briefcase to take to Ben's on Friday.

Lying in bed that night, I thought of them as spirit guides. They would speak to me of what they'd learned in life, perhaps. They'd lived in a time, after all, filled with danger, in a part of history that spilled blood like ink over each year's page. Maybe they'd explain to me why I'd suddenly forgotten how to live in a polite society, follow a passive path strewn with John's unique version of primroses.

Fuck John, I thought, and fell asleep.

At midnight the howling began. I jumped out of bed in my nightgown, went from window to window in the dark house.

The moon was just a sliver and had already risen high enough to gather its trail across the water back into itself. I had to scan the lake by dim reflections.

The simulated war cries bounced around, came from one place, then another. Eerie. I wished I didn't know for sure that David wasn't out there, taking up his vicarious struggle again, against the white man. But it was Wednesday and David was in school, in Warsaw. And this was a man's low howling.

I wished for Reason's gun. Ben had said he'd used one to keep the coffee klatsch matrons at bay. It must still be here. I shivered. Unless the thieves had taken it with whatever portable booty they'd found, before I came.

When the war whoops finally settled back into whatever hole their maker had crawled from, I decided to search the house, first thing in the morning. The computer print-out, my rough draft of the MacKays, could wait.

I finally got back to sleep by wandering mentally through the house, searching for a hidden gun cabinet. Reason had been devious in so many ways. The hunt must have gone on in my dreams, and merged into morning with a constant examination — of everything — as I brushed my teeth, drank my coffee. Each wall was considered, every seam in the carpet looked at. I walked around the outside of the house with my bowl of cereal, and that's when the realization came.

There had to have been a back door. Inside, I knew, the far wall of the hall that led to the bathroom and bedrooms, was blank. It was a varnished, knotty pine; paneled, like the rest of the house. I opened the shed and peered over the spider-webbed wooden barricades into the gloom. There was an outline of a high corner, a line lower down that could be the frame of a door, obscured by the piled-up furniture.

I went back inside to the hallway, and felt around the crevices of the paneling, inserted a screwdriver into any likely cracks, and pried. It was the whole section of wall that swung inward on hinges, set close and tight to the carpet. But it was a door, or had been, once. One side was covered with knotty pine and left unattached at the ceiling and floor. Inside, a panel humped over the other side of the door frame, forming a cavity. And here was Reason's gun.

I looked at the edge of the jamb and found a mechanism to lock the door. Reason hadn't needed a screwdriver to get to his gun. He'd simply installed a light switch that wasn't a light switch. I'd wondered why that particular switch didn't do anything. I realized I'd been locking and unlocking a secret door, and started laughing. I flipped it on now, and saw the metal bar swing down out of the jamb, and latch onto the empty air.

I shut the door, and discovered a convenient hole in the knotty pine, just big enough for a fingerhold.

Amazing. And simple, just enough to do the job, but wonderfully deceptive. I grinned at the devious nature of my grandfather's mind, and got ready to print out my charts.

While the printer ticked away, I gathered up the things I'd take into town. All the laundry, the clothes I'd worn of Reason's, and my own much-used blue jeans. My grocery list. And I'd stop in a sporting goods shop, have the gun checked and cleaned, perhaps. I'd even buy shells and have someone show me how to load it.

Maybe then the whooping and howling in the dead of the night would stop.

Reason's old blankets could stand washing, too.

I already had furniture refinishing supplies on my list, a trip to a hardware store. I'd stay busy, work on the furniture in the shed, clean out the back bedroom. I would look at a new mattress, I decided, and worked out how I would get one down the hill and over the lake on a pontoon.

The printer spit out the last of the twelve pages of charts, and the meager pile lay on the tray, thin as a noodle. Five and a half weeks of work, and this was all I'd accomplished. Well, this and moving in, cleaning up, rooting around in Reason's grocery sack, saving a boy's demented life, arranging a new career for myself — manual labor, dirty work.

I added the charts to the contents of my briefcase and fixed myself a sandwich with the last bit of peanut butter and a crust of bread.

I wandered around outside, eating it. I never seemed to sit at a table any more, for meals. Maybe I was going native: reduced to wearing Reason's baggy jeans, rolled up around the ankles, the last of his clean shirts and, finally, his boxer shorts, cinched in with a safety pin. No bra left to wear, except the one I was keeping clean to wear tomorrow. A laundromat and a grocery store would be priorities, after the meeting with Ben.

The lake was quiet, a little wintry today even in the noon-day sun. Spring was here in fits and starts.

Only one rowboat was on the water, and I hadn't seen the coffee klatsch. After a minute of munching contentedly, I realized that the rowboat was making for the island. I choked on the dry bread, wiped my mouth with Reason's sleeve, looked down at the faded fabric of Reason's jeans, threadbare over the knees. Its belt barely kept the pants up over my hips. Company?

It was Adam Andrew. He called out to me and waved.

I couldn't run and change, there was nothing to change into, except the clothes I'd saved for the trip to town, my business suits. Besides, he'd seen me. Oh God.

I waved back.

"I see you've survived," he said, a few feet away from my dock.

He'd stopped rowing, as if he was waiting to see if I was going to be friendly.

"Of course," I said, chilly.

He grinned.

He wasn't easy to offend. And there was something about him, not just his extreme good looks, that attracted me. Or maybe I was simply happy to have company, a warm body, someone my age. I smiled back.

Apparently, he took it for an invitation. "I saw you out here, walking around, and decided it was time you had a tour of the lake." He spread his hands, nodded at the other seat in his rowboat.

"You've got good eyes. Didn't you say you lived at the promontory there?" I said, pointing.

"Got me a spyglass." He was grinning again. "I can see what color underpants old Sally Hayes is wearing, any time I want. The old broad can't get in and out of her paddle boat without flashing a view."

"You're a voyeur," I said. "Do you watch me too?"

"Any chance I get. You're easier to look at, though. Too bad you always close the curtains." He laughed, threw the hank of blond-brown hair off his forehead.

"City living," I said. "I'm used to avoiding perverts." But I looked back at the house and realized that I lived in a fishbowl, with only a fringe of hideaway hedge.

"Come on, get in. I'll introduce you to all the other perverts on the lake." He made an attempt at leering. "I'm not alone, you know."

It was impossible to be serious with him. I stood looking at him, considering, but not for long. On Monday Ben had said, "It's an island, not a cloister," and since then he'd been the last person to set foot on the island. Besides, Adam Andrew felt safe, despite his binoculars.

"Hang on, and I'll lock up the house," I said over my shoulder.

"Hey, don't bother," he yelled after me.

I did anyway. I even took the time to wedge my briefcase into the space inside Reason's secret door and latched it. And I locked the front door, tucked the key in the pocket of the baggy pants, then carefully stepped into the boat while Adam held it against the dock.

"Not used to boats yet, are you?" he said, laughing again.

"You can tell?"

"Getting any better with the pontoon?"

"I'm a pro with the pontoon," I said. "You *have* been spying on me!"

"Told you I had. But not all the time."

"Oh yes," I said. "Your other amusements take time, of course."

He grinned and pulled on the oars. "Haven't seen you on the lake yet. I bet you don't even know about the old man's fishing boat — it's still propped behind the shed. Got weeds growing around it."

"Oh?" I looked. Sure enough, there was the pointed bow sticking out behind an upside down old raft. I'd noticed the raft. It had a frayed old rope attached to a coffee can full of cement, a different-colored barrel strapped to each corner.

"Yeah. So you need a tour, right?"

"I'd love a tour," I said. "You're right, I haven't been around the lake."

He started rowing hard with powerful, deep strokes that pulled the fabric of an old flannel shirt tight over his shoulders. It didn't seem to matter what he wore, clothes couldn't conceal — maybe just couldn't contain — his physical presence. There was something superhuman, abnormal about him.

"Do you know, Adam," I said, "you have the only normal name I've run into, on the lake."

He smiled, as if accepting his regular portion of praise.

"Not my real one, towngirl," he said, and smirked.

"Oh?"

But he pointed back to the island, said, "Better check that old rowboat over, before you put it in the water. The old man used it last summer, I saw him out a lot in it. But you never know . . . "

"I didn't even know it was there."

"So it was either take me up on my offer, or let the

pontoon loose and pole it around the lake, huh?''

I laughed.

"Yeah, well. Let me know if you do it. I wouldn't want to miss a sight like that. Better than Mrs. Hayes's orange drawers.''

He started pointing out the lake houses, telling me who lived there, who came only on weekends, adding embellishments where he could, bits of gossip that proved he'd put in time with his binoculars. All the while, he rowed. At the neck of the lake he gestured to his cabin, perched over the edge of the pointed ridge.

"On our way back, you can meet my roommate, Saul. He's at work now. I'll tell you about him, later.

"But now, you got to hear about Peter. I call him Peter Peeper, he's worse than I am — insatiable, really. He's a judge. Wears these bifocals that, I swear to you, he lets slip down his nose so he can pretend to stare at you when he's really eyeballing your bust. Not that I've got much of a bust," he added. "But towngirl, look out for yours.''

He kept it up, this outrageous banter, as we slipped around the point and into the bigger section of lake.

"Hey. What's this?" I said, looking around as another wide shoreline began arcing off behind the promontory.

"Papakeechie, towngirl, the lake you live on. Need a map?''

"Adam, I can't see this from the island. I didn't know this part was even here.''

"Okay, so you get the ten dollar tour, the one with the history lesson thrown in. But you owe me.

"See, there was this British townboy, liked making good in the paradise market, came up from Indianapolis after the century kicked over. Name of Sutton, or Sudlow, whatever. Had a place on Wawasee.

"All the land here, and Wawasee too, used to belong to the Indians — Papakeechie and Wawasee. Only his name was more like Wawo-aussie, something like that. Waubee, maybe. Well, the Indians gave over their land to their skinny old Uncle Sam, and Sam, see, he sold it to pay for the Wabash and Erie Canal. That was great for the white folks, 'cause Wawasee was truly a piece of paradise, and right behind it were these six big fishing holes.

"Well, Sud-whatever gets this idea, see. He was in the business, selling land right and left, and he knows an opportunity when it's smack behind his summer place, kicking him in the butt.

"He gets a bunch of like-minded money-bags in, gets it all organized, buys up the land. Then they drill wells to flood it. Bang. Lake Papakeechie. Bang, bang — six little fishing holes are now three big ones."

"Whoa. What happened to the Indians?" I said, thinking of David.

"Didn't belong to them anymore, anyway. The aforesaid uncle set him up a village for his little band of mates, gave Chief Papakeechie a brick house. He looked like a king. Sam didn't give out too many of them brick houses.

"So now we got us a private lake, no motor boats allowed, and a governing body, too."

I raised my eyebrows.

"The Papakeechie Preservatory," he said with his nose in the air and his voice low, full of fake awe.

"Is that like a conservatory?"

"Yeah. Preserves, conserves and marmalade. Good thing."

"Why?"

"Well," he said, "I think we need protection from people like your grandfather. They make wills, put the lake in danger . . . "

I cocked my head and stared at him. He produced a dramatic glare under his scrunched-up eyebrows, stared right back.

He shrugged then, and went back to rowing. "But Saul thinks . . . " He paused, lowering his voice. "He's a peon, poor thing — a physical therapist — we have to forgive him. He thinks it's the Preservatory we need protection from."

"What on earth are you talking about, Adam?"

"He thinks they're all self-serving bastard hypocrites who'd like to run their own little scam."

"Yeah?"

"Yeah, towngirl."

He was grim, all of a sudden, and the change was drastic. He'd been making me laugh at his quirky neighborhood tour, and now I felt like an enemy. He started glowering at me, as if I was personally responsible for the safety of the lake.

"Look, Adam. I don't know the neighborhood. I don't know the politics. I'm new here. Why the hell do you think I need the tour?"

He relaxed. "Sorry. It's the politics, all right. They've caused a lot of bad blood, here on the lake. There was a lawsuit, see. The State wanted to claim Papakeechie as a public lake, and the case drug on for five years.

"Judge finally threw it out." He rolled his eyes, and the twinkle I'd begun to recognize was back, suddenly.

"See, the fish come through under the road there." He turned around and pointed.

We were back out of the portion of lake hidden by the point, and headed into the large section again. I followed his finger to see a road dipping between ridges, crossing a low spit of land swamped in lily pads and cattails.

"All that behind the road is state land, a wildlife preserve. So the State must have figured, why goodness me, fish pass through the marshes, in and out of the lake, why it must be a public lake."

"Okay, Adam. So what?"

"So if it's public, towngirl, any beer-guzzling bozo can

stick a boat over the edge of that road there, where it dips." He snorted. "No privacy. Bye-bye Papakeechie."

"I guess I'm beginning to see your point."

"Just stay your six months, Belle. Keep all the greedy bastards off that island and those lots of Reason's. There's just enough land there for parking lots, some kind of damned public access."

I let him row, for awhile, and calm down.

"Adam," I said finally. "How do you know so much about the terms of my grandfather's will?"

"Oh hell! He went and told Zillah, down at the store. Same as putting it on the front page of the paper."

"Oh," I said.

What had Reason gotten me into?

The rest of the tour was more serene. Adam didn't know as much about the people at the west end of the lake, so he talked about the birds, the Canadian geese and the herons, about their nesting in the acres of protected habitat, the way they herded over to Papakeechie in the summer, skimmed the water, and the banging noise they made. He loved the lake, obviously, and loved talking about it.

"Paradise," he said. "Never crowded. No noisy ski-boats, no scummy oil on the water."

Maude Beanblossom had told me motors weren't allowed on the lake, but not why. Preservatory, preserve... If the waters of the lake were connected to the waters of the preserve, gas and oil would contaminate the breeding grounds.

We'd gone all around the lake by now, were nearing the point where his house sat, and where my clover leaf section of lake joined the waters of the other two.

"We can't have motorboats because of the birds?"

"Yeah, and the fish. Propagation."

He was fighting a current now, where his spit of land dipped below the lake, and he had to pull hard for his dock. He made it, slipped a noose of rope over the pier support, and wiped a flannel sleeve over his forehead.

"I need a beer," he said, and hopped out of the boat, turned to extend a hand. He grinned, added, "Saul will be home. You have got to meet Saul."

"Why?"

He hauled on my arm, yanked me out of the boat as if I was some sort of luggage, laughing. His eyes were dancing.

"Saul," he said, "is a very unusual fellow. And he won't mind your party clothes."

I looked down at myself, ruefully, then up at the cabin. It was handsome, modern, and thick-paned picture windows were set like a sidewalk, reflecting the gray of the water, all the way around the front room. The logs were a rich golden red. They'd been sealed or stained, surely.

Adam whispered, "Have you ever seen the result of a blond German and a big black African?" He giggled.

"Both good-looking cultures," I said, noncommittal.

"An unusual combination though, you have to admit." He watched my face, and laughed. "By golly, I think she's got it," he said.

I almost blushed, as if he'd really caught me forming a picture.

"I enjoy different cultures," I said, defensive.

"I know you do, towngirl. You'll love Saul. Come on, let's do it."

I followed him up a scruffy path, listened to his cross between a cackle and a high-pitched giggle, wondered if I was wise to enter this den. He was odd, but he was the only real ally I had so far, on the lake.

What the hell, everybody was odd. At least Adam had got himself a normal name.

He climbed a short flight of steps and, still grinning, held the door for me.

"I," he said with sudden dignity, "extend hospitality to very few." He bowed. "You are chosen, towngirl."

I made a return bow, in the throes of courtesy. "You honor me," I said.

He giggled, then shrieked, "Saul!"

Saul came through the dining room to greet me with his hand out, confident, composed. He threw a smile at Adam, shifted it, shook my hand and studied me. I looked at both the men, trying to decide which was better looking. Adam, with his light hair and eyes, almost effervescent with enthusiasm and mood swings, or Saul; Saul was darker, well-muscled and well-controlled, in a conservative light-weight sweater and khaki pants.

Saul took charge, showed me to an antique velvet divan, and suggested a strawberry daiquiri.

Adam played host while he was gone, pointed out the view to the east, where my island floated at the end of the lake. He moved around the windows and bragged about getting the sunset and sunrise views I'd thought he would have. He talked about how he'd found this property at the tip of the promontory, and grabbed it.

I listened, and watched him move around, and enjoyed the mix of furnishings; there was a blend of college dorm junk and mature sophistication. When Saul returned with the daiquiri, I was staring at a beer can pyramid, tucked like a giant golden ant hill behind a polished, upholstered Morris chair.

"Unusual, isn't it?" Saul said, sweeping the room with his eyes and one casual hand.

"Well, eclectic maybe."

"This crazy person," Saul said, sighing, "likes contrast."

"I am an artist," Adam said, tapping his chest.

For some reason, this was no revelation. "What medium do you work in?" I asked. "Do you use the camera in your work?"

Saul settled himself in the Morris chair and sipped at his drink. "He's a nature photographer," he said, "and good at it. Freelance.'' He turned to Adam and asked, ''What did you find today?''

I felt a word left off the end, almost as if Saul had bitten off an endearment. Then I had to bite my own tongue, stop an ''Oh'' from sliding out.

Adam was roaming the space around the inside of the windows. I got the feeling that this was a habit of his, and realized all the furniture was arranged on an oval hooked rug in the center of the room, like a medallion in a frame. It formed a run, and Adam used it as a lion would at the zoo, for pacing.

''A Great Blue Heron.'' He frowned at Saul. ''But not a beer.''

''Get it yourself,'' Saul said, and shrugged.

I clamped my throat on a threatening giggle.

''How do you like life on an island?'' Saul asked smoothly.

''So far, I like it. But I'm not fond of the night noises — all that howling.''

He laughed. ''They're just dogs, you know. There's nothing more dangerous than geese, in the preserve. Of course, Adam has been out on the lake when they fly over *en masse*; he thinks he should charge environmental hardship pay.''

''I'm always getting dumped on,'' Adam said, coming back with his beer.

I smiled. ''It's not the birds, making noise,'' I said. ''I don't mind them.''

''Course not, you work inside,'' Adam said.

''It's at night, all that whooping and yowling. Haven't you heard it?''

They looked at each other, and they both shook their heads.

''It's not the dogs?'' Saul asked.

''Human.''

Nobody said anything, and the silence began to be

uncomfortable. I finished my drink, leaned back on the divan and savored the effect of alcohol on my tense shoulders.

"I'm surprised we haven't heard it," Saul said.

"How would you hear anything," Adam said, "when you sleep with that damned subliminal stuff?"

I raised my eyebrows, and Saul took pity on me.

"My little experiment," he said. "I think it's possible to exercise the mind while one sleeps. At the moment, I'm using rain forest sounds."

Adam snorted. "Last week, he thought he could learn Italian!"

"*Cretino.*"

"You looked that up!" Adam hissed.

Saul grinned, and turned back to me. "What time does this howling noise happen?"

"Around midnight, for the most part. But I don't always think to check the time."

"Ah," he said. They exchanged glances. "We never go to bed before midnight. I got a set of classical CD's for Christmas, and I've been trying to bring some culture into the cretin's life."

"He plays this drivel — loud, towngirl, loud, every damned night! And then he puts on his subliminal stuff, with those stupid earplugs."

Saul threw a look of scorn at him, and Adam snickered.

"You'll have to stop now, Saul. We'll have to keep an eye on the lake. And an ear."

Saul nodded. "Well, I couldn't go on much longer anyway, with the loud music. The townies are coming back already. Summer's almost here."

"And the Judge has complained three times," Adam added. "Although we enjoy annoying the Judge."

"Everything's different here, in the summer?"

And they told me, as if both were anxious for a more cheerful subject.

Relief relaxed me more than the daiquiris, more than

conversation with the people whose lives were arranged in cycles made naturally by the seasons. Both Saul and Adam launched into accounts of the summer people, who created still more cycles in their culture by the ebb and flow of their arrivals and departures. But just knowing I had neighbors, and that they were aware of the jerk out there, howling across the lake, was the greatest help and relief of all.

Adam and Saul bickered and snapped at each other like dogs competing for their territories, and Adam was definitely odd, moody and opinionated. But somehow, I felt I had friends on the lake.

Until that night, when I knew for certain that the howler was playing his act for me. Because he grew even bolder.

~ *NINE* ~

I cracked open only one of the bedroom windows that night before I went to bed. I'd discovered that I enjoyed the incredible noise all those insects and frogs — or toads — made in their mate-finding frenzies.

I'd snuggled into a sweatsuit and lay cradled in the center of Reason's mattress, in the pouch formed by his body over the decades he'd used this bed. And I listened to the sounds he'd heard every spring, since he'd come to live on the island. I was wondering what had occurred to him through all those springs, in all those years of listening. But I lay in his place and laughed, realized he'd probably have said, "The earth talks too damned much."

I laughed into silence, and suddenly I *heard* the silence. There was nothing. Where before there been an absolute din of sound, there was now every variety of nothing. My laughing hadn't stopped that frenzy of noise, surely.

I held my breath, felt my fingertips grow icy. And then there was a knock, and I relaxed. Maybe Adam. Had I forgotten anything? It wasn't late, after all.

I'd almost thrown off the covers, got up to answer the door, when there was another knock, and then another. Then they were coming fast, and moving.

The banging hit at my head, bruising behind my eyes, in my ears, raising welts of threat. First, I grabbed my comforter and threw it over me, and then in a muffled, wild rush I jumped off the bed and let out a scream.

Someone was out there, running around the house, banging low, high, on windows or walls, whatever would make a noise.

The blanket slipped off my head and I kept on screaming for another minute or two, long enough for me to realize that this tune had to be changed quickly. So I yelled, "I'm calling the police, asshole!" instead.

I dropped the comforter, and yelled some more: "And I'm getting my gun!" at the top of my lungs.

The rush of mixed-pitched knocks stopped, for a couple of seconds, so I yelled about the police and the gun again—I had just about got it all out, when the knocking started over.

"Asshole!" I shrieked.

That did it. There was total quiet again, and then a hint of sound, like a wary animal creeping away. I stood still, listening, and heard an oar dip, but no other noise. He was trying very hard to be silent.

It took me several minutes to actually get out Reason's gun and head for the phone. I had to stand there and listen to replays of terror; I had to rewind, relive a concert, shaking like a conductor's baton in a failed crescendo. My whole body jerked, kept time with the knocking, kept time with the screaming, the yelling.

Then, gripping the shotgun, I slid along the walls into the living room by the light of the four-watt bulb in the hall. I tested my voice, picked up the phone, dialed nine-one-one. Somehow the phone got away from me and landed upside down. When I picked it back up the connection was broken, so I slammed the whole thing back together, and it rang.

The noise hit me as hard as if the knocking was back and had made it inside the house. I stared at the ringing, had to will myself to grab at it, silence it. I set the gun aside, made one of my hands cup the other over the receiver. I picked it up, and my eyes kept moving around the dark room, over each faint set of drapes, as if I could see through them.

"Belle?"

I croaked out something.

"Belle, are you all right?"

"Who . . . who is it?"

"Who — who?" the voice said. "Saul, Belle, it's Saul."

There was a pause. "Saul, your neighbor," he added.

"Saul?"

"You left our house, a couple of hours ago, remember?"

I cleared my throat. "Yes."

"I thought I heard something, kind of a faint screaming. Just thought I'd call, make sure you were all right. Was that the howling you were talking about?"

"No. No, Saul, that was me."

"You were screaming?"

"Uh-huh. Somebody was outside the house, running around, knocking on all the walls and windows."

"No."

"Yes."

"Have you called the police?"

"I'd just dialed. Then I . . . I dropped the phone, and you called."

"I see," he said. "Listen, call them again, right away. This should be reported. Do you want us to come over?"

"No, I'll be okay. I've got a gun."

"Hang on," he said.

I heard a muffled argument, and then he was back.

"Adam says he's coming anyway, that the guy might come back."

I felt normal again, suddenly. "Tell him I've had

enough company, for tonight."

"Okay. But you'll call the police?"

"Uh-huh."

I put the phone down and dried my hands on my sweatpants, lifted the receiver, and dialed. The operator insisted on sending someone right away, even though I reminded her that I lived on an island.

"They'll find a way," she promised.

And they did. Within twelve minutes a deputy sheriff was there on my short pier, and the man he left in the rowboat was off again, to check out the other island and watch for any movement on the lake.

I felt foolish and gratified, stumbled through my story in conflicting moods. I'd been terrified, but I thought it was probably a prank. I was fine now.

There was no need to mention Reason's gun — Reason didn't seem the type to have gotten a permit for it, if one was needed. Besides, I hadn't found any ammunition. It probably wasn't even loaded.

I found myself telling this florid, chunky deputy all about the cottage having been ransacked, when I arrived in March. And I rounded out the evening by feeling like an idiot, because I'd never reported it.

"Wish I'd had a chance to have a look around," he said, "before you cleared it all up."

"Yes. I should have called. But the phone wasn't hooked up, yet."

"Number of people in the area, year-round. Most don't mind helping out."

"Well," I said, "I guess I thought, well, an island, you know . . . "

"All part of the territory. Plenty of islands, around here. Trouble doesn't keep itself to shore." He stood, scribbled in his book, and muttered, "Part of the job." Then he headed for the door.

I walked down to the dock behind him feeling properly

chastised, although he'd done nothing but give me a stern look, for not reporting the break-in. I thought of David, briefly. But it had been me, caught at obstructing justice, worrying that David had wrecked the house, deciding not to call the police.

The man in the rowboat was back, and he'd seen nobody on this part of the lake, no sign of a boat at the other island.

"Appears to be no immediate danger," the deputy told me. "We'll have somebody out in the morning to have a look. Meantime, don't disturb anything, don't walk around the house."

"I won't."

"Make sure your windows are secure, lock the door."

"I will."

"Call, if there's any more trouble." His eyes glittered, reflecting the faint glow of his partner's flashlight. "No reason for this sort of thing. Good little community here, but I know where to ask some questions. 'Specially now, since the summer folks aren't back yet."

Was David considered a part of the summer, or the year-round people, I wondered. But it wasn't David, I reminded myself. David was in Warsaw, sound asleep in bed. The knocker was the other one, the weekday howler. It had to be.

"Thanks for coming," I managed aloud.

"Done it before, Ma'am. Judge keeps a boat ready for us."

The judge keeps boats ready for lots of people, I thought. I watched him step into the judge's rowboat, asked, "What else has happened, to bring you out on the lake?"

He laughed, for the first time. "Oh, we get the calls, sure enough. Got one over on Wawasee, the other day. Bunch of boys, getting in practice for graduation, they said.

He sat down, steadied his bulk in the boat, added, "Don't quite see how getting naked in the middle of the lake prepares 'em for life, but . . . "

I watched the boat slip away over the dark water, heard the steady creak of the oars, and realized the weekday howler must have greased his oarlocks. He'd made only that one dipping noise, when the oar skipped briefly, before digging into the water. If I could just row around the lake, look for heavily greased oarlocks . . .

I walked back up the path and into the house. I locked the door. Maybe the howler had a canoe. Maybe it wasn't a rowboat, after all. I checked every window twice, slammed and locked the open one, in my bedroom.

I went to sleep, and dreamed that Chief Papakeechie was out there on the lake, doing his dance. Then he was falling, falling. It took forever for his body to swing through the air, and he was calling out to me. The words were strange, and made a pleading sound, a hopeless singing trickle of syllables. I saw myself listening harder, felt my eyes strain to hold him there above the lake, long enough to hear him.

Kah-twah-when-jee, I thought I heard. *Katwaawendgee,* David had said, too. It meant, 'why'.

And he disappeared under the black surface.

The deputy sheriff was back in the morning. He brought both a male and a female officer with him to search around the outside of the house, but they didn't find anything. Cantweld — I caught his name this time — didn't think much of my 'greased oarlock' theory, but promised to keep it in mind.

I got the laundry bundled up in Reason's old blankets when they left and loaded it onto the pontoon. I slipped my briefcase out of the hole in the secret door, locked the house up, tight. I was wearing my own clothes, an actual bra and underwear, one of my silk office blouses and a pair of pressed dress slacks, a matching lightweight jacket. I walked the boat across to the shore, euphoric to be going to town.

The professional cut and feel of my own clothes felt like luxury. Before I pulled onto the road at the top of the hill, I checked my make-up in the rear view mirror. It seemed so many ages ago that this look had been habitual.

Ben seemed impressed. He greeted me with amused admiration, saying only that I looked well. Maude was less discreet.

"My goodness, dear. You look very nice. Lovely to stay in fashion, even on an island."

I laughed and reminded her, "You know I don't. You saw me in grubby jeans when you visited."

"I didn't notice, dear."

"The trunk of my car is full of dirty clothes. I even started wearing Reason's old things."

"I'm sure he wouldn't have minded."

"But my dear," Ben said, "you need a washer. I never thought . . . "

"No, no," Maude said. "Reason had his laundry delivered. She's on an *island*, darling, the septic would never stand a washer."

"He did that? Had his laundry picked up?"

"And delivered. Light starch on the collars, dear." Maude smiled at Ben. "I know he got Kessler's to give him a call, bring everything down the hill."

"Kessler's?" I said.

She nodded. "I'm sure they'll do it for you, too."

Ben snorted. "If they did it for Reason, they'll do it for you. Reason couldn't call in a favor anywhere in the county."

"Except with you," Maude reminded him.

"Yes, well . . . " Ben said, and cleared his throat. "Let's get to it, then. Come in Belle, come in. Makes no sense standing here in the hall."

He stumped ahead of me into the enclosed porch, settled himself into the same old rattan wing chair. Maude said something about tea and left us alone.

"Now then," he said. "Notice you brought your work. Good."

"Yes," I said, and looked out over the tame expanse of Lake Wawasee, the tended lawns, the motorboats bobbing at neighboring piers. Papakeechie was so different, often moody, or rowdy, with scowling waters. "Ben, the other day you mentioned that my grandfather said if I survived, the first five weeks . . . "

"Yes. Reason was concerned. He knew it wouldn't be easy."

"What was it, exactly, that he was afraid of?"

"Hah! I don't believe Reason was ever afraid of anything."

I narrowed my eyes, let my eyebrows express my doubts. I needed answers, and this kindly old man either hid a concealing nature or truly didn't know the questions.

"Ben, why did he ask you to check on me every five weeks? And why are there people out there trying to scare me?"

"Now, Belle, why would anyone want to run you off?"

He closed his eyes. That had been a trick of John's, when he'd made a slip. "That's what I'm asking," I said softly.

He made a dismissive gesture with his hands. "Folks around here are a bit prickly with newcomers, that's all. They'll get used to you." He sighed. "Remember, dear, you're accustomed to an entirely different culture."

"The house was ransacked, Ben, when I got there."

"What? Are you sure?"

"I'm not suffering from culture shock, Ben. Reason seems to have been pretty methodical; he wouldn't have lived in that mess. The house had been wrecked, and quite possibly robbed.''

"Why didn't you call me, call the police? You should have told me, Belle.''

Again, that small, but valid point. I leaned back in the cushions, trying to think what to say. It occurred to me that I might have seized on David's possible guilt to avoid calling anyone. I'd been the only person in the world, in March, and maybe I'd simply wanted it that way.

"You should have gotten right back in your car and come here, Belle. We would have helped.''

Ben frowned at me. I guess I'd hurt his feelings, by not running for cover under his competent wing.

"I'm sorry. I was tired, so I just piled everything up and went to bed. The next day I got it all cleaned up, and moved in.''

"You should know better, Belle.   No evidence, no fingerprints. Good gracious, that was foolish. You're to let me know if anything more happens, understand?'' He folded his arms over his barrel chest and gave me another paternal frown.

It was time to tell him about the howler.

"Just like your grandfather,'' he said.

I looked up.

"Always thought he could handle anything. A very independent man, Reason was. Didn't trust anyone. Probably right, wanting us to check up on you every five weeks.'' He scowled.

"Did he think I'd give up?''

"Not at all. Just cautious, that was Reason. Besides, he'd made up his mind that if you did give up, it wouldn't make any difference to the land, because you weren't good enough for it.''

"Good enough?''

"Sure. Reason had some, ah, abnormal views. He figured the land was its own, shouldn't be passed along, or traded for cash. Your forefathers worked it — many more acres, actually, than what little Reason had left — so he figured you might treat it better than someone else, that's all.

"But you weren't to have it without giving something back. He'd go on about it being his sweat and their sweat, that went into that piece of earth . . . that the fruits of the land were only theirs for the moment, that they'd consume the harvest and give back their sweat and their toil to the land. And then they would reap the fruit once more."

"Very poetic," I said.

"Very Indian. Very native American, I should say." He nodded to himself. "Reason had his own odd reasons."

Ben let out a scoffing noise, and I blurted out a defense: "Because of his Indian ancestors, don't you think?"

"Ah. Yes."

We sat there for a moment. Ben was lost in thought I suppose, in memories, and I . . . well, maybe respect for my odd grandfather was growing amid the confusion.

Ben broke the silence. "So," he said, "let's see Reason's genealogy, then I can give you a bit more in the way of direction."

"What kind of direction?"

"First things first, my dear," he said.

I took the charts from my briefcase and handed them over, watched as he leafed through them. He took his time.

"Very organized. Not what I would call the normal system of charting, though," he finally said.

"I've never seen a genealogy, normal or not. I can do it over. This was just an initial compilation."

"There's no one way, my dear" he said. "And we keep forgetting, Belle, referring to it as Reason's. It's really yours, you know, your family. Do it however you like."

"He didn't leave any guidelines, then?"

"Not about structure. Just about content. Which brings

me to the encouragement I spoke of.''

He handed back the charts and heaved himself out of the chair. And again the ancient desk in the corner produced Reason's offerings. He came back with an envelope and ceremoniously handed it to me.

''As you can see, it is sealed. Just as Reason wished.''

I laughed. ''He didn't trust his own attorney?''

Ben didn't smile. He resettled his bulk in the chair, looked out over the bloated waters of Lake Wawasee as I ripped open the flap. Inside was another bundle of assorted receipts, curling around each other in a rubber band.

''Most houses have a front and back door,'' I read from the sales slip on top. ''Well, Ben, I've found this. He had turned the back door into a sort of secret compartment. His gun was there.''

Ben covered his eyes with one gnarled hand and clamped his mouth tight.

''Are you okay, Ben?''

His chest heaved, and Maude made a sound from the doorway, ran to his side, fluttered over him.

''You're just laughing,'' she accused. ''What's so funny?''

''Reason,'' I told her when Ben started spluttering. ''He left me his gun.''

''Old fool,'' she said, and stomped out.

The next two slips were stapled together. Nothing was written on their backs, and they appeared to be just what they looked like; two grocery store receipts stapled together.

''What does this mean?'' I handed Ben the receipts.

He controlled himself enough to look at them, flipped the top slip over two or three times.

''I told you that you'd get to know your grandfather, Belle,'' he said, and his belly heaved, which knocked his cane to the floor. He struggled with his face, lurched sideways to retrieve his cane and cleared his throat. ''Money was important to Reason. Most of us older folks get that way. Has to do with clinging to life, hanging onto what we've got, I suppose.''

"Yes?"

''I think this is exactly what it looks like. The top slip is from the large grocery store in town. The bottom slip is from Uriah and Zillah Sopwell's shop, here between the lakes. Been there yet?''

I nodded. "Uriah offered to open an account for me.''

"He would," Ben said. "He's been after me, ever since Reason died, to say if you were coming. Tell him anything, Belle," he said, "anything at all you want to pass along, to everyone in the county.''

Adam had said that, too. "So what do the receipts mean?''

"Look here, Belle. See what a can of coffee costs, here? And see this, the same brand, but a dollar cheaper?''

"That's all? Reason was worried that I'd waste money?''

"Not your money, Belle. His money.'' He reached into the pocket of his voluminous sweater vest, pulled out a check, handed it to me.

Five thousand dollars. My jaw dropped. It was made out to me, from Ben Beanblossom's private account.

"This comes with the five weeks' check-in. Remember, I said he wanted to give you some encouragement. I had to add it to the taxable amount of the total inheritance, and if you didn't come, I was to deposit it into the account for the Preservatory.''

"I thought you said he didn't trust anyone.''

"Well," Ben said, serious. "It always does come down to picking someone, someone to trust.''

Yes. It always does. Ben could have kept this money. I looked at him, suddenly, and my thoughts must have been obvious.

Ben chuckled. "Yes Belle, I could have received twenty thousand from old Reason, and given you five of it.

Matter of fact, that's exactly what I did.'' His belly began heaving again, and he spluttered, ''Twenty — yes — twenty!''

''There's more?'' I asked, astounded. I had my savings, but when six months were up I'd be broke, no matter how careful I was with money. Or how often I avoided Sopwell's store.

''Oh yes,'' Ben said. ''There's more.''

''I didn't realize Grandfather was wealthy.''

''When your grandmother cleaned him out with the Wawasee property, Reason got serious about money, collected it like a pack rat. Saved all his income from his family's investments, turned it into more, lived on his earnings.''

''What did he do for an occupation?''

''He liked to fish. He didn't earn anything, when he was younger.

''His father was fifty when Reason was born — see there, you have the date on your chart. While Reason matured, his father was selling off land for development. Place was getting to be popular, with the Indianapolis crowd. Hiram and Reason, well, they argued a lot apparently, so Reason would go off and fish. Didn't even marry till he was late into his thirties.

''After Isabelle left him, he got himself trained as a surveyor. He started developing his ideas about land then, spent a lot of time debating the points of property ownership with anyone who hired him. Funny thing was, most of the land he surveyed was part and parcel of the land his grandfather settled in eighteen thirty-five, back when the Indians still legally owned much of it. Hiram had sold a lot of it off. Guess Reason felt entitled to rant and rave.''

Ben stopped his lecture, looked idly out the window.

''You miss him, don't you Ben?'' I blurted.

''I do.''

Then he snapped back into his business mode, said, "Well, Belle. About that ten week check-up, that you've already breached. You said you found some notebooks?"

"Yes. Taped inside his chest of drawers." I pulled them out of my brief case and handed them over.

While he leafed through them, I looked at the bundle of receipts Reason had seen fit to 'encourage' me with so I wouldn't waste his money. There was a laundry receipt from Kessler's, showing delivery charges. Nothing was written on the back, though. I suppose Reason hadn't wanted the cleaners to overcharge.

"He couldn't bring himself to buy stationery, could he?" I said.

Ben's eyes twinkled as he handed back the books. "One of his little economies," he said. "These seem valuable, by the way. Shouldn't you leave them in my safe, until you're ready for them?"

"I've been anxious to get the charts done and start reading them. I'm ready now."

"At least make copies, Belle. You've had a burglar, after all."

"I will," I promised.

I forgot to make the copies. I'd added the opening of a bank account to my list of errands, and didn't get back to the island till almost dark. I was loaded down with groceries, supplies, clean laundry, the freshly-oiled gun. I did the only thing I could think of. I tucked my briefcase back into the cavity in the hidden door, with the gun.

It had been a long day. I bundled the stacks of folded, clean clothes into the spare room, put only the groceries that needed refrigeration away, left everything else in bags on the counter, and collapsed on the old davenport. I finally made myself a sandwich and ate it while I watched the news on television. Then it was all I could do to pull on a clean nightgown and fall into bed.

A peaceful night, I realized, when the morning sun reflected off the water, past drapes I'd forgotten to draw closed, fell like raindrops on my eyelids.

Saturday. David was coming. I bolted out of bed, grabbed Reason's old jeans and the rayon shirt I'd worn Thursday off the bedpost, dashed into the front room. I could see a boat rounding the little island. It was seven forty-five, and he must be anxious to show up on time. The little brat.

I had just enough time to brush my teeth and run out the door, yanking a comb through the tousled mess of my hair. I put the comb in Reason's breast pocket and waited on the pier.

David's father was rowing, David was grinning.

Juda Kinzie glanced at me, and an expression of shock dented his face for just a moment. I looked down at myself. God, I must look awful.

"Good morning, Ms. MacKay," he said.

I stuttered out a decent response and studied his movements, heard the smooth, greased quiet of the oarlocks as he maneuvered smoothly up to the pier. David hopped out while his father tied off, and I stood there staring until he dropped the mooring line.

"What's the matter?"

"Nothing."

Juda Kinzie could barely keep the smirk off his face, but the once-over his eyes gave me was enough. "Well then," he said. "Nice day."

His eyes lingered at my waist, at the bunched-up fabric belted there, and the corners of his mouth tilted. Nasty. It was so obvious, the way he struggled with his manners.

"Dressed for work?" he asked, and vaulted out of the rowboat, stood up straight.

He was ten inches away and talking down at my nose, but the amusement in his eyes, that smirk, made me stand my ground. I was blocking the way to the island, hands on my hips, and unless he became a hell of a lot pleasant, he'd have to stay perched on the edge of the pier, over the water.

"Yes," I said. "I am." I suppose he thought he'd be invited in, shown over the place, offered coffee.

"I see," he said.

I could tell that he did see, because his eyes became wary, and his mouth turned serious.

"Let's start over, shall we?" he said. He pushed his hand out in the little bit of space between us. "I am glad you're here, on the island. Reason was a good friend to my son."

I moved back a pace casually, put my hand in his and gave it a squeeze more firm than I meant to. But I'd decided pretty quickly that our phone conversation had given him the wrong idea. Reason's clothes had given him another wrong idea. Screw him, I thought, and smiled sweetly.

David yelled at his dad from the door to the cottage, and I turned to look, still blocking the way. "Go on, Dad," he said. "I can walk home. You'll be late for your date."

"It's all right son, Jennifer can wait a few minutes," Juda Kinzie called back.

"Jennifer doesn't like to wait," David insisted.

"You shouldn't keep Jennifer waiting," I said, and gave him my best professional chill, the one I used to reserve for felons.

He stood there and began another appraisal of me. I was glad to see that his attitude was gone, that he'd figured out he was not on my 'A' list, and he was puzzled.

I put my hands on my hips, stuck one foot out and posed like a dainty model, smiled.

"You mustn't keep Jennifer waiting," I reminded him.

He threw me a startled look and gave up, got back in his boat, picked up the oars.

"Uh. No need to give David lunch, he can come home

for a sandwich,'' he said.

I had him on the run. And I'd enjoyed the nonverbal conversation we'd just had, so much more than the lopsided one we'd had on the phone. This was one good-looking guy that had gotten mud on his expectations.

I could afford to be magnanimous and warmed up my smile, put syrup in my voice. "David will be fine. I've planned to give him lunch, and I promise not to indulge myself in amateur psychiatry.''

His eyes narrowed slightly. "Okay," he said, and he took a mean stroke to the water, splashed himself in the face.

I didn't laugh, though I'm sure he expected it. I just stood there and watched him rowing away. Who did he think he was? A tall, dark, good looking answer to every girl's prayer, I supposed. Jennifer's prayer. I'd seen enough of control freaks — John had filled my quota for a century at least — screw 'em. Screw 'em all. No, I didn't feel like laughing.

I wiped the palms of my hands on Reason's jeans, and realized they were damp, and shaking. Maybe because he'd reminded me of John. That air of total confidence, of superiority, vitality. The potency of their gazes. The feel of their skin: both had warm hands, pulsing hands.

I wasn't about to take any shit from David's father.

"Belle?" David yelled.

"Coming.'' I turned around and headed for the steady ground of the island.

~ TEN ~

We pulled out the dusty, mildewed, four-poster bed from the shed, David and I, and I set him to work cleaning it while I drank my coffee, took my shower. Then I put the groceries away and fixed hot chocolate for him. We had a snack and decided together what to do to prepare the gardens.

David knew. He'd done much of it the year before, for Reason. We'd pull all the old plants today, start a new compost heap. Then we'd shovel the dirt from the old heap into the cart, hitch it to the tractor, and begin the process of shuttling compost up the hill to each of the terraces.

We went over on the pontoon and I backed the garden tractor out of the shed. It was a gear-grating event, and more than a shadow of a doubt crossed David's face.

"I guess I'll be doing the mowing too, huh Belle?" he said.

"I can learn."

"Good thing Reason's got a little tiller. He wouldn't let me use it last spring. Said I was too young. Showed me how, though."

He went to the shed and pulled out a long-handled machine, perched on vicious metal claws.

"See?" he said. "Chews up the dirt, mixes and mashes."

"I bet it could chew up a pair of feet, too," I said.

"Nah. Reason's got some old boots I can put on."

He seemed to realize what I was wearing suddenly, and smirked at me, just as his father had.

"You got Reason's clothes on."

"Your dad seemed to think they were good to work in."

"Yeah. You look good, too."

Then he stood and considered me, as if he might change his mind.

"Never mind what I look like," I said quickly. "And you won't be getting your feet and your fingers anywhere near this machine."

"I won't get hurt. Honest," he said.

"We'll see."

He was different, anxious to please, pleasant. Not at all like the little boy I'd pulled, kicking, from the lake. The suicidal little boy. If he was grateful to me, for backing up his story about being hired to work Reason's gardens, he showed it only with steady labor.

I decided to get that issue out of the way, when we went back to the island for lunch.

"Why did you tell your father I wanted you to do the gardens?"

"'Cause I already had the job."

"What?" I put his sandwich on the table and crossed my arms, frowned down at him.

"Well, Reason told me last year."

"Okay . . . But then he died."

"So? I knew you'd want to keep his word. Reason always kept his word."

I just looked at him.

"Besides," he said,, taking a bite, chewing while he spoke, "you told me I could work for you."

"David . . . " Well I had, sort of.

He looked up, his eyes pleading, his jaw stopped in mid-chew. "And you told my dad," he said.

"I was maneuvered into it, David. We both know that."

"And Reason said," David spluttered. His whole body tensed, waited.

I gave up, went and got my own sandwich, sat down, smiled at him.

"All right, David. I just wanted you to know that I'm allergic to being manipulated. Don't make a habit of it."

He grinned, and took another big bite.

"You are a good worker. I guess Reason knew what he was doing."

"Reason knew everything," David said, content.

We spent all afternoon across the water, pulling weeds on the side of the hill, spreading compost. I got better at driving the tractor but David was terrific at it, and did most of the shoveling too, while I raked the compost over the black, spongy earth.

When the sun dipped above the land link between Papakeechie and Wawasee, David put the tools away and headed for home. He yelled down at me from half-way up the hill, shouted that he'd be back early in the morning.

I could hardly believe I'd done a whole day of this, and wasn't looking forward to keeping up with David tomorrow. I pulled myself across to the island with aching shoulders, trying to remember the boy from the midnight drowning, the boy who thought he was a dead Indian chief. There'd been no sign of that boy, today.

My last drop of energy went into covering up the four-poster David had cleaned, tucking the musty old tarp around its rope-twist legs. I left it lying on the patch of grass and went in for a long, hot bath and a late supper of salad and sardines, the best I could do.

And then I went to bed, determined that Juda Kinzie would never again catch me looking as I had this morning. I'd be up at dawn, arming myself against his amusement.

* * *

I was. Up, properly dressed in my own fitted jeans and a shirt no one could mistake as a man's. My wild hair was tamed, a loaf of bread was rising, the coffee was on.

My lips felt dry, so I put on lipstick and stared at myself in the mirror. It was nearly eight in the morning, and I was looking at a face with bright eyes, a flush of pink in her cheeks. I'd peeked out the window three times. What in the hell was I doing? I grabbed a tissue and rubbed the lipstick off.

I heard David bolt through the door, and went out into the living room. Juda Kinzie was leaning against the door frame.

It was as if I had multiple personalities; another woman took over my mind. That wasn't me licking my lips, shining up the remnants of lipstick. *I* wasn't the one smiling, inviting Juda Kinzie into the house for coffee, strutting to the coffee pot, pouring out into my mother's best cups and saucers. I felt invaded by an advertisement, by a television commercial.

He pulled out one of the chrome and yellow vinyl chairs, sat looking expectantly, waiting to be served in that nineteen-forties chair, like a nineteen-forties poppa with a willing, well-dressed wife.

The oldest game a man and a woman had ever played. And I was eager, apparently, to play it. Oh God, let me get a grip.

David was watching. He made a snorting noise and walked out the door.

Thank you, God. It snapped me out of my personal Twilight Zone, dumped the other woman back into the bowels of my brain.

I plunked the cup and saucer on the table, slapped down a napkin so he could mop up the coffee I'd spilled. And I tried with every bone in my back to keep my eyes on the bread pans as I put them into the oven, sit down and sip

from my cup, as if I used fine china every day of my life.
I didn't trust myself to smile, so I simply stared at him.

He finished swabbing the decks, and grinned at me.

"All the elements of civilization," he said, "but a bit
lacking in delivery."

I shrugged. "Don't drink it."

"Of course I'll drink it. I'm always grateful for coffee
in the morning with a beautiful woman."

I choked slightly, felt some warmth in my face.
"Plenty of practice?" I asked.

"Nothing," he said, and he paused, smiling deeply into
my eyes, "to prepare me for this."

Damn. He was flirting with me. And I'd asked for it.
Or that other woman who'd become me had, before I woke
up and smashed her face in. Now I couldn't think of a
thing to say.

David walked in again, thank God, saved me again.

"I can smell that bread clear outside," he said. "Can
I have some?"

"Me too?" Juda Kinzie asked.

I ignored *him.* "It's not ready, David. I've just put it
in the oven." I got up and bent over to look in at the bread.

Juda Kinzie sat there and watched every move I made.
I could feel his eyes, the new assessment he was making.
But it was my own response that frightened me. The
tingling at the roots of my hair, pulsing blood in my
fingertips. Worse, why the hell had I got up and looked
into the oven?

I turned around and caught him, glared at the approval
in his face. I put my hands on my hips and stared him
down, watched the gleam fade from his eyes like shutters
closing out the light. We kept having these nonverbal
conversations, Juda Kinzie and I.

A twinge of anger shot between us, ricocheted back
and forth.

He pushed his cup and saucer away and I swiped it up,

carried it to the sink.

"What's the matter?" David said.

"Nothing at all, son." Juda Kinzie sighed, pushed his chair back and got to his feet.

I smiled over my shoulder, tried to be casual, said, "Time to get to work, David."

"Thanks for the coffee," Juda Kinzie said.

He managed a small quirk of his lips that might have passed for a smile.

I returned it. "Not at all," I said.

The tension went out of my body as he went out of the door. Funny, the anger had bitten me hardest when I saw the appreciation, the gleam drain out of his face. I must want a fight, I realized. I hadn't known I was still so bitter, so confused about John and myself that I'd go flipping personalities around, play the sexuality game. Damn.

David was back in the doorway.

"You don't like my dad?"

"Of course I like him. I just don't know him."

"You aren't very nice to him."

He was right. But I wasn't about to add shame to the emotional mayhem.

"Not like Jennifer. She's very nice to him."

So why is he flirting with me? Maybe he did deserve whatever I threw at him. A little "come on," a little "get lost" — what the hell, of course he deserved it.

I shrugged.

"So, what do we do today?" I asked.

He stood looking at me, and I could see his thoughts in his face. He was pairing his dad and me up, working it all out. I shook my head at him, and he grinned. Good grief, this ability to discuss things without ever saying a word must run in the family, just like their shared capacity to accept whatever they liked as reality. David was good at it, too.

He gave up. "Well, it hasn't rained for days," he said.

"Reason told me to till when the dirt's dry. And we got all the compost on. I guess now we mix and mash."

"Okay," I said. "But I can't go over till I take the bread out, so what about working on furniture for now?"

"Sure, if I get some of that bread first," He waited for my nod, and added, "Nothin' better than bread, with the butter melting, all gooey."

He helped drag out the old dresser from the shed, and then set to work cleaning it while I started applying a refinishing treatment, to the bed. Then we took a break, ate warm bread and drank hot chocolate. He sat there gobbling, dripping crumbs through a foamy marshmallow mustache, and talking about the chest he'd been wiping down.

"Bet that stuff's old," he said. "And it smells funny."

"Mildew," I said. "There's a little bleach in the water you're using to clean it. That'll get rid of most of the mildew. Then we'll let it all dry and I'll oil the drawers, take the old finish off the outside . . . "

"Guess that stuff," he interrupted, pointing at something behind me, "prob'ly belonged to them."

I pushed my chair back and looked into the living room, realized that David was pointing at the two portraits I'd hung back on the wall, my first morning on the island.

"David," I said, staring back at him, "I don't suppose you know who those two are?"

"Sure I do. Reason told me. That's his mom and dad."

Hiram and Anna Galway MacKay. My great-grandparents.

"Thank you, David. I checked for names on the back of the pictures, but there weren't any. I'd no way of knowing . . . "

He snickered. "I know about him. Bet he had a twig to walk across on, when he died."

"What?"

"You know, a twig."

"No, David, I don't know."

He sighed. "When a Miami Indian dies, see," he said, drawing out the words slowly, "he's got to cross this river. If he's done some good stuff when he was alive, he gets to cross over on a big fat log, and all his ancestors come to meet him, and give him strawberries."

"Strawberries?" David, I wanted to say, I don't think so.

"Yeah. But see, if he's done a lot of bad stuff, then he gets a branch to cross on. If he's been really bad, the branch is really little, like." He made the snickering noise again, and pointed at Hiram. "Don't think he ever got his strawberries."

"Oh." It was all I could think of, to say. Strawberries.

I looked at David, trying to see even a hint that he was making all this up. I watched him slurp the last of his hot chocolate, swing an arm up, wipe his mouth on his sleeve and heave a great, satisfied sigh.

"Ready?" he said, and his eyebrows went up like upside-down little happy faces.

"Uh, sure," I said.

The rest of the day was a dreary repeat of the one before. Both of us tried the tiller, trading Reason's heavy boots back and forth between us. We didn't stop for lunch until one o'clock and, afterwards, we went straight back to the terraces. It took all afternoon to work our way down to the bottom tier of the gardens, and by then we were both pretty good at using the tiller. But I was exhausted, and even David was beginning to drag. It took both of us to roll the claw-footed monster back into the shed.

"Don't you have school tomorrow?" I asked.

He nodded and took his baseball cap off, shoved springy brown hair like his father's back over his head, and replaced the hat.

"Maybe this is too much for you, David. I shouldn't be

working you so hard.''

"Nah. Besides, this is the hardest, getting it ready.''

"It's all hard. I don't know about this, David. I don't know anything about gardening, maybe we shouldn't be doing this.''

He pursed his lips and frowned up at me. "Reason said.''

"I'm not Reason. And it's an awful lot of work for just you and me.''

He turned away from me and picked up the envelopes of seed from the box on the shelf. "I can do it,'' he said softly, and leafed through the envelopes.

"But there's weeding, David. There's planting and digging and more weeding, and then there's picking, and selling.''

"Don't weed. There ain't no weeding. All we gotta do is shove leaves and grass and stuff up under the plants. I know how. I can do it,'' he said again.

"David . . . ''

"Here Belle,'' he said, handing me some of the envelopes. "Look what Reason got for you. We never planted none of this last year.''

The top envelope was labeled 'moonflowers' and had directions on it, in Reason's handwriting. The next envelope was full of something called four o'clocks, and another held columbine seeds. There was another labeled 'cleome.' They were all marked 'island,' and held together with a rubber band, just as the bundles of receipts had been.

David handed me another bundle of envelopes, all marked 'market,' and all flowers.

"Guess we're supposed to plant these here on the hill, and sell 'em,'' he said.

I sighed. "David, just because Reason wanted to plant these, well, it doesn't mean we have to.''

"Reason never planted flowers.''

"So?"

"He got 'em for you."

"David, maybe he liked flowers. There are tulips and daffodils on the island."

"I know. He got me to plant 'em last fall, just before school started. Got 'em for you."

"David . . . "

"He did. Got 'em for you. Told me so." David snatched the envelopes back, returned them to the shelf, pulled his feet out of the heavy boots and then tucked them into a corner of the shed. He was out the door and waving good-bye before I could swallow the concept of Reason, offering a bouquet of anything but poison ivy.

"Hey, wait! I haven't paid you."

"Reason didn't pay me till he got his first money from the market," David called over his shoulder. "Said if we didn't do a good job, we wouldn't get nothing for it."

He waved again, and kept going. I watched him up the hill.

I couldn't help thinking, Reason, you reprobate . . .

I picked up the flower packets that were intended for the island, tucked them in my pocket.

I walked the pontoon back across in a daze. Reason had known that he was dying, had prepared the way for me, softened the view with flowers. But he hadn't given, really given much, outright. Almost everything had a chore attached. It was as if he was saying over and over, "Do something. Make it your own, earn it." Each of his little gifts was a hidden treasure, smuggled inside a job. My head was swimming, each thought a lily searching its way up, through choking pads.

It got lonely during the week, when David was in school. Spring was raw again, and not many people had been out on the lake. By Friday I'd only seen the coffee klatsch twice, so when I saw Adam heading for the island

I was ready to stop work early, take in some conversation.

I'd accomplished a lot; I'd worked on reading the handwritten notebooks, got the bed finished and brought the pieces in. I'd even set it up, and found that someone had already adapted the antique frame to handle full-size bedding. For a moment, I wondered if Reason had cherished some sort of unrealistic dream. There'd never been another chance of course, with Isabelle, and he must have known it. The bed had probably been stored away when my father died. Nevertheless, I ordered a mattress and box springs for it, from a local store. Now, perhaps, I was making it ready, setting it up for my own unrealistic dreams.

The bedding would be delivered on Saturday, and David could help me bring it across to the island.

The dresser was still humped under the tarp, out on the grass, and I couldn't move it alone. So I dragged Adam out of his boat and made him help carry it into the house.

"And what do I get paid for this manual labor, towngirl?" he asked caustically.

"A shot of my grandfather's bourbon," I said, and laughed at his look of disgust.

"I won't help you again, not unless you keep a stock of decent beer," he said, and snarled.

"You know . . ." I put down my end, propped open the door. "You waste a lot of energy pretending to be ferocious."

"I am ferocious."

"Uh-huh."

We maneuvered the heavy dresser around corners, through into the back room, and went back out for the drawers.

When they were slotted in, both of us stood back and admired the handsome old furniture. I'd used an easy dissolving agent and steel wool pads, then simply brushed on a urethane finish. The rich reds and mottled auburns blended silky into brown.

"Mahogany?" Adam asked.

"Who knows," I said. "Cherry, maybe?"

"How'd you get all this down the hill?"

"I didn't. It was stored away in the shed. All I had to do was clean it up. David bleached out the mildew."

"David?"

"David Kinzie. A kid on the lake who's been helping me out."

"Got you a manual laborer? Already? Good God, towngirl. But hey, what's wrong with using me?"

"You'd have your hand out."

His eyebrows were up, and I'd begun to expect drama in every one of his versatile expressions. I enjoyed it, and watched him pose, hands on hips, giving me a regular once-over with fabricated shock on his face.

"I am slashed," he said. "Cut to the bone."

"David's only a boy, Adam."

"And I . . . I am a man." He puffed his chest out. "Got any more man-type work?"

"Nope," I said. "That was it. All done. No need for men around here."

He snorted, and patted my back. "You are such a capable little cowgirl. Next you'll be out shooting venison."

"Got me a gun," I said, nodding.

"Oh my dear!"

"Yep."

"But, I'm frightened."

"Wanna see?"

"Sure. Guns are so disgustingly macho."

I'd forgotten. It was in the secret door. So I shook my head quickly, unwilling to share Reason's hiding place.

"Nope. Changed my mind. You'll hurt yourself."

"Hey!" he wailed. "Not fair! You said you'd show it." He grinned, and bolted for the door. "Bet it's under your bed!"

I couldn't help it, I giggled, and followed him into my

bedroom. He was on his knees, his head covered by the trailing king-sized comforter, his yelling muffled.

"Where is it? Come on, cowgirl! Where's your gun?"

I grabbed his arm and yanked, and he flew up at me, flipped me onto the bed, pinned me. Suddenly, nothing was funny.

"Where is it, doll?" he said softly.

There wasn't a trace of an expression on his face, nothing at all to guide me.

"Adam, you're scaring me."

His hands were off my shoulders as soon as the words were out, held in mid-air, hovering like his face, undecided. His eyes seemed to glaze, and he stared at my mouth. Then a spasm yanked through him, straightened his spine. I closed my eyes in relief and breathed. When I looked again, he was leaning against the bedpost, smiling.

I shivered suddenly, and got up off the bed unsure. Had he meant to kiss me — or beat me up? I stomped out of the bedroom, shaken, with a show of outrage.

He followed me. I poured myself a shot of Reason's bourbon, splashed in some Coke. Ice was rattling in the glass, ever so slightly, and he stood and watched it tinkle.

"Didn't mean to scare you, Belle," he said.

I took a sip. Not enough Coke.

"I do get carried away. I'm sorry. But I was just joking, towngirl. You been hurt, that's what it is. Some man, in your townie past?"

I looked at him quick. He was nodding his head like some smug guru. "So what the hell are you?"

"But you don't have to be afraid of me, Belle. Really, you don't."

"You're supposed to be my friend, Adam. I thought so, anyway."

"Yeah, well. I am your friend, towngirl. But don't be going around thinking I'm perfect. Saints and angels don't live here, on the lake." He grinned.

My lips turned up in an automatic reflex and I smiled. I didn't have much experience with friends, but I'd never expected anyone, ever, to be an angel.

"Can I have one of those?" He eyed my drink.

"I thought you only drank beer."

"You don't have any beer."

The bottle came down from the cupboard again, and I poured some bourbon out for him.

"Not too much pop," he said, and went to sit on the ancient davenport.

I brought his drink, sat down on the green chair and watched him, wondering about friends, about men. Maybe I should try to find a female friend. Could I offer a bourbon to the ladies in the coffee klatsch? Of course not. It would be fruitcake or cookies, for them. A gurgling bubble burst, low in my throat.

"What's so funny?"

"Fruitcake," I said.

He looked puzzled, and then he shrugged. "You've done a lot with this place," he said.

"Have you been here before?"

He grinned, and all those volatile expressions chased across his face, again. "Not me, no."

"So how do you know you like what I've done?"

"Hey, towngirl. I'm trying to be polite, here. Friendly. You know."

"You never came to see Reason?" I asked, persistent.

"Reason." He looked forlorn. "No, Reason didn't like me much."

"How come?"

"Hah. Who knows?" He wrinkled up his forehead, pained.

"Reason had no tolerance. Not for the odd camera jockey, anyway. Probably thought I'd sell his picture to the tabloids — call it, 'old man has shotgun medically grafted to his arm'."

"Did he shoot at you, too?"

He laughed. "So you've heard how he used to go and scare off the old ladies?"

I nodded.

"Like I said, no tolerance for cultural abnormalities."

"The ladies don't seem abnormal to me."

"You don't know those ladies," he said.

"It's you, taking pictures of their underwear, now that's abnormal."

Adam choked on his drink, came up laughing. "All right, towngirl. Enough! I admit it, I'm strange."

I gave him my very best 'holier than thou' look.

"But Belle, those ladies! You have to understand, they try to get you married. I know just how Reason felt. It's like their *raison d'etre,* or something. Like they've got to verify their lives by making damned sure everyone they know is miserably married off." He sank into the cushions and sulked.

I laughed at him. "Just stop taking the weird pictures, Adam. Really, it's beneath you."

"Hey, I make money on my nature pics — real money. I don't have to sell the weird ones. They're just for entertainment. And revenge."

"Adam . . ."

"Okay, okay, towngirl."

"Quit sulking, Adam." I got up and took his glass, went into the kitchen to fix him another drink. "So you didn't get along with my grandfather?"

"No tolerance."

"You? Or him?"

"I told you — him. He didn't like Saul, either."

More and more, I wanted to know Reason. He'd left me clues to his personality, and intolerance didn't seem to fit.

"I know he was set in his ways, opinionated," I said. "But for a man who was proud of his own mixed heritage,

I would never have thought he'd actually dislike someone because of his genes. I mean, he seemed intelligent.''

Adam smirked. "He was smart all right."

I handed him the glass, caught the gleam in his eyes. He was smug, as if he was keeping a secret. I knew that patronizing look, had seen it often enough on John's face, when he was fawning over an especially rich widow, or had sniffed his way into any extra, even legal, cash.

Adam must have sensed another dose of suspicion. His face went bland.

"How are you coming on Reason's little history?" he said.

"You know about that, too?"

"Sure. Told you when we were out on the lake. Reason told Zillah, down at the store. You're supposed to do this historical survey, an in-depth kind of genealogy." He lowered his voice and added, "Compiling corpses."

"So he told Zillah — what, everything?"

Adam jerked a shoulder up. "What's everything?" he asked.

Why had Reason spread this around? For a cautious man, a close-mouthed man, it seemed odd.

"Why would he do that?"

"You mean tell Zillah?"

I nodded.

"Maybe he wanted people to know, so you'd have a chance at keeping the island."

"What do you mean?"

"Maybe he distrusted the people here, towngirl, even more than he distrusted the Preservatory. Maybe he figured you'd have a better chance if the folks here knew you weren't letting the land go."

I shook my head. "It doesn't make sense."

"Just put in your time, towngirl. Then you can get away fast, like a quick little city cat."

"Adam, you turn confusion into an art form."

"I know, I know. Give me another drink, next Friday.

No, no, give me a good lager, and I'll try to explain. It'll take weeks and weeks. You'll have to put in a couple cases of beer, just for me. I'll come every Friday, and drink 'em up." He nodded solemnly.

"Adam, you have a real mean streak. Does Saul know? I think, as a friend, I have a duty to point out to him the exact shade of ugliness it puts on your personality."

"Sure towngirl. By all means, tell him."

"It's my duty."

"I'll bring him with me, next Friday. It's time to plan our annual ceremonial, anyway."

"Ceremonial?"

"Every year," he said, "we have a Shooting of the Breeze Party, when Memorial Day comes and shoves all the city folk down our throats, for the summer."

"What do you shoot the breeze with?"

"Our weapons," he said. "Now, let me see what you've written. I truly hunger for the culture and education you bring to this forsaken, pervert-ridden land."

"Enough speeches. You speak much and say nothing." I got up, rifled through the papers next to my computer.

I handed him a few pages of the draft I'd managed this week. "Read!" I said. "And eradicate ignorance from your bosom."

He looked down at his chest, bulging nicely under brown flannel. "Sorry," he said. "My ignorance isn't home."

I laughed at him and got up, went into the little arm of the kitchen to let him read. I'd like an opinion. I was used to John's constant direction in the writing I'd done for him, the scrawled comments he made in the margins. It seemed hard to focus, to build my case with only the dead for a reference point.

The words rolled through my mind as I stood at the sink and washed up the dishes from lunch. My case.

I realized that this was really the story of any pioneer

family. Each must have formed a survivalist culture, just as they wove fabric to replace their worn-out clothing; each story would be as individual as its maker, but would follow the same process of warp and woof threads . . .

Success, survival, would have come only by adapting to new surroundings, by maintaining an acceptance for other cultures. An ancestor of mine had married into the Miami Indian tribe of Papakeechie, and had given me a distinct dichotomy of adverse cultural backgrounds. It was a background historically tragic, defined by death, by the struggle for homeland.

It all seemed oddly current. I seemed to still be living that struggle.

My 'case' would bring diverging cultures together and form Reason's unique blood line. My blood line.

Polly MacKay and John Hiram MacKay — they were the warp and woof of this particular heritage. Papakeechie was Polly's father, and a powerful Miami chief. I'd read about him before coming here, to the lake. And I knew a bit of history, too. In eighteen thirty-eight, many natives of what was now the state of Indiana were gathered to begin marching down the Trail of Death to Kansas. Papakeechie, and many others of the Miami Nation, refused to go westward or to sell the remains of their land.

Papakeechie, I knew, had something like thirty-six sections of land in eighteen thirty-four, reserved to him from the treaty of eighteen twenty-six. His village was home to about seventy-five, and his brother Waubee, or Wawasee, had a similar village nearby.

Papakeechie had been granted a fine brick home, which blew down in a tornado in eighteen thirty-four. Bricks were flung through the wild winds, and one had struck his wife, Anougons, killing her. Papakeechie's once potent band of over two hundred and fifty had been decimated by disease, by liquor, most of all by the overwhelming odds against sustaining its culture.

There had been a reduced number of suitors available to Henziga, Papakeechie's daughter, she whom John Hiram called Polly. So when John Hiram offered gifts to her father and asked to marry her, Papakeechie may have accepted more out of necessity than approval.

The chief was a broken man anyway when his wife died, and he'd died soon after her. I'd found no mention of David's claim that he drowned in the lake, but Reason's notes on receipts mentioned Papakeechie's orphaned young son, Kemoteah.

His name meant 'Whispering Winds,' and he, too, had a tragic end. He'd grown up and married, and his wife had been killed by the suitor she'd rejected when she'd chosen Kemoteah. Kemoteah killed the suitor, and the suitor's brother, Nagget, killed Kemoteah. A band of furious Miami then killed Nagget in revenge. Kemoteah had become their chief when a man named Macose, who was chief after Papakeechie died, drowned.

I wondered if Macose was David's 'dancer on the water,' and smiled, dried my hands on a dish towel. I wasn't sure I wanted to discuss it with David. It might remind him of that night.

Reason's receipts were sprinkled with nuggets of fact, and the notebooks made fact come alive. The journal had been written by Hiram, my great-grandfather, he whose picture hung on the wall. His thick, stiff sheets of paper were brittle and worn, smudged by time and by a little boy's dirty fingers. I could almost see him learning his letters as he related the events of his days. Often this week, I'd looked up at his aged face and saw the boy he'd been, scratching his stories down in a cramped hand, in a mix of biblical and childish phrases.

The other notebook contained the 'Dear Brother' letters, which had forced my decision to chart these names. 'Dear Brother' turned out to be Hiram's father, John Hiram MacKay, who'd married Minerva McFarren. He'd come to Indiana in the early eighteen hundreds and had traded with the Indians, had eventually filed a claim for a tract of their land. When Minerva died in childbirth he'd married Polly, and his parents had not approved.

"Belle?"

I dropped one of Reason's old cups and it clinked across the floor.

Adam laughed. "Caught you thinking of means and motives?"

"For what?"

"Well, you're painting a case for the Injuns here, cowgirl. All I see is outrage. Thought this here was supposed to be a history of the family. Where's your white-eyed side?"

"I had to start somewhere."

"Hey, don't go all defensive on me."

"Sorry," I said. "Actually, I do need a critic. Do you really think it's a lopsided start?"

"Depends."

"On what, Adam?"

"Well, it's like photos. Depends on the market. You want to antagonize white folks, here?" He winked at me. "I often stick a firearm somewhere in the frame when I'm doing a shoot for the hunting trades. But see, if I'm after environmentals, why, I put the instruments of terror away. Get it?"

"Don't patronize me."

"Hey . . . " He shrugged. "Read it whatever way you want."

I stuck my tongue out at him, and he grinned back. "Okay," I said. "So you think I've got the balance off."

"Yep."

I walked back over to my green chair and sat down, leaned back and closed my eyes.

"It's not like it's going to be published, or anything," I said.

"Right."

"But I'd rather put it into perspective, try to get at the value of the merged cultures. I certainly don't want to antagonize, even if I'm the only one who ever reads it."

"Hey. People get mad. If they don't see anything, they don't learn anything. No input. Same as no input."

"You're right, Adam."

"You're kidding! You mean you understood that?" he said, pretending astonishment.

"I'll rewrite."

"Wow! Because of me, of what I said?"

"You're no dummy, Adam. And I told you I needed criticism."

He got up, puffed out his chest, waddled around the floor. "I can teach a towngirl, I can teach a towngirl," he sang.

"Oh my God," I said.

"What?" He stopped waddling.

"Well, I've always prided myself on my appreciation for different cultures. I just realized I'd completely biased myself against my own — the one I grew up in, anyway."

"You're a traitor, Belle," he said, sadly.

"And you're weird, Adam."

"Not me. I appreciate everybody, if they appreciate me."

"And I like weirdos," I said.

I looked over my shoulder, and winked up at Hiram.

~ *ELEVEN* ~

Another day of physical labor lay ahead. It was a glorious day; the morning air was crisp and the sun was dripping diamonds on dew.

Watch it, I told myself. Spring fever. All those singing insects are riddling your mind with romance. I shaded my eyes from the glittering water, from the sparkling leaves on the island's bushes and trees.

I'd worked late on the history after Adam left, had overslept this morning, and now I had little time to dress before Juda Kinzie and David arrived. But I knew myself better now, and purposely pulled on a pair of Reason's jeans, rolled up the sleeves of one of his many rayon shirts, yanked a brush through my hair without checking myself in the mirror. I put on a pair of old suspenders, adjusted the straps to fit, let the shirt hang out in ragged tails between the clips.

The hell with men. I made instant coffee and sat at my little desk waiting, determined not to watch for Juda Kinzie and David.

The desk was at the window, so it was hard not to look out and enjoy the glittering water. Too soon, the sun would be over the treetops on the hillside, high in the sky. It would stop scattering rays over the prism of lake, refracting, washing the cottage in waves of light like billowing silk.

I saw them coming, in the canoe this time, instead of the rowboat. I saw David jump out and up onto the dock. Saw Juda Kinzie pick up his paddle and push off. His hair glinted iridescent in the early sun, like the inside of a sea shell. His profile was sharp against the backdrop of shining water. I watched him leaving.

The hell with men.

"Hey! Where's the bread?"

It was hard to get energetic about another workday.

"What?" I said. "I'm supposed to make home-made bread for you, every weekend? Is it part of your wages, or something?"

"I like it," he said, pouting.

I sighed, and took another quick look out the window.

"Speaking of wages, David, we need to get this settled, at least keep some kind of record."

"Reason said if you count the hours you work on the land, they count against you."

"I'm not Reason, David."

"No, but you're her."

"Her?"

He poked his toe at the carpet, dragged it around a curling fern in the ancient rug's pattern. "Nothing," he said, and walked back out the door.

I followed him. There was something about the way he'd said that. It reminded me of his wild eyes, the night he'd done his tap dance routine on the water.

"Tell me," I said.

He'd stopped at the back of the house and was poking around at the boat that sat propped there, smothered in weeds. "We got to get this out," he said, "maybe paint it up."

"Tell me, David. Who's 'her'?"

His eyes streaked up at me, then back at the boat.

"I'll make bread," I said.

He smiled then, a quick little quirk of his lips. "You

will?''

"I will."

"Okay, but don't laugh. Promise?"

"Promise."

"See, Reason told me all about her. Called her Pollyanna, said he called her that cause she was such a 'diehard opterist'."

"Opterist?'

"Yeah. Opterist. Somethin' like that. She was always happy . . ."

I laughed. "Optimist, David. You mean optimist."

"Yeah. Well, she was happy. Like you."

Like me? Somehow it shocked me. I wondered, was it true? I sure thought I'd been miserable, running from John, from that blind sort of faith I'd been pretending was love. Running from a fabricated life.

David turned the boat over, began dragging it through the weeds.

"You're not finished, David. Come on. You want bread, you got to pay the baker."

He groaned. A strange sound from such a small boy.

"Okay," he said. "So you remind me of her, that's all. Of the stories Reason told."

"And who is 'her'?"

"You should know. Thought you were doin' Reason's history. She was Chief Papakeechie's girl."

"You mean Polly, then."

"Sure. Her uncle was Wawaesse, the old chief who wore the silver ring in his nose. Unless," David confided, "the visitors weren't so important. *Then* he wore a fish bone, just to show 'em their place." He gestured under his nose, and put a superior look on his face.

I smiled, a little relieved to see David acting like a regular kid.

"Okay, so I remind you of Polly, Papakeechie's girl. So how do you figure this?"

"Pahedketeha," he said.

"Excuse me." And hadn't *he* just said Papakeechie?

"That's okay. White people never can get the names right."

"Oh? And what are you, then?"

"*I* know." He turned his nose up, pursed his lips.

"Okay David, so what's this about Polly?"

"You're her incantation."

Oh-oh.

"Her re-incantation." He looked serious.

I shivered. Being me was hard enough.

"Yeah, that's it," he said.

Enough. "I am *nobody's* reincarnation, David. I am me, Belle Regina MacKay."

"Reincarnation, that's it. Don't you know?"

"David, I know who I am."

"Don't you know Regina means 'queen' in Latin? Reason told me. So you're her, the daughter of the king."

I was getting exasperated. "David, did Reason tell you I was Polly MacKay, reincarnated?"

He looked at the ground, pursed his lips. "No," he said.

"All right then. Look, David, I'm glad for your help around here, but I'd appreciate it if you didn't make me be somebody I'm not. And I'm not, David. I'm not Polly."

I stood glaring at him till he sneaked a peek up at me.

"Okay," he said.

"Good," I said. "Then I'll go make your bread."

I turned to go inside, trying to control the sudden shakes that twinged up from my knees. I heard David skipping along behind me, chattering about the boat. He was saying something about Reason having bought paint to do the boat this spring, and he went right to a cupboard under the sink and pulled a can out, went back outside, whistling. I pulled out the flour, the sugar, the yeast, mixed the dough and began banging the lump around the counter until I calmed myself.

I would call Juda Kinzie, I decided. I'd tell him to get his son some help.

But then, maybe it was me. Maybe I shouldn't be so unnerved by this. Maybe he was just pretending. I was too close to all this history stuff, the ancestors were getting to me, maybe that was all. Maybe.

I kept an eye on him all morning, while the bread rose and baked. He seemed normal as he cheerfully washed, dried, and painted the bottom of the boat. He cleaned his brush in turpentine, then soaped it in the bathroom sink and propped it up to dry in the sun. He even washed his hands. Then he sat, drooling, and watched me take the bread out of the oven. He gobbled and talked at the same time, all about what we would plant today, how I should water while he was in school, which of the seed should wait on warmer weather.

He was fine. Not a trace of oddity, no gloom, no doom.

A delivery truck crept down the hairpin curves of the driveway just as we were finishing our lunch, and David and I took the pontoon over, watched the men unload the new mattress and box springs. They said delivery meant putting the pieces onto the bed and, obviously determined, hauled the bedding onto the boat, even held the pieces upright as we lurched across to the island.

One of the men kept cracking jokes about my 'mule-drawn' mode of transportation, and commenting on my living in the dark ages. I'd had enough of his snide remarks before we ever got to the island, and told them to leave the mattress and box springs leaning up against the outdoor light pole.

"Can't do it, ma'am," he said.

"I'm telling you to do it."

"I'm tellin' you, girl, boss won't like it."

"I don't think we'll worry, boys," I said sweetly,

"about what your boss likes, now that your customer is quite satisfied with your services."

For several seconds I thought he'd simply heft the mattress, and go on up the path to the house. Plum-colored shadows under his eyes seeped into his already ruddy cheeks, in behind his outraged, flaring nostrils. I put my hands on my hips and stared, curious, as several of the larger pores on his face gorged themselves on color.

"Hey, come on, Bert," the skinnier man said. "You said you'd help with all the deliveries."

Bert's gaze transferred briefly to the other man's face. He grunted, took his hands off the mattress and tipped the sides of his mouth up.

"Yo-kay," he said, and shrugged.

They went ahead of us onto the sloping pontoon pier and Bert nearly slipped, yelled back at me "Ya need to get this fixed, ma'am," and hopped onto the boat.

David and I grinned at each other and took our usual surefooted path, along the high edge of the lopsided pier. I ferried the men back to shore, thanked them for their trouble, watched the truck crawl back up the hill.

"What a turkey," David said.

"He did complain a lot, for someone who seemed so eager to help.'

"Don't need him. You and me'll do it."

All afternoon we planted peas, sliced the stored seed potatoes and hunkered them down in the earth. He outlined his plans for the garden: where the herbs went, where we'd plant flowers for the market. When we'd plant what.

"I hope you're this good at school work, David. Do you save any brain power for spelling?"

"This is easy," he said.

"Not for me."

"That's 'cause you weren't here, and I was. Reason told me what to do."

"Maybe he should have paid you ahead, too," I grumbled.

David grinned. "He did!"

I stopped what I was doing, and stood up. My back

ached.

"Gave me somethin'," David said. "Gave me somethin' valuable."

"What?"

"Somethin'. Said you'd pay me too, though, if we got the crops to market."

"That reminds me, David. If, and I do mean if, we get anything to grow, where do we take it to sell?"

"Uriah and Zillah always let Reason sell it over in the lot next to their store. Lots of people go on Saturdays in the summer and sell their stuff. Reason had the best stuff, though." David leaned on the hoe he was using to dig holes, and puffed his chest out. "*Me* and Reason had the best," he said.

"Okay, so I'm a stall-woman now."

"We got a big umbrella, and we got a folding table, and a coupl'a chairs. It's fun," David insisted.

"Right," I said. I'd seen a moldering canvas umbrella and what looked like a recycled, rusting old yard table, in the shed. Both of them should have been left to molder away decently and in privacy, at the dump.

We finished up for the day, and David put the tools away. This was fast becoming normal, I realized, as I locked the shed. He headed up the hill and turned to call back instructions, just as he usually did. I sighed, bone-weary. As usual.

"And tomorrow we'll do your flowers," he was saying. "On the island." He grinned, trudged the rest of the way up the hill, sprinted the last few yards to the top, and was gone around the bend of the road.

"Sure," I said, and dragged my weary body back to the cottage.

Maybe I was too tired to sleep well.

Calling the police had been a good idea, because I'd had plenty of nights completely devoid of disturbance. Unless those singing insects and all those "harumphing" frogs, coming in on the bass notes, counted. But the howler seemed to have been scared off.

Anyway, it was a weekend night, and I'd been seeing to it that David was a worn-out manual laborer on weekend nights. Since he'd been the weekend howler, I should have been guaranteed a good night's sleep.

Or so I thought. I kept assuring myself of these facts, each time I tossed in Reason's lumpy mattress.

It also occurred to me, one of the times I woke up, that perhaps I'd take the new mattress David and I had dragged into the spare room, trade it with this one.

Finally, it seemed to me, I was asleep.

I must have been sleeping, because I was walking uphill in a dense green woods. And I knew I wasn't, not really.

There were lovely smells, leaves stroking my cheeks, breezes whispering in my ears, the sounds of singing; they all combined in a refreshing rain of sensation that folded arms around my body, warming me. Then I was at the top, with a carpet of treetops rolling gently downward. A string of water winked far away, dove under branches, resurfaced over and over. I began running through the woods, leaping over moss and rocks easily, as if I knew every wildflower underfoot, every jagged, jubilent surface of the path.

Soon the string of water lay ahead, boiling wide like coiling ropes of pearls, all gurgling light and life and white-water dancing. The water seemed to rush up at me, and I couldn't stop running, running. Then my feet left the ground and began treading air, reaching for the surface, touching bare-toed, licking at it like tips of flame.

And I saw the woman. Smiling, at the edge of the water, eating strawberries one by one.

I knew if I awoke, if I so much as blinked a hint of waking, I would sink there in the depths of the white, roiling water. I knew I had to dance all night long, dance with a cascade of pearls, lilies leaping for air between their pads.

The woman put down her strawberries, reached out a hand, and the light reflected off the lake and crashed over my eyelids. Another beautiful day, another laboring day.

The dream dissolved like hysteria into weeping. All I

had left was aching legs and feet so heavy they fell to the floor, throbbing, when I swung my body out of bed.

I'd never get used to all this bending, and digging, and scrabbling in the soil. It had taken a full week of sitting at my computer, to get over last weekend.

Reason's clothes, the ones I'd worn yesterday, had been filthy, had gone directly into the hamper. I didn't have the energy to figure out the best way to make myself look as if I didn't care. So I wore my own jeans, dragged myself into the kitchen, made an entire pot of coffee.

One cup was helpful. The second got me off my butt and over to watch out the window.

Juda Kinzie and David came, right on the dot as usual. But they sat together in the boat, seemed to be having an argument. Juda Kinzie was wearing an old felt hat, like a relic from some decrepit trunk. He had on a wrinkled hunting jacket, the kind with rumpled-up pockets everywhere, and his glasses clung to the bridge of his nose, and bobbed as he shook his head. He looked completely different, intense, and totally focused on the conversation with his son.

Suddenly, he smiled. Dimples cut the long planes of his cheeks. A trick of light off the lake flashed on his glasses, off the gash of teeth, and he threw back his head and laughed.

I watched, almost mesmerized, as his hat fell and he grabbed it, swept his hat-flattened brown hair off his forehead, fingered the dark bristling mustache, grinned at David again. That flash of joy unnerved me. And dimples! My God, the man had dimples. He had laughter in him.

David jumped out onto the dock, and I watched warily as Juda Kinzie followed him. He was coming up the path, fast.

As usual, David bolted in, rambling on about something like he always did, energetic, flushing out words just as if he wanted to watch them swirl around in the bowl of the room.

I didn't seem able to hear. The words got garbled up in the rushing sound that was pouring through my brain. My face felt hot, as if I'd gotten caught eavesdropping, had heard something I shouldn't have heard.

And the man stood there and grinned at me. Close-up, the dimples were deep gashes on either side of his mouth. When he realized I was staring he laughed again, and his square jaw dropped down, his head made that tilt back again, and the glasses flashed light from the window behind me. God, he was attractive when he laughed.

It was my first coherent thought, and it steadied me. I put a hand up and wiped my face with it, as if it would help. I watched him take that ridiculous hat off, hold it politely.

"David wanted me to come in, to tell you he had to get off early."

"We're going out for dinner," David said. "But take a look at my dad, Belle."

"David wanted you to see my get-up."

"Yeah. See? Dad can wear old clothes and look good, too."

They were making fun of me. I opened my mouth, but nothing came out. Instead, I felt my face go warm again.

"No, no," Juda Kinzie said, waving his hands. "It's not what you think."

"Dad and I think you look great in Reason's old clothes."

"I always wear this stuff," Juda Kinzie was saying, "my father's old hunting clothes — to go out in the preserve."

I watched him move the hat back and forth between his hands, and realized he was actually embarrassed.

"But David, well, he . . . he wanted you to see." He turned towards the open door.

I folded my arms across my chest. "I think you look great," I said.

His face went pink. I couldn't believe it. He'd stopped, smiled at me from the door, and I saw the flush.

"Want some coffee?" I said. I got up as casually as I could, walked into the kitchen, poured him a cup. He still stood at the door, twitching the hat between his fingers.

David looked back and forth between us with a sly little smile, and then bolted out the door.

Juda Kinzie seemed to make up his mind. He walked to the table, pulled out a chair, sat in it. He was tentative, as if he hadn't thought he'd get away with something he'd done. And he was smiling.

"So," I said, sitting down at the table. "You hunt?"

He shook his head. "No, no. I just walk around back there, watch the Canadian geese. Sometimes there's a heron or two."

"Sounds nice."

We smiled at each other, two teen-agers before their first kiss, I thought. Oh God.

"David told me I must have been rude. He said you only get mad at him if you have a good reason."

"Yes," I said.

He pursed his lips under the dark brown mustache. It occurred to me that it was my turn to be apologetic. But I was too busy watching his mustache conform to the planes around his mouth.

He tried again. "Thank you," he said, "for being so good to my son."

I remembered my concern for David, and bristled. "Your son is easy to be good to," I said. "Anyone would appreciate him."

He frowned, and reached for his cup.

"Really, he's phenomenal. He's painted the boat, got the whole garden planned out, did most of the preparation." I looked down at the blisters on both palms, blown full of fluid overnight. "He's amazing. I couldn't have done it without him. Wouldn't have done it . . . "

He reached over and took one of my hands. "Let me see," he said idly. "Good Lord, that looks bad."

For just a moment, I could feel nothing but my own hands. A banging pain had erupted in my palms, seemed to be playing leap-frog just under my skin.

His right hand reached, and a long finger touched the skin near one of the bubbled-up blisters. His whole body seemed poised, all his energy concentrated in examining my hand.

I looked at his face, so close, so intent. The black stubble he hadn't shaved, the smell of him, the brush of dark brown over his upper lip were fascinating. I watched his eyes travel up from my hand and over my mouth, up, till we both were caught, stunned into a shock of muffled terror, reactions delayed just a moment too long.

I don't know which of us was frightened more. I only know I recognized his fear, because it was so like my own.

He dropped my hand and gulped at his coffee, got up. He practically ran to the door. Then he collected himself and said a proper good-bye, thanked me for the coffee.

He closed the door and I laughed aloud. I'd just seen total lunacy in both of us.

For the first time it occurred to me that perhaps it was me and not John who had been afraid of commitment. I, who'd run from love. Why else would I ever have been attracted to John? Perhaps we're drawn to what we need at the time. Perhaps I'd wanted a different kind of security, one that protected me ultimately, from love, from real caring.

I knew with Juda Kinzie there'd be no tolerance for games. If . . . if he played, he played. But if he loved, he loved.

David and I took that day a little easier. We planted flowers around the house; the cleome, the four o'clocks and moonflowers in what had been the tangle of weeds behind the shed. Then I raked loose soil over them while David went across on the pontoon, and watered the seeds we'd planted on the hillside. I was still puttering in the dirt when he got back to the island.

He watched me for a minute and then volunteered, "Got some boat paint left. I'll paint the rest of the rowboat. Work on the raft next weekend."

"You don't have to do *everything*, David," I said. "I'm working you too hard."

His face flashed panic. "No you aren't," he said quickly.

"I'm glad you're taking off early, today."

"I won't, if you need me."

"David, for heaven's sake. Go out to dinner, have a good time."

"My birthday's next week, is the reason. Dad wanted to do it on the weekend, so we could stay out a little later. But I don't have to." David put a little pucker of disapproval on his lips. "Besides, Jennifer will be there."

"Oh." Jennifer again. "David, why didn't you tell me it was your birthday? You should be taking the whole day off, going out in the woods with your dad."

"Nah. I like being here." He grinned at me. "You don't mind?"

"Of course not."

We were interrupted by an "Ahoy there!" of all things, and both of us jumped, looked up to see Uriah Sopwell, the shopkeeper, coming around the corner of the house.

I gave one last tamp to the earth over the moonflower seeds, got up off my knees and began to put my hand out. It was covered with dirt, so I wiped it off on my jeans.

"Planting, are you? Good, glad to see it. Reason loved his flowers and such," Mr. Sopwell said.

"He did?" David and I looked at each other.

"Place was always decked out, come summer." He smiled, showed off a glint of gold in his teeth. "Here now, I didn't come to be talking over old times, young lady. Came to drum up support."

"Certainly," I murmured. "Anything I can do . . ."

He beamed down at me.

"Now, I'm not talking Veterans of Foreign Wars, or the Papakeechie Beautification Committee. Although, young lady, I understand your father was a Vet — you're welcome to join, down at the Legion." He flashed his gold tooth again. "And you're sure pretty enough to be on the Beautification Board." He winked.

I blinked up at him, realized that without his canvas apron on his clothes exposed a bowed-in chest, as if he was sentenced to perpetually bend, to look people in the eye.

He smiled, looked around at the heap of decaying weeds, the upside-down rowboat.

"No, I'm here to lobby, for personal reasons." He

laughed out loud, bending his tall frame backward with the effort. "Reasons — that's good."

"Mr. Sopwell," I said. "Are you running for an office?"

He controlled himself. "Well, that I am, young lady. You're very — what's the million-dollar word? Astute, yes. You're very astute, to have made the connection."

I sighed. "What are you running for, Mr. Sopwell?"

"Uriah, young lady. Call me Uriah, like I told you at the store." He smiled again, and stuck out his hand.

I swiped at my jeans once more, took his hand, gave it a little shake. It was limp, as if he hadn't expected a firm grip, then the fingers tightened.

"I'm Belle. It's been awhile since I was a young lady, Uriah."

He laughed loudly, and I caught on. This was a comedy routine. I laughed with him, for a moment.

"Uriah. What are you running for?"

He spluttered to the end of his merriment, and blinked at me.

"Papakeechie Preservatory, Belle. I think we're in need of a strong hand, and I mean to provide just that. Your grandfather was of the same mind, I might add."

"I'd be glad to support you, Uriah, if I agree with your assessment of the issues."

Behind me, David made a small snorting noise, and jogged off with a watering can to the spigot.

"Glad to hear it young, er, Belle. Glad to hear it."

"What are the issues, Uriah?"

He looked down at me, and a frown smudged his eyebrows.

"Well now, not being here too awful long, you may not understand, exactly. They're complicated, tied up in our history hereabouts."

I smiled sweetly. "I'll do my best," I said.

"You see, Belle, we've just come off a long battle with the government. It cost too much and dragged on too long. Now that's all water under the bridge, but I never did agree with Mr. Hayes — that's Tom Hayes, and Sally, over to the west side of the lake. Don't think he handled it properly. To our best interests, you know.'' He nodded at me.

I tried not to smile, but I couldn't help thinking of Sally-of-the-orange-drawers-Hayes, and how she tried to get the bachelors of the lake married off, according to Adam. I managed a solemn nod to match Uriah's.

"Are you in favor of making the lake public, Uriah?''

His eyes gave him away.

"Well now, I see you know a bit about it,'' he said.

"I've got no problem with the verdict. Fair's fair.''

"Fair's fair?''

He shrugged. "Your grandfather thought things should have been handled different, that's all.''

"Is that so?''

"Why, sure.'' Uriah put his hands on his hips, swiveled around to take a long look at the island, the hillside away over the water. "Why else would he have set up his will like that? He must have figured public access was the right thing to do. Reason had views on ownership, you know.''

"You must have been a good friend to my grandfather, Uriah, to know him so well.''

He glinted a flash of gold at me. "Me and him were old buddies. Told me to look out for you, he did.''

"And he was going to help vote you in, as what, Uriah, President of the Preservatory?''

"That he was, Belle.''

"When is the election?''

"Come next spring, term's up for Tom Hayes. Then he'll see what kind of brew he's cooked up.''

"Early, isn't it Uriah, for campaigning?''

He grinned again. "Never too early for a veteran to be looking out for the mess his country's in. Now wouldn't your daddy have said the same, Belle?''

I cocked my head. "I don't know, Uriah. I never knew him.''

"Well, you can count on it, Belle. Your daddy, old Reason, they were never johnny-come-latelies. Knew your daddy, I did, before he went off to Indianapolis with Isabel.

Had spunk, your daddy did. He'd have done the right thing.''

"And what is the right thing, Uriah?''

He stared at the ground, mashed an earthworm with his heavy boot, dragged his wide, clear blue eyes back up to my face. "Why, public access, ma'am. It's for the good of the country, for the good of the lake. Can I count on your vote, come next April?''

"I'll think about it, Uriah. I haven't been here long enough to form an opinion.''

"But you'll be here, come April?''

"I plan on it.''

"Then you'll be doing the right thing, Belle. Doing what old Reason wanted for you, and you've got a vote coming." He stared again at the perimeters of the property. "Valuable land, this. You could turn a dollar easy, when you've put your time in. Could go anywhere, do anything.''

I couldn't believe my ears. "Uriah, you just said Reason wanted me to stay.''

"Why sure, Belle. Better for you to realize the profit, than the Preservatory, after all. But he knew this was no place for a girl, not for living on in. Hell, no one knew better. Why, didn't your grandma up and leave?''

I nodded. "But, why did he go to so much trouble, to set it up so I had to stay?''

"Oh, that. Why, he wanted to see you grounded, girl. See you got off to a start, with your family behind you. Aren't you writing the history, and all?''

I nodded.

"How's it coming?''

"Okay, I guess.''

"Now Reason's history, that was important to him. You do a good job for him, you hear?'' He smiled, a paternal, melancholy sort of smile, and added, "Reason had lots of kinfolks, I know. Used to tell me about them. Hell, back then folks raised kids like crops, to help on the farm, you know.''

I nodded again. Maybe your folks did, Uriah, I wanted to say.

"I'll be off then." He lifted a finger, and shook it under my nose. "You're a lucky girl, to have a grandpa concerned for your future. Look out for Reason's interests, now, don't up and sell to the first Tom, Dick or Harry comes along. I'll be glad to find a buyer. Matter of fact,' he said, considering, "I know just the man."

"You do?"

"Why sure, Belle. You leave it to me."

He glinted his teeth at me again, turned and headed around the corner of the house. I followed him, reminding myself to check the sound his oarlocks made. But he was heading for a rubber dinghy, bobbing next to the pontoon. He waved, hopped onto the pontoon, crossed it and swung his long legs over the railing, folded himself up like a puppet on strings, and dropped into the tiny boat. It belched, rolled, and Uriah grabbed a miniature paddle and stabbed through lily pads into the muck at the bottom of the lake.

"Oh hey," he yelled. "You want the paper? Told Brian, that's my boy, that I'd ask."

"Sure," I said.

"Fine. I'll see it starts first thing in the morning. Box'll be up at the road." He waved again, slipped a short rope off the pontoon railing, tossed it in the dinghy and began paddling away.

I stared after him.

"What did he want?" David asked.

"You know, David, I thought I knew. But now I don't."

David snorted. "Yeah," he said. "Reason couldn't stand him. Said he never could figure out where the hell he was coming from."

"Don't swear, David. But you know, I think Reason was right."

I watched as Uriah reached the shore and shoved himself into the shallows. He stepped out and pulled the rubber boat after him, dragged it bouncing behind him uphill — the cocky orange plumage of a strange, flightless bird.

"I'd like to know," I said, "how he got over here without us seeing him."

David shrugged.

We grinned at each other, and I reached out and messed up David's hair. A bit of pink came into his cheeks, and he turned away.

"Gotta go," he said.

I took him across to the hillside, and as I pulled on the overhead wires I wondered at our similar conditions, wondered how much of David's neuroses were related to losing his mother. If anyone knew how that felt, I did. So often, David just seemed like a lost little boy, anxious to please, begging approval.

"Happy birthday, David," I said softly, when he jumped off the pontoon.

He laughed. "Yeah. Another day older, another day poorer." He jogged off up the hillside.

What? Was that something else that Reason had said?

Just a very strange day, I told myself, on the way back across the lake. Every time I thought I understood each of these situations, each of the personalities I encountered, I ended up dead wrong.

Uriah — he had a funny laugh, like a girl's, almost a giggle, really. And David's laugh was a deep baritone tumble.

Juda Kinzie. Well, his laugh was like David's, boyish and deep, and this morning I'd found out just how his laughter made me feel. My fingers tingled on the wire as I replayed the scene at the kitchen table, watched his hands examine my blisters, his eyes focus again on my own. And then that spark of recognition that flashed, fatalistic, between us.

Oh, hell. I couldn't let myself think like this. I was lonely, I lived on an island, for God's sake. It had been, what, eight weeks since John and I . . . That was all this was; I was used to a very full, erotic, fulfilling sex life, and I missed it.

I jumped onto the pier and tilted, balanced myself to accommodate its slanting level. This dock had to be fixed, before it slumped entirely into the muck. Like me.

At least today, thanks to David, thanks to Reason, something positive had been accomplished. Flowers had been planted all over the island, the time-honored female equivalent of staking a claim. Like a dog marking off his territory, I thought. Now all I had to do was wait for the flowers to grow, and I'd no longer need Reason's gun to tell whoever it was who'd tried to scare me, tell them I was staying.

Yes. Despite Uriah, who hadn't known Reason at all. He thought Reason always planted flowers on the island. I nodded at each of the new beds we'd made out of weedy plots, and smiled at them. Reason would not have left seeds for me, set tulip bulbs out, found a boy to help me, if he'd wanted me to sell his place.

Uriah seemed to think that Reason came from a line of big families. But I knew I was the last of a series of aging parents, who'd produced only one seedling, late within each of their seasons.

This bit of land had trickled down to me, and Reason had wanted me to work it. He'd got me all dug in for a fight, left me his gun, money in case I had none, heirlooms to prove my pioneer stock, a battalion of dead relatives to comfort me. Plenty to do, too; plant the market garden, write the history, care for his disturbed young friend. He'd left me more than enough to build a life. And everything he left me required an effort, a token sweat to water the land his ancestors — our ancestors, had worked.

I'd start in the morning. I'd rework without bias, the words I'd written. And I'd try to tie the cultures in my background together. I'd earn my keep.

I walked around the island, wallowing in the satisfaction of work completed, for the day.

Far out on the silent, late-afternoon, sunshine-dappled lake, a fisherman reeled in his line, pulled up his anchor and dropped it with an audible thwack, into his boat. He picked up his oars and rowed, oddly gentle. Dipping, quietly stroking, making for home, I suppose.

~ TWELVE ~

In eighteen hundred and thirty-five, John Hiram and Minerva McFarren MacKay arrived in Indiana, the nineteenth state formed in these United States. John was the son of David Reason and Angennetta MacKay, of Fayette County, Pennsylvania, and the brother of Clara. He came in search of a space in the wilderness where he could work and earn a living, for himself and his hopeful young bride. He came, too, to escape religious tyranny, and to embrace the liberty of mind available within the vast interior of a new nation.

In Pennsylvania, he left his young sister and a father and mother who had brought with them from Scotland a religion he was disinclined to respect. Thus, he cut himself off from his forebears and attempted to form his own concept of morality and of ethics, and to build his own brand of freedom.

John MacKay found, in the region known as the Indiana Territory, a people and a theology he could honor.

He found a tribe of the Miami Nation, a people in the process of being routed from their homeland by an ever greedy government. A people in turmoil.

And he found friendships, a fellowship in his reverence of Mother Earth. Theology became to John a matter of understanding, an unquestioning acceptance of the uniqueness inherent in life. Religion, God, became to him a matter of caring and appreciation for all men, and a love for the land, despite the conception of primitive, cultural aberrations he'd been raised with.

I stopped composing for a moment and looked up at the wall, to the face of John's son, Hiram, who'd written so well and clearly of his father's temperament. It had seemed unnatural, to me, when I read Hiram's journal entries. I couldn't imagine ever writing anything so flattering about any father, had never known anyone who'd done so. Until now. I studied Hiram's face, his deep-set eyes and intense gaze, the unyielding set of his jaw.

Hell, even his beard seemed prickly, rigid and judgmental.

I hadn't known my father at all, and it occurred to me now that he may have been just this intent on proclaiming, or renouncing, his father, Reason. Ben had told me that Reason and Hiram hadn't gotten along. Now it seemed that a pattern had been formed long ago, in Pennsylvania. It appeared to be a MacKay tradition to analyze paternal competence. A MacKay must approve, or stand firmly against the eccentricities of prior MacKays.

I found myself winking again into Hiram's light eyes, telling him out loud, that I must have been spared.

Men from John's own race were pushing acquisition of Indian lands. Men from his own environmental inclination, from within his former religious affiliation — men who had abandoned their own homes in search of their freedom to worship — were instituting restrictions upon that same spiritual necessity, for their native hosts.

It was a grotesque, perverse period in American history. Lands were given, taken back — concepts as foreign to the native inhabitants as theft is to a gift.

The people who inhabited these lands were accustomed to migration. They accommodated the seasonal changes, the variants of weather, even the contaminating influences of war among themselves. But never was land purchased, bought and paid for with so much bloodshed, for so alien a cause. Respect for the land, for the rights of usage, this was a motive with worth. But the white man's cause was inconceivable. And his cause meant death — the complete and total cultural eradication of an entire nation.

Many treaties were bandied about, so much flotsam on the fast-flowing stream that swept away any sense of self, of continuance.

The hunting grounds were slashed and burned, the hunters became the hunted. Annuities doled out by the government attracted flocks of carrion-eaters, to dine upon the souls and the monies of their prey. What was given by the government often traded hands a short distance away. Whiskey was obtained, quarrels ensued, and each man dead meant a loss of bloodline, a cultural genocide.

John Hiram MacKay watched men of his own race stalk the Miami. He'd left home to avoid oppression, and instead the seeds seemed to him to have trailed with him, sprouted here among his friends. It became his hope to merge these cultures, take the best of both and form life anew. And so he salved his conscience by securing sections, keeping access open to his neighbors in the adjoining reservation of Flat Belly, in the new-formed county of Kosciusko, in what had become the state of Indiana. And he absorbed the force of all the confusion, interpreted the bitter truth in dosages less dangerous to the culture he'd embraced.

In eighteen thirty-one a resolution of the Legislature of Indiana had requested an appropriation by Congress for the extinguishment of the Indian title to lands within the state. It was forwarded, the Secretary of War commissioned it, and it became an object of extreme importance: to extinguish the title of the Miami to their lands. After all, these lands were surrounded by white settlers. They were in the heart of the state, on the line of the Wabash and Erie Canal, then under construction.

This resolution took time to implement. Some negotiations were successful, and John MacKay watched the Trail of Death wind down in the summer of eighteen thirty-eight, when a fifth of the Potawatomi died en route to Kansas.

His friend Papakeechie, or Flat Belly, of the Miami, had been granted a fine government-built brick house in the Treaty of Eighteen Twenty-six. Thirty-six sections had been reserved for him at the edge of his dwindling village, near the lake that now bears his Anglicized name.

But in eighteen thirty-four a tornado struck, and flying bricks from his fine brick home killed his wife.

In that year, Flat Belly's name led all the rest of the seventy-two Miami chiefs who agreed to cede land to the government, including Flat Belly's thirty-six sections. His brother Waubee was the fourth signatory.

John witnessed the desecration of the timeless character, the soul of a nation. He, too, had suffered personal loss. His wife, Minerva, had died two weeks after their baby was stillborn; it was a cruel repetition of a common pioneer fate. In eighteen thirty-five he married Papakeechie's daughter, Henziga, whom he called Polly. In eighteen fifty-five, twenty years later, she bore him a son, Hiram. Within this one small soul, John attempted to place his dream of preserving a culture.

Or so said Hiram, John's son.

I pushed the print key and waited while the first pages of my new, improved history of the MacKays spit themselves out. As soon as page one dropped onto the tray, I grabbed it.

Within moments, I knew what Adam would say: It was prejudiced. The new, improved version still reeked of a biased viewpoint. This time, though, I'd managed to spread the bias around.

Hiram's journal had referred to Papakeechie as "Pahedketeha," just as David had. And David would probably approve of my less-than-subtle condemnation of those antiquated governmental mandates.

But I was dramatizing the story, fabricating reality to my

own tastes. And so what? There was nobody else to please. I was all that was left of this family, why shouldn't I write the history to suit myself?

I stood up and paced the room, looked out windows, idly noticed that the fisherman of yesterday was back. My words shouldn't count, I mouthed through the window at him. His head cocked slightly, so I pretended he was listening, and went on, aloud: "My words are only an interpretation. I should write these events as the people who lived them, saw them."

I sat back down, and stared at the still-chugging printer.

That's what I'd do. Instead of homogenizing their words, I'd simply transcribe them, let them write their own story. Then I'd interject with bits of documented historical data, cite chapter and verse. It would mean presenting opposing opinions, but what was black and white? What, historically, wasn't just a series of disagreement, misunderstanding? That's what war was about, after all.

I turned around and looked out the window. The man in the boat seemed closer, so I asked him, "Isn't it?"

His response was, apparently, to catch a fish. I watched him lean back in his boat and reel in, intent on his own answers, or the question of his own dinner. I smiled, and thought that Reason must have looked much the same out on the lake, often alone.

Reason's receipts would guide me. I'd go to all those libraries, collect copies of all the data he'd scribbled notes for, instead of merely condensing Hiram's account.

After all, Hiram's journal had also contained a recipe for squirrel stew, which hadn't seemed the least bit appetizing.

It was almost noon, Monday. Tomorrow, I could drive to the different libraries Reason had noted on all those receipts. I'd make another attempt at an unbiased history on Wednesday, and set myself a theoretic deadline. Maybe there would be a good start on yet another version of my history, by Friday.

Adam could be induced to read for me, if he'd been serious about coming over and bringing Saul with him. Maybe I'd call and invite them both, plan a little party.

I'd sacrifice two hours to the laundromat, tomorrow. Pick up some fancy beer for Adam and something Saul might like. I wanted to thank Saul too, for calling, the night he heard me screaming. I'd clean the house Friday morning, while I printed out whatever new material I had.

Deadlines forced my brain to jog along to the beat of a routine, and cheered me, made me actually giddy with optimism. I searched out the cord and plugged in Reason's ancient radio, turned it on, revolved the knobs until I found a station. And then I grinned at its hulking art deco face.

When I'd walked in the door that first night, this radio had been buried under books, its back ripped off. As if it had been angry ever since, a high-pitched scream trebled out, settled into a cascading series of sound, up-beat, melodic. A voice punctured the foam of the beat and I turned the volume up, did a few twirls around the room on my way to the kitchen to make myself some lunch.

The sun sparkled off the water, the coffee maker giggled at me. They were cohorts in a conspiracy, and I gave in. I put my sandwich down and danced again around the room. Even the next song, a love's lost, lyrical sort of tune, couldn't walk off with my mood. I thought of John, often. But by now I felt good about leaving, empowered by my action, and each of my days here made me less inclined to cry.

David had thought me happy, like Reason's 'Pollyanna.' I grinned and twirled once more. Maybe he was right. Maybe I'd been leading myself on, pretending to myself that I'd been betrayed. Maybe I'd been looking for betrayal all along, as if it were all I could trust. And maybe now I trusted me.

I turned down the volume, grabbed my sandwich and

walked outside to eat in the open air. Then I watered the new beds, went across to the hillside and watered more seedlings, came back to the cottage and picked up the latest, still-biased draft of my history. There was a drumming sound coming from the radio, a low, ceremonial chanting of revolution, of destruction.

Appropriate. I would cast out prejudice, destroy preconceived notion. I would rip up this draft before Adam ever saw it. And I would vow to listen to all the ancestors, pledge an open mind at the library tomorrow. I'd let guidance come when it would, instead of chasing it down, gnawing at the meat of an idea until it fit my guidelines.

I took the piece of mask from the mantel and began ripping, began yelling at the paper, dropping bits of the history onto the floor. The arrowhead-sharp ceramic point of the ceramic mask streaked across my left hand and I cut myself, squealed, and came to my senses.

I must be crazy. And with the howling, and the knocking on doors and windows, and above all with these dead relatives, corpses to — Adam had said — compile, I had plenty of reason.

"Okay, Reason," I said. "Here's my blood, your blood, and I'm giving some back." I let a few drops from my palm drip onto the heap of shredded paper on the floor, and giggled.

"I hope you're happy now," I added, and cleared up the mess.

That night I dreamed of being guided, through long dusky corridors of thought. It had to be like a hallway, because each time I had an idea, I'd knock on another door. Sometimes the door would open, and then I'd say my idea out loud. When that happened there'd be a laugh, dumped through the doorway like a bucket of water on an unsuspecting guest, and the door would slam shut. The guide would take my hand, lead me on to the next door, faster and faster. Soon it was *knock, idea, laugh, bang; knock, idea, laugh, bang.*

I was definitely going crazy. I opened my eyes, smiling, and heard the banging on the door.

I grabbed a robe and made my way down the hall, wondering if I was even awake. A strange male face ogled at me through the little diamond window of the door, and behind the face the light of dawn peeped in. The eyes in the face never blinked, watched me all the way across the room, so I simply stood at the door and stared back.

"Belle?" he said, muffled by the heavy old oak.

"Yes."

"I'm Brian."

"So? What do you want, Brian?"

He finally did blink.

"Pa said you wanted the paper," he whined.

"Oh." That Brian. Brian Sopwell. I opened the door, and he handed me two papers, bundled up in rubber bands.

"Here's today's," he said. "And yesterday's. You didn't pick it up. It was left in the box all night."

"So it's what, the crown jewels?" I shrugged.

"Somebody could'a come along and stole it."

"I forgot," I said.

"As long as I'm here, I'll go ahead and collect."

I peeked outside, around the slightly stooped, tall figure of Brian, who'd obviously inherited Uriah's lean frame. Light was beginning to glint off the water, casting a premonition of day onto the lake's calm, morning surface.

"A bit early to collect, don't you think, Brian?"

It was his turn to shrug. "Usually get it, first thing. Gave you a paper yesterday, but the money for the month's supposed to come up front."

"Don't you bill?"

He frowned down at his watch, squinted back up at me. "Put the envelope in with your paper, half through the month," he said.

I turned away to get my purse, and heard him step inside. Hell. I went back, gently shoved him out, said, "Give me a moment," and shut the door.

When I opened it again with money in hand, he looked like a kicked dog. "Sorry, Brian," I said, "It's a bit early for me, for company."

It must have mollified him, because he grinned and said, "That's okay, Belle. Reason was always a lot meaner, when he forgot to pay."

"I didn't forget, Brian. I just didn't know." I got ready to shut the door in his face again, and suddenly it occurred to me. "Hey Brian, how did you get out to the island?"

"Got my rubber boat. Keep it in the trunk." He grinned again, flashed his teeth just like his dad, minus the glint of gold.

Hell. No woman can be an island. It's not allowed, on Papakeechie.

I watched out the window in the predawn gloom, as Brian tucked his long legs into the pitiful little blow-up boat, paddled furiously for shore, loped up the hill to his car.

The papers were there on the table, when I got back late Tuesday.

I'd made copies of the notebooks, copies of all the articles Reason had scribbled page numbers and sources for on his receipts, from libraries within a thirty-mile radius. I barely had the energy to fix toast and read the damned papers.

I made sure I did one thing though, before I went to bed. I rebound the old notebooks in some plastic sleeves I'd bought, put them into new binders, and then slid them inside the secret door. It was the closest thing to air-tight that I could manage, and I crawled in under the covers at midnight, pleased with myself for making sure they were safe from further deterioration. I'd use the copies from now on, to enter information into the computer.

I was groggy, almost asleep when the howling started up. The weird dream of the night before, blending into Brian, banging on my door, forcing me awake too early and therefore tired all day long and now this, made me swear aloud. Then I lurched out of bed and ran for the hidden door, grabbed Reason's gun, took off out the front door in my nightgown.

I went tearing down the path to the little pier in the moonlight with the gun in a two-fisted grip — a finger on the trigger, my left hand aiming the barrel wildly. My bare feet skidded on the dock's planking and I swore again, loudly, and pulled the trigger. The noise scared me awake. I'd forgotten that the gun was loaded, didn't even remember cocking it.

I nearly dropped the thing in the lake. And the sound of it was reverberating through my eardrums, setting up a sort of chanting noise, audible. Or was it? I cocked my head, listening, willing the strands of sound to come again.

They came softly, in a gentle, female song. Pale, muted affirmation, lasting only seconds, drifting back to vapor.

Or returned home, to my own imagination. But the blast, and maybe the sight of me in my swirling white gown, waving a shotgun around, had startled the howler into silence. I must have looked like a madwoman.

And if the fool out there had a real grudge, I was also a sitting duck. There's always a bigger gun, and a person who knows how to shoot it. I felt like an idiot, ran quietly back off the dock and back into the shadow of the house, holding the gun carefully by its neck, like a dead duck.

After about ten minutes of what felt like astonished calm, I went back into the house. There was nothing to see and my own unlikely behavior had scared me as deeply as the howlers'.

I put the gun away and decided to leave it alone. The planting of flower beds was a much saner method of territorial defense.

Still, with the covers pulled back up under my chin, and my whole body shivering, there was an undeniable smirk on my face, a satisfaction somehow, to have met the fearmongers on their own turf, with a weapon they seemed to understand.

Flowers just might have been too subtle for the bastards.

~ *THIRTEEN* ~

Whack. Thwack-thwack.

What now, I thought, and jumped out of bed. I'd made it all the way to the door before I realized, it wasn't the door getting this particular pounding.

Thwack-thwack-ka-whack.

I could see a lone Canada goose through the diamond pane in the door, and then another taking off from the water, by the little island. There it was again, that noise, as a third slapped at the water, using its surface as a sort of liquid runway, smacking out a series of banging, lift-off notes.

But it was morning and time to wake up. Just a rather odd sort of alarm clock to get me out of bed.

I was awfully smug for a couple of days, at least until Thursday. And I was happy. The self-imposed deadline, indulging myself in the newspaper every morning and in music through the day: they meshed perfectly with a couple of good nights of uninterrupted sleep.

I began putting the words written in Hiram's youth into the computer, adding passages from the book of letters, which I'd photocopied along with Hiram's journal. This was the better route, I was sure, understanding their lives from their own perspectives.

I will practice the words my father speaks, Hiram wrote, only he used an unorthodox spelling of *speaks* and *words,* and his handwriting had been horrible. *And I must read of the Good Book, write of the Good Words. He say I am a good son. Mother say I am the boy-child she call Wasatch. This mean great beauty. She say I am like to the Great Pahedketeha, in his young blood. But I know he was very fat. Mother say he fat when he die, not when he was young blood.*

Today a man come to our home. He speak to Father, ask what squaw here for. Father say Polly good wife, no squaw. Good mother. Good food maker. I do not understand why that man call squaw and show teeth. Squaw is not good word for Mother. Squaw mean private part, I think.

It was difficult reading the younger Hiram's words, but soon they were better formed, the spelling precise, if antiquated. There was a lot here written in his youth that I'd ignored in the draft I'd just ripped up.

The entire copy of the journal, all the copied letters, would go into the index of my history, of course. The originals should be kept in an acid-free binder, in a dust-free, light-restricted environment for posterity.

Posterity? I had to have a child, to achieve posterity. I laughed out loud. Not likely, not without a sperm bank handy. Unless — maybe Juda Kinzie would volunteer? That made me laugh harder, picturing his look if I asked him for a donation to benefit the cause of MacKay posterity.

Mother says her Wasatch grow in beauty to match his name. Father says my name, Hiram, is a good name, an old word meaning most noble. He says is good name for boy child of noble family, who come from daughter of chief.

My grandfathers died before I was borned. Mother tells me stories of her father, who was proud to be called by the name Flat Belly, although it was not true. I can see the years when Flat Belly and Waubee were young bloods, in my mind. They were like a river running in setting sun, golden, sharp and fast, Mother says. I am sad not to know them. Flat Belly, he was full of the white man way later, in his house of brick. And Mother says he called on the spirits of our old fathers, and drowned in the tears of the ancestors.

Mother also tells of Monoquet, a Potawatomi chief who fought with Tecumseh at Tippecanoe on seven November, eighteen hundred and eleven. He was an old man in eighteen hundred and thirty-six, and died after several days with a young woman from a Michigan tribe. His tribe blamed her and she fled north, but was chased down and brained with a tomahawk by two young bloods of the old chief's band. His people then put his body sitting down, and built a crib around him with his dog, his horse and his weapons. They refused to go to their new lands in the west until their chief's body had fallen. Years went by and the chief sat on, and the people stayed. Then some white settlers grew tired of this, and poked at the chief's body and pushed it over. The Potawatomi then removed to their lands in the west.

Mother tells many such stories. She tells me I must remember. Sometimes, I believe she tells me stories to teach me of the good and the evil which lives in all things, in all men. So she tells me stories and says to me "look out for all things Maalaawee, all things bad."

Father is home again. He says he will stay, that he is old, and broken by the past. My mother does not believe he will live long with us. She says he will travel soon, to the spirits. Today I will help make his cyder and sugar, and put milk from the cow in, and bid him sit by the fire.

He must rest, and not go to see the spirits before they call him.

I shivered, and looked up the date of John Hiram's death. Hiram had been right. His father had less than a month to live. The year was eighteen seventy-one. Young Hiram was sixteen years old.

Poor John Hiram. He'd lost his first wife, Minerva

McFarren, who died two weeks after the stillbirth of their baby, a girl he'd named Christina. Difficult times. And the MacKay men had begun a history of losing women.

Except for Polly. The MacKays never lost her. She'd lived on, into the turn of the century.

Hiram married late, and his wife had died young. Isabelle hadn't died on Reason, she'd merely left him. And my mother . . . I didn't know about my mother. She'd simply left me alone, with Isabelle.

I flipped through Hiram's journal. The last entry was made in eighteen ninety-two, and was a fluid account of the matrimonial rites performed for him and one Anna Galway.

Hiram and Anna suffered a series of infant mortalities. I knew from Reason's bundle of receipts he'd been the one surviving child of Hiram's middle age. And Reason married late, into an age growing accustomed to divorce. His wife had left in the contemporary manner, dragging her young son with her. And then my father's wife left him, after he left her, to go into the Armed Forces. Good background, I thought, very good genes for matrimonial longevity.

I went to bed that night thinking that I might want to take my sperm bank idea seriously, and had some strange pictures in my mind when I woke up. Juda Kinzie, offering up a cup — John Schaffer, looking dismayed at the puddled contents of his spent passion.

At least I woke up smiling. I wondered what John would have said as he handed me the cup. "Cheers?" It made me laugh again.

It reminded me to call Adam and Saul, and invite them to come to the island Friday afternoon, for a party of three.

Adam and Saul hadn't been home, but Juda Kinzie called Thursday evening. He was pleasant, and said he wanted to thank me for letting David off early, last Sunday.

"I was happy to let him off," I said sweetly. "If I'd

known it was his birthday, I would have insisted that he take the whole day off.''

"Oh no, Belle. He would have been miserable. He's crazy about this job.''

Crazy. Well, *he* started it. "That reminds me . . . ''

"What?'' he said.

"Don't you think I should be allowed to know what the doctors say about his condition? I mean, in case of trouble?''

"What condition?''

I sighed. "David's mental instability, of course.''

"What are you talking about? Has anything happened?''

"Mr. Kinzie, your son is sick. We've discussed this before.''

"*Ms.* MacKay, yes, we have. I thought you agreed not to pry into a situation you neither understand nor have the qualifications to administer treatment for.''

"*Mr.* Kinzie, I'm concerned with his fixation on American Indians, *dead* American Indians.'' I shivered, remembering last Saturday, when David had told me I was the 'reincantation' of Polly.

"It was your grandfather, you know, who got him started on all that, told him what books to read.''

I choked, and stared over at the stack of papers next to the computer, all pages from books that I'd copied using Reason's rubber-banded receipt file. Everywhere I turned, Reason was there first, poking his head in, feeding David bits of nonsense that scared the daylights out of me.

"And I'm delighted, ma'am, that he shows an interest in the cultural influences of that heritage, instead of guns, drugs, whatever the current fad is, at school.''

"Guns? You said guns?''

"Yes. I said I was glad he had no interest in them.''

"And you, Mr. Kinzie, do you have an interest in guns?''

"Certainly, to a degree. Why?''

"A degree?" I said.

"Yes, my father taught me all the skills I'd need. He was an avid hunter. But David's not the slightest . . . Ms. MacKay, I thought we were discussing David's condition."

"Right." I pushed Tuesday night's realization that the howler might come up with more than war cries to shoot over the lake, out of my head. "Exactly what is his condition?"

"Nothing," he said, pouncing on the question. "He has no condition, no abnormal condition, nothing unusual for a kid who's lost his mother."

"That's what the doctors say?"

"Yes."

"They're wrong."

"Have you considered, Ms. MacKay, that it may be you, who's wrong?"

I hung up on him. I couldn't think of a thing to say without stuttering, spluttering with anger. I stomped around the room for a good five minutes, making "ai-yi-yi" kinds of sound. Juda Kinzie simply would not listen.

His face popped through my frustration, the look he'd had at my kitchen table last weekend; his eyes staring cannily into my mind, seeing my fright, reflecting his own. It occurred to me that maybe he couldn't see David's instability because he had his own, and for the same reasons. They both missed the wife and mother who'd died. Juda Kinzie, however, was dating a woman named Jennifer, and did not appear to be grieving. The face in my mind suddenly grew dimples and grinned.

I pictured him touching another woman, his hands feeling her blisters, throbbing through her torn skin, pulsing. The hazy person named Jennifer dissolved, and there I was, feeling his hands again for myself, weakening.

"Ai-yi-yi," I yelled again to the empty room. This was not working. He was an ass, plain and simple — couldn't hear the truth about his own son.

Another day older, another day poorer, David had said. Was that one of Reason's comments? He did parrot a lot of Reason's words. Odd words for a boy, to say about his birthday.

David's birthday! I'd forgotten to get him a present. It came out of nowhere, the answer: I'd give David whatever he could earn from one of the terraced gardens and I'd let him choose whichever garden he liked.

I sighed and dropped into the over-stuffed green chair, suddenly drained from the pacing, from the anger, relieved to have found a gift Reason would have been proud to give.

But sleeping was filled with confusion Thursday night. Thoughts swirled, faces — especially Juda Kinzie's — formed up in my head, debated all the aspects of insanity. I didn't need fake war cries to drift me in and out of nightmares, that night.

They came anyway.

The words I'd put into the computer that day deviled me, even the recipe Hiram referred to as his Mother's squirrel pot pie: *Skin, then put them clean into water and let to boil. Roll and cut your dough into two inch squares, remove the squirrels from the broth and put into the oven. Drop the dough in broth and cook. Serve the pot pie with hot potatoes, squash, Father's pickles, and berry pie or any other type pie for dessert.*

Father calls this 'Polly's pot pie,' but Mother says she is adding what Father likes to food her people have always prepared. This is squirrel soup, she says. There is a tradition, among her people, to have a soup always warm in the Council House, to serve and nourish guests.

Mother would give me the brains of the squirrel, a very great delicacy, but only if I had done my chores and letters.

Juda Kinzie reappeared in my dream, grinning at the cup in his hand. He offered it to me, threw his head back and laughed. I watched those dimples cleave both his cheeks as the *haw-haw-haw* rumbled over his tongue. The cup was full of squirrel brains, not sperm, and I burst into tears.

A woman came and comforted me. She stood over my bed and sang to me in words I'd never heard, in a tune low and melodic and loving. I thought she must be Indian, because she wore a sky blue cape like a European Madonna, but it was decorated on all its edges with round silver disks, illuminating skin which glowed warm, brown hair . . . I thought, no, Indians had black hair, and then I forgot to worry, and I listened to her song.

It was deep into the night when I woke to the howler. I just lay there in Reason's bed, and let him perform. I might have been too tired to chase down to the pier tonight, in my nightgown, with Reason's gun. Or maybe I was really asleep and thought I was awake.

It didn't matter.

The woman's song started up, from the pier outside. It grew strong and took on a deep, chanting tone, cast itself over the water to the howler. It must have reached him mid-way through a shriek, cutting him off, forbidding him access to my ears, letting my eyelids slide shut and dropping me back into dreaming.

And for the hog we used all but the whistle. Hog lung was cut into squares and browned on each side, covered with water and thickened with flour and milk.

Hiram's words woke me with a shiver at five in the morning, and I gave up on sleeping. I couldn't help wondering again what a "whistle" was, and decided to finish getting his words into, and out of, the computer. Maybe then it would stay out of my mind at night, and I'd get some rest.

Motivated, I sat at the computer in my bathrobe and finished transcribing the sections of the journal as the dawn washed over the lake, behind me.

I hoped Adam would come for the promised Friday critique. I'd bought beer for him, lugged it across from the car, and put in a couple of bottles of good red wine, Italian, which Saul might enjoy. Reason's bourbon was still in the cupboard, and the refrigerator was full of food from Tuesday's trip to town. I could both wine and dine any guests, even Ben and Maude, who might choose to appear this weekend.

I hit the print button and slumped with relief. I'd look it over and decide where to insert the historical data Reason's receipts had supplied. Hopefully, they would balance, and bring rationality into my biased viewpoint.

The new history began spitting out of the printer and I saw myself, twenty years from now, rereading, perhaps still learning from the experiences of my forebears. But I would never, never eat squirrel brains.

I let the chair squeak back, swirled around to the window, watched the dawn falling over the lake and set my next deadline.

On Monday, I'd begin transcribing the letters from the other notebook into the computer. When they were all in, I'd cut and paste info from them into the history, too.

Then I'd add the genealogical charts, and insert the documented historical facts I'd copied from the libraries. At that point, everything would be in the computer, so I'd simply cut and paste my way through summer.

I could feel a groan building up inside, when I realized it wasn't all that simple. I had to add the work of a market garden, a stall in the parking lot next to Uriah's store every weekend, and the summer was edited away. Like a boss with a perpetual time card, Reason had forgotten to schedule a vacation.

But today, today was for having fun, having company, I hoped. For laughter and music. Tomorrow, I'd see Juda Kinzie, have David here again. I'd take a break, try to learn the pleasures of the lake.

I'd forget about dreaming, and howling, and hog's lungs, whistles, and cups brimming with fluids. They were making me crazy.

All day I cleaned and primped the house, baked bread, watered seedlings. I switched bedding with the guest room, in the hope that bad nights were a direct result of an ancient, lumpy mattress. I showered in the early afternoon, washed my hair, found nice clothes to wear, listened to music and felt excitement building into joy. I was like a neglected puppy wagging his tail, hoping to get himself petted.

Adam came at three-thirty. I had the music up and didn't hear him knock. He walked in and tapped me on the shoulder just as I was taking the bread out of the oven. I screeched, and he bent over nearly double laughing at me.

I dumped the loaves safely out to cool on the counter, pretended to frown at him.

Still grinning, he grabbed my waist and whirled me around the room in a sort of old-time waltz.

When the song was over he stopped, let his arms slacken, put on a rueful face.

"Ah, towngirl," he said. "Music pouring across the water, from the old man's cabin. Such a nice change."

I took his hands and shook them off my hips, steadied my breathing. He just stood there, eyes twinkling, and tilted his head, appraising me.

"You need more exercise," he said.

"Reason's seeing to it that I get plenty. By fall, I'll have muscles as big as yours."

He extended an arm and made a fist, eyed the bulge on his arm, fondled it.

"Well, maybe not," I said, laughing at him. "Want a beer?"

"You bought me beer! Bless you, towngirl. Bless you."

He followed me into the kitchen, peered over my shoulder into the refrigerator. He held the door and nosed around while I opened the bottle for him, and he itemized the food out loud, naming the cheeses, the fruits and the sliced Italian bologna.

"Where did you find *prosciutto,* Belle? Saul will go nuts."

"I called the IGA, asked them to put it on their order for me."

He looked impressed. "And they actually did? Who's all this for, anyway?"

"Why Adam, you said you'd come. And it's my turn to treat you. Besides," I said, "I wanted to thank Saul."

"What for?"

"Remember? He called, that night he heard me screaming." And then it occurred to me, looking into Adam's bland, smiling face: The howler had shown up again. I'd even run down to the pier and shot off Reason's gun, but neither Adam nor Saul had called. Softly, I added, "I wanted to thank you both."

"You're having a party! For Saul and me! Belle, you should have told me. Three's too many for a date — sometimes."

I smiled. "I tried to let you know, last night. Nobody was home."

Adam tilted his beer up, swallowed, said, "Oh yeah. We were out."

"Where is Saul? You said you'd bring him."

"He's just getting home, I bet. I'll call and remind him." He lowered his eyelids, and drawled, "I wasn't really sure, towngirl, that I wanted him to come . . . "

I laughed at him.

"But, since you bought prosciutto, and beer, and you've got all this food . . . "

"I live on an island, Adam. I've got to have plenty of food, whether company's coming, or not."

"Are you sure you want me to call him, towngirl?"

I smiled at the look on his face, and drew out the moment, pretending to consider. "Oh well, why not?" I said finally.

"You've got no imagination at all, do you, Belle?"

"I've got enough to spot a fake, my friend."

He grinned, shrugged, and walked over to the telephone, accomplishing one of his swift mood changes by the time he reached it. I was almost disappointed. Play-acting wasn't all bad, especially when one had been spending too much time collating corpses.

"I'll tell Saul to bring something to stretch the menu. Squid? Do you like squid?"

"Adam, where's he going to find squid?"

"You," he said, rolling his eyes, "would not believe what he's got in that freezer." He dialed, and grinned at me while he waited.

I barely heard Adam babbling at the phone, stood there wondering, instead, if he and Saul had been gone Tuesday night, too. He hung up, and did a little dance, singing "Party! Party! Party!"

He stopped dancing to take a swig of beer, and then he smiled at me, twirled around the room again. He couldn't be the howler, he was too mercurial. And how could I suspect Saul, either? After all, Saul had called too soon after the howler quit, to reach a phone. But why hadn't they heard the gun at least, on Tuesday? "You said you went somewhere last night," I said, "but you act like you never get out."

"Ah, towngirl. We are starved for anything that passes for culture in these backwaters." He frowned at me. "Why you think we likee you?" he said, in an accent of indeterminate origin.

"Maybe you like me for me. Or for my *prosciutto.*"

"For your beer," he said, and tilted his bottle again.

I laughed at him. "Actually, Adam, I like you for your intuitive services."

He raised an eyebrow.

"I printed out another version of the history early this week. And I kept thinking you were right, last Friday, about my biased viewpoint. So I gave up writing about the political situation, and just put in pieces about the people. It's all on my desk. Will you look at it for me?"

The play-acting vanished again, and he walked over to the desk and picked up the stack of papers. "Sure," he said.

"Great. I'll run up and get the mail while we wait for Saul."

I left him standing there, studying the first page, and I practically ran to the pontoon, whisked myself across the water, and jogged up the hill.

Most of my mornings started by going up for the paper and the mail from the day before, moving the sprinkler if it hadn't rained in the night, watering another tier of the garden while I read the headlines. It was becoming routine. But this morning I'd finished Hiram's journal, instead.

I came out on the top, onto the road, stood in the afternoon sunshine and admired the neat terraces stretching down to the lake, and the sweet, sprouting new plants. They were indeed the fruit of my labor, and of David's, and I turned to get the mail in a satisfied daze of pleasure.

The mailbox had been the first thing I'd fixed, of Reason's, and its simple, sturdy shape always reminded me of my first day on the lake. It had signaled Reason's driveway, dangling like a drunk from a post.

I let the flap down now, put my hand in expecting the emptiness I usually encountered. But it curved around something cold and smooth, touched something furry. I yanked my fingers back and bent to look inside. A sweet stench reached me first, delivered the revolting news to my eyes. A styrofoam cup, and inside, a dead little mouse.

A shaking rolled through me, fast, and I stumbled to the edge of the woods, swiped my hands through a tuft of long grass, scrubbed.

Then I walked back to the mailbox, carefully gripped the bottom of the cup and heaved both coffin and tiny corpse across the road, into the preserve. I slammed the lid of the box shut, and shuddered again. And I looked in the plastic newspaper box before I put my hand in for the paper.

Then I was scattering gravel on the run downhill, my legs were shaking on the pontoon, and my first jerk on the wire dropped me to my knees. I got back up, forced my legs stiff, started walking the boat across.

Adam was waiting to tie off the pontoon for me. I centered my gaze on his face and buried the mouse in the back of my mind, long enough to make it to the tilting pier. Then I had to throw the rope to him, maneuver over the high edge of the slanting boards. As soon as I was on level ground, I dropped.

"Yo, towngirl. What happened? You okay?"

He was standing over me, reaching. He had a whole new look on his face, actual concern, maybe. "A-dam-damn," I said, and stopped, gulped, opened my mouth again. "Damn," came out.

"Yes?" He said, and started smiling, seemed to think better of it, dropped down beside me.

I shivered. "There was a mouse, Adam. A m-mouse in my mailbox."

"Got a cat in my hat, want to see?" He grinned at me, but his arm moved up, and he patted my back with odd little, hesitant taps. "A mouse, okay," he said, "was it dead, like?"

"It wasn't *like* dead, Adam. It *was* dead."

"Ah, yes. The bigoted buffoon has struck again."

His cheeks seemed to have sunk into his lower jaw, denting in, clenching, shoving his chin out. I ducked my head to look up into his eyes, squinted to see if he was taking this seriously.

"Now and then, Belle," he said slowly, "I find myself uncertain about the wisdom of living here. Naturally," he added, "there is nowhere entirely free of fear."

"What?"

"We, Saul and I, have ourselves been the victims of the bigoted buffoon. For our benefit, he chose to dissect a Great Blue Heron, a studly fine specimen of bird-dom. Left it right on our doorstep, lest we ignore his message."

I winced, and Adam continued patting my back in little quirky jerks.

"You, towngirl, have garnered only the smallest of reprimands. You must ask yourself, is this a comment on me, or on the company I keep?"

He meant it. I could feel the sincerity, something I'd only seen in Adam once — that day he'd rowed me around the lake and told me to stay my six months. And then I realized that he thought the mouse was delivered, dead, because I'd been seen in his company.

"Oh, I don't know, Adam," I said. I tried to smile. I'm good for a mouse comment, all on my own, don't you think?"

"Are you, towngirl? Are you already causing trouble?"

"Of course," I said, making my voice smug. I shrugged his hand aside, pushed myself to my feet.

We trooped up the path to find Saul, lounging in the doorway.

"Reinforcements," Adam hissed.

"Hello, Belle," Saul said. "It seemed you were having a private moment, so I went on in and put my dish in the oven. Hope you don't mind?"

Adam draped an arm over my shoulders, said, "He has a real gift, towngirl, for making himself at home."

"I don't mind."

Adam gave me another little pat, and then an abrupt hug. He stepped away quickly, turned around and stared across the water. Saul and I stood silently, watching his throat work.

"The Bigoted Buffoon of Papakeechie has struck again,

Saul,'' he said softly, finally. "Left Belle a mouse carcass.''

"*Cretino,*" Saul whispered.

''I know that word,'' Adam said, and threw Saul a quick smile, turned back to stare over the lake again.

''We all know that word,'' I said.

''I thought you both seemed a bit moody, sitting down there at the pontoon when I arrived. But Belle,'' Saul said, ''Don't take it too seriously. He wins, if you do.''

Adam had been scanning the lake, and he pointed at a boat that was anchored near the promontory, directly across from his house. ''Hey, Saul,'' he said, ''did you happen to see that guy, when you came over?''

''Yes, he was a bit farther out, though.''

''Who is it?''

''I've no idea,'' Saul said.

''For God's sake, Saul. The animal corpse guy could be anybody. You got to keep your eyes open.''

''I'm not in charge of watching the lake,'' Saul said, and shrugged. ''But I did notice that the judge is on his way over.''

Adam whirled, took a few steps so he could see around the corner of the cottage, and whistled. ''Oh shit! Belle, have you had your music up loud? What the hell does he want?''

''Cordial, Adam,'' Saul said. ''Remember, be cordial. He's a nice enough neighbor. You simply antagonize him.''

''He's the one agonizing!'' Adam insisted. ''He agonizes over everything, like it's his fucking duty!''

Saul sighed, and shoved his hands deep into the pockets of his pressed, cotton pants. ''Adam . . . ''

''Oh shut up.'' He stomped off, down the path to the good pier, where both he and Saul had tied up their boats. He stood fiercely, feet apart, facing the judge's rowboat.

The judge was making a slow processional out of his

rowing. He'd lift one oar, dip it in, lift the other. All the while he was taking in the island, the cottage and Adam, standing there, with curious, sporadic glances. The boat waddled forward, cross-hatching itself across the water.

"We'd better rescue the judge," Saul said. "I don't know what gets into Adam, sometimes."

"He thinks the judge looks over his bifocals, uh, funny," I said.

'Of course he does. Ever looked through those things? There's no other way to look through some of them." Saul headed down the path, added, "It's Adam who looks at things funny, and he doesn't even wear glasses."

"Yo, Judge, want a drink?" Adam was already yelling. "Got a beer, here, with your name on it."

The judge paused, let his gaze wander over the three of us, dipped again.

Saul took hold of Adam's arm and pulled him backwards, stepped in front of him. "Hello, Judge Farwell," he called out. "Have you come to meet our new neighbor?"

The judge nodded.

He was close enough, now, to look around for a space to slip his boat in. Except that my back door dock was already crowded. He dipped and pulled again, and then he started a slow backstroke shuffle, running in place in a race with turtles.

"Shall I move a boat over, tie you off?" Saul asked.

"No, not to worry, Saul. Just here a moment, to say hello to Reason's girl."

I stepped up next to Saul and cleared my throat. "I'm, ah, Reason's granddaughter," I said. I'd almost admitted to being Reason's 'girl.'

"Know you are." His eyes went up and down, peering over his glasses in a kind of myopic glare. Having taken stock of me, he nodded to himself. He grunted, moved his gaze over to glare at Adam, then Saul.

Behind me, Adam giggled. I looked over my shoulder and caught him winking at the judge, looked back praying that the judge hadn't seen it.

"Now boys," the judge said, unconcerned, "we'll have none of your games, here, with Reason's girl. You behave yourself, young man. As for you, Saul . . ."

I was right next to Saul on the dock, and could feel his arm twitch, but he smiled.

"Could use your help, tomorrow," the judge went on, "with Mrs. Farwell."

"Certainly," Saul said.

"That's fine then. Well, Belle, wanted to welcome you here, to the lake."

"Th-thank you," I said.

"Come to visit, when you can. My wife would be pleased to meet you."

He actually smiled, and his eyes crinkled at me above his glasses before he dipped and turned his boat, creaked one oar, then the other into the water.

"Whew," Adam said under his breath.

"What is the matter with you, Adam?" Saul demanded.

"Offering the judge a beer."

"Loosen him up?"

Adam laughed lightly, and the noise joined the sounds floating across the water: *smack, ha-ha, creeeak, splutter, smack, creeak . . .*

I stood on the dock, staring after the judge. "You know," I said slowly, "The judge has the only boat on the lake that hasn't had its oarlocks greased."

~ *FOURTEEN* ~

In the morning I was showered, dressed in the best-looking work clothes I could find, had the bread dough proofing for David, the radio on softly, and was on my way across the lake to fetch the paper by seven-thirty. I practically danced up the hill.

I'd fixed a big bow on a stick and bent down to push it into the ground, on my way uphill. David could choose whichever terrace he wanted, and move the stick to mark his territory. I wondered if he'd want me to make him a cake. I wondered if I *could* make him a cake.

Sure I could. I'd given my first party last night, until Saul got a call on his portable phone, and had to run off.

I remembered Adam making a grab for the phone as Saul put it back in his pocket. Saul had slapped his hand away.

"Saa-wal, no," Adam whined. "You're off duty. Let Randy take this one."

"She's not Randy's patient, Adam. You know that."

"God. You're such an upright piece of manhood."

Saul smiled. *"Assolutamente."*

"Saul!" Adam hissed. "There's a lady present."

"Cretin, I said 'absolutely'."

"I can understand English," Adam had said.

I'd managed to find out, later, that they'd gone over to Lake Wawasee, Tuesday night. I smiled at all the fuzzy, green sprouting things on the terraces, and remembered

Adam's tale of planning this year's 'shooting of the breeze' party, with a friend. And that they'd gotten home very late.

I told him that I'd done some shooting myself, that night.

He'd gotten serious immediately, and I'd been dragged down to the dock to see if I could show him which part of the lake the howling had come from. After that he'd gone home, and I realized too late that I'd never thanked Saul for his phone call, the night he'd heard me scream.

I went back across with my paper now, thinking how much fun it had been having friends over, gobbling up conversation. Saul had managed to spice up dinner with his squid, served in an Italian sauce made of, predictably, onion, garlic, olive oil, mushrooms and tomato.

At eight o'clock on the dot, I was outside plucking weeds from my new flower bed near the short dock, looking for David and his father.

The ladies went by on their paddle boats, three abreast and chatting, sipping from those wide-bottomed mugs.

I remembered the judge's welcome, figured I could use all the friends here I could get, and made an attempt. I waved, called out: "Good morning."

The woman in the middle nearly dropped her cup in the water, recovered, began steering close to shore. She had on a house dress of sorts, and her plump thighs peeped with every stroke of a pedal. Mrs. Hayes of the orange drawers? I smiled.

She must have mistaken my thoughts for honest good cheer. She called out a greeting, nudged the crony on her right closer to the island.

I'd never before been the kind of person who thought about people's underpants, and I was embarrassed enough to try to be gracious. I waited, and the three boats plodded closer.

"Hello there!" she said, beginning a backpedal, humping a quick forward stroke and then another backpedal.

She was running in place and needed it, from the looks of the oversized house dress, the skyward tilt of the unoccupied side of her boat.

I controlled my grin, wondered if Reason had been so cruel.

"You're the old man's granddaughter?"

I nodded. "I'm Belle MacKay." At least she hadn't called me Reason's 'girl'.

She gestured right. "This is Jeannie DeVane, and here's my friend Mary Cott; she's just here for the summer. Jeannie and I live here year-round, though." She took a breath, rushed on. "We've seen you about the place, this spring. I'm Sally Hayes. Knew your grandpa."

I choked. I'll bet you knew him. Knew him well enough, anyway, to steer clear of his target practice.

"I'm glad to meet you," I said primly.

The ladies looked at each other. Mary was slim and pretty, in a light-weight running suit. Jeannie was plumper, with shorts and a sturdy jacket, sensible shoes and yellow socks. All three ladies had primped and curled hair sprayed onto their heads like helmets, but Jeannie's had a blond cast that matched her socks.

"We get around," Sally said. "If you have any questions, just call Jeannie or me."

"Sally's husband heads up the Papakeechie Preservatory," Jeannie said, in a gravely voice.

"Jeannie here handles the Beautification Program," said Sally.

"We can always use help with the Beautification Program," Mary said.

I was supposed to ask how I could help, I realized.

"There's a bake sale coming up . . . " Mary added.

"Well," I said, "I'm getting better with bread."

"Lovely, dear," Sally said. "Not at all like your grandpa, are you?"

"I'm afraid I didn't know him."

The three exchanged glances again. Jeannie snickered, and covered it quickly by taking a sip from her mug.

Sally clamped her pink-tinted lips tight, forced a little smile.

Mary said, "Nice meeting you, dear. We'll call about the sale." She began paddling away, and Sally and Jeannie nodded at me and took off after her, taking up their positions; Sally centered and heading the flotilla, the other two forming a wide arrow in the water.

I could hear the muffled voices drifting back in their wakes. "They aren't so bad, Reason," I said aloud.

No one else was on the water. From where I stood the little island blocked my view of Juda Kinzie's house, so I wandered around toward the pontoon dock and scanned the empty water there. I pulled a few weeds from the new flower bed on that side of the island, and finally went back into the house.

The bread was ready to punch down, knead slightly and put into pans. I worked on it, and kept glancing out the window, wondering why David was late. Wondering why I felt duty-bound to carry on Reason's antagonism towards the coffee klatsch ladies. It was a defense mechanism probably, a barrier I put up to keep from getting close to anyone. I slapped lumps of dough into the waiting pans, told myself not to fight with Juda Kinzie.

There was a pattering sound outside, and David shoved open the door, grinning, followed by his father.

"Sorry I'm late," he said. "Stayed in town, last night." He ran over, sniffed at the bread I was about to cover, and took off out the door.

Juda Kinzie cocked his head at me, and leaned against the door frame.

"Coffee?" I asked, and turned too quickly for the cupboard, grabbed a mug, headed for the coffee maker fast enough to bump into the counter, yelped.

"Sure," he drawled. "Are you all right?"

I nodded, kept my back to him, concentrated on pouring. I heard him walk across from the door, pull out a chair at the table, scrape it over the floor.

I held the mug with both hands, set it down in front of him carefully. Then I turned quickly and checked the bread, opened the cupboard doors and began putting the dishes from last night away.

"It looks as if you've had company."

"Yes," I said, but the word sounded squeaky. I cleared my throat and added, "I had two of the neighbors over, for dinner. Adam and Saul. They live in the cabin on the peninsula. Do you know them?" Awfully long-winded. Shut up, I thought.

A sipping sound stirred up the silence.

"Adam and Saul?"

It was the slyness in his voice that calmed me down. I walked to the table, sat down across from him and looked him in the eye. "Yes," I said.

"You had a party, with Adam and Saul?"

He asked it innocently enough, with wide-open eyes and brows that tipped up over his glasses.

"Yes," I said.

He shrugged, tipped his cup and took a sip, set it down and smiled at me.

"That's nice," he said. "By the way, I thought you'd like to know I took David back to see that specialist in pediatric psychiatry, the one he went to last year."

"Oh?"

"Yes."

It was his turn to be nervous. I watched as he squirmed a bit, in his chair. He cleared his throat. I waited.

"That's why we're late. We stayed in town to see Dr. Monroe last night. Late hours on Fridays, you know."

I nodded.

"He, uh, he wants to see him again."

It was my turn to raise my eyebrows. I took full advantage.

"It's perfectly normal, you know, this delayed type of reaction. Dr. Monroe said so."

"Ah," I said.

"It's simply a sort of role-playing, an acting out. It releases repressed grief."

"So. I decided to be more helpful. "The doctor decided there was cause for some concern?"

"Well, perhaps a little."

"Hmmm," I said.

"Nothing too serious."

I jumped up from the table, put my cup and saucer in the sink, reminded myself not to get mad, not to fight with Juda Kinzie. At least he'd taken David back to see the doctor. David walked in, right on time, and grinned at each of us.

His father scraped the chair backwards, over the floor, got himself up to his feet. "I should go," he said. David dogged him out, and slammed the door.

I slumped into the nearest chair.

David didn't let me off easy, that Saturday. We'd dragged the old raft, with its four different-colored barrels, its cement-filled, coffee can anchor out from behind the house last week, before pulling the weeds and planting the flowers. Now it sat humped near the edge of the island, bleaching the grass underneath. So David came slamming back into the house with a verbal list of chores, and moving the raft into the lake was first.

"But how?" I said, remembering the spiders I'd found under it, the shoving, grappling with the raft's weight.

He rolled his eyes. "Got the rowboat ready. So we get it in the water and we tow it out."

"It'll sink," I said.

"Geesh. Come on, Belle."

He brought me Reason's old waders, dripping with tufting, snagged webs from the residents of the shed. He brushed at them casually, wiped his hand on his shorts. And then he expected me to put them on. I peered into the black holes and carried them out to the dock, rinsed possible spiders out of them before I stuck my feet in.

Then we hauled and shoved and dragged till I saw the wisdom of having a man around, on occasion. I stood in the water and pulled, David pushed, and finally the thing fell over the edge of the breakwater and slapped water in my face, rode the wave it made, knocked me over.

David laughed, first. Then he grabbed the anchor rope and notched the coffee can between rocks of the breakwater. I pulled myself up onto the raft, dumped the water out of Reason's waders, wondered why I needed a raft, anyway.

Then we launched the newly-painted rowboat and towed the raft along behind, wove back and forth across the lake in front of the island, argued briskly about currents, depth, seaweed. Neither one of us knew anything about it.

"This is it," David said. "Reason put it about here."

That clinched the matter. Besides, I was hungry, and I'd waited all morning to give David his birthday present.

He tried to eat his way through my groceries, and at last I got him headed over to check on the gardens.

David saw the red ribbon right away, poking up from a terrace of bean seedlings.

"Pick a garden, David," I told him. "Pick any one you want, for your own. For your birthday."

He looked up at me.

"Go on. Whichever one you want, you get anything you can earn from it." I smiled. "I figured Reason would give you something like this."

He looked at his toes, scuffed at the dirt.

"What's the matter, David? You don't like my present?"

"Reason already gave me one, gave me one ahead."

"He already gave you a garden?"

"No."

He continued kicking at the dirt.

"What, then?" I said. I bent down, and peeked under his cap, realized his eyes were wet.

"David. What's the matter?"

He made one grating, throat-clearing noise, then another. "Some-something for you, too," he said to the ground.

I waited, already suspicious.

"Gave me something — something to give you."

It was hard to be patient, to let him get control of his squeaking voice. Reason's gifts were always so obtuse ...

"Told me not to give it to you, right away." He looked up, and added, "You won't like it."

I knelt down on the ground, took one of his hands and looked up into his teary eyes. "It's all right, David. I haven't always liked everything I've been given. Have you?" I smiled. "After all, I've just given you a bunch of work on a piece of dirt."

He choked out what might pass as a chuckle, and his face lost some of its sharp tension.

"So don't worry about it. We don't have to like every present."

"Not a present," he said.

"Okay," I said.

"Papers. Bunch of papers. And a letter."

"Reason gave you papers?"

"Nope. Gave *me* his silver fishing cup. Got a lid on it, and it's big — like this." He measured out space a foot high and several inches wide in the air, with his hands. "Said after I gave you the papers, I could put stuff in it." His face fell, and he toed the ground again. "Already did, though," he said.

I shrugged. "So I won't like these papers. So what. Thanks for warning me."

"Okay," he said, and smiled. "And you don't mind?"

I stood up, dusted my hands off on my jeans.

"You don't mind, I put stuff in, before I gave you your papers?"

"Well, that depends," I drawled. "What did you put in with them — a frog, worms maybe?"

"Nothing smelly," he said.

"Oh. Well, okay then."

He gave me a weak smile, and I reminded him to pick a garden. "Since Reason already gave you his gift, this is from me, I guess. A whole patch of dirt for you to turn into spending money."

He picked the bean garden, where I'd stuck the bow in the ground, and cheered up slightly. We worked side by side all afternoon, weeding, pruning out weaker seedlings, mulching around the strong ones, watering.

I couldn't help wondering what it was that Reason had put on David's scrawny shoulders. The papers must be awful, or frightening: death certificates? If Reason hadn't already been cremated and his ashes scattered, I'd have been tempted to dig him up, right now, and shake him. Damn fool. He had to have known about David's mother. Had to have seen that David was too young, too fragile in his own grief, to handle Reason's special mix of, well, of bullshit.

Damn. What was he giving me next?

I slept deeply, undisturbed by dreams, and there hadn't been a hint of the midnight howler for days. But I felt distinctly apprehensive, irritable, grumbly. There'd been no more dead rodents in the mailbox either, thank God, but I'd never shove my hand in again, without looking.

The sky was overcast, and there was a faint mist in the air. I could see by the damp, dripping hillside that it had rained in the night. I walked up the hill for the paper, thinking that a Sunday without sun was a legitimate excuse for grumbling.

On the way back across the lake a fish jumped, splashed

back into the water and scared the daylights out of me. I dropped the newspaper and it plopped onto the wet deck. So there it lay, getting steadily damper, blotting water around the fold of its meager bulk. It reminded me of the shallow, moldering motivations of the people who lived here, who didn't even have a decent-sized Sunday paper. Small-minded folks, who played childish pranks and made weird noises on the lake.

Back in the cottage, I flung the soggy paper onto the table and, chilled, sipped at my coffee before I thought to add sugar or milk. I spluttered, swallowed quick.

"Damn," I said aloud, and sat down, unfolded the soggy paper and stared at it.

Juda Kinzie knocked, opened the door, strolled in and over to the table. He sat down.

"Don't you wait for people to invite you in, in this part of the country?"

"Sorry." He smiled at me.

"I'm supposed to jump up, get your coffee?" I asked.

"Sorry," he said again, and grinned.

"Goodness me. Aren't we cheerful?"

"Well I am, anyway."

I frowned at him.

"I'd like coffee, if that was an offer. Bread too, maybe, with a little butter and jam."

I sighed, added an exaggerated, weary groan for good measure, got up and poured a cup of coffee for him. I smacked a plate on the table, just hard enough so that it wouldn't break, slapped a loaf of bread on it, handed him a knife. And then I sat down again, across from him.

He sliced a couple of thick slabs and looked up hopefully, said "Butter?"

"In the refrigerator."

He grinned again, got up and rummaged around in the 'fridge, came back to the table with butter and jam.

"David has brought over Reason's old trophy to show

you."

I put my head in my hands, and my shoulders slumped obligingly. Yes, of course. David had warned me, and now I wished he hadn't.

"Reason won a lot of contests, you know. He was quite a fisherman in his youth."

"Ah," I said, and watched him spreading butter over his bread, dipping the knife into the jam jar, dripping it over the Formica tabletop, slavering it on top of the butter.

"But this was his nicest trophy, and he was quite proud of it. I'm sure David's been telling you . . ."

"Hmm."

He shoved his glasses up on his nose, held the slice of bread in both hands and gave it a satisfied nod. He opened his mouth, closed it over a large portion of heaped-up, lumpy red globules. His teeth ripped the bread apart.

I wondered how he managed to act so boorishly at home, in my house. Next, he'd be wiping his face with his sleeve like David did, letting out an "Ummm," of appreciation.

"Ummm," he said. "Anyway, David says you gave him one of the plots, all he could earn from it.

I nodded.

He smiled at me, took another bite, chewed it up and swallowed some coffee. "Trouble getting to sleep, last night?" he asked, and prepared to take another bite.

David pushed the door open, shoved a tarnished silver trophy inside, and took off again. I heard him trooping down the path, singing a song to himself.

"Actually, no."

He smiled. "You look a little, well, peaked, as my housekeeper would say."

"And you look a lot like your son, when you eat." I gave him a look that should have made him aware of his manners.

He ignored it, opened his mouth for another bite of jam

and bread, chewed.

I sighed again, gave up on him and looked over at Reason's trophy.

David had left it lying on its side on the floor, and the rippled effects of oxidation winked silver to black, sly. It held secrets, secrets I wasn't sure I was prepared for. I'd spent my life blinking out my past, letting it tarnish, letting it rot and fester.

"You remind me of Reason," Juda was saying.

I looked back at him again, watched his cheeks collapse in dented craters, as he chuckled. He took another sip of coffee and I dropped a hand from under my chin, left the other to prop it up, tried to look idle, and waiting.

"Of course, David talked about him all the time, last summer. Now he talks about you. So, naturally, it would be obvious."

"What would be obvious?"

"Why, the resemblance. You're very like him, hasn't he told you? It's why he felt so comfortable with you, right from the start."

He felt comfortable with me, I wanted to say, because I'd dragged him out of the lake, kicking and screaming.

"Reason would have these morose spells, I guess. David always called them his 'old grump days,' and now it seems they're an inherited trait, rather like eye color."

He was teasing me. He leaned back, looked blankly across the table. All of a sudden, I realized that Juda Kinzie thought he knew me because of things David had told him. That would explain why he felt free to walk in, unannounced, make himself at home . . .

"I inherited his gun, too," I said.

"You are in a mood today."

"Mr. Kinzie," I said, "David really doesn't know me well yet. Even I don't know me well yet."

He grinned, and scraped back his chair. "Well then," he said," I guess the pleasure will be yours."

I watched him walk across the room, still cheerful, open

the door and wave at me, walk out.

My hand went up to wave back, but the door was shutting, and Reason's trophy rolled and clattered the few inches to the wall. I felt prickly, and shivered.

He was right, I was grumpy, had been since I got out of bed, walked the boat across in the foggy morning. The worst of it was that I wasn't sure why.

And what had I meant, when I said I didn't know myself? My memories were filled in with a foggy, pleasant lethargy, like pieces of a dream. Early in life, I'd developed a habit of reconstruction, building on all my events until they gleamed pretty under a haze of fabrication, like the frilly netting on a doll's dress.

Both my prom dates had been handsome and attentive. Neither of them tripped me, as we danced under the mirrored ball. They hadn't had pimples on their noses. No. And my father had never died, he'd probably just lost his memory and lived on, dazed, in some veteran's hospital. Mother, well, as soon as she knew that Grandmother was dead she'd be back, to gather me in her arms, smother me with love.

Grandmother. Reason's wife. Perhaps the papers had to do with her. She'd searched for Mother, said she loved having me but that every daughter needed to know her mother. I didn't. And I'd been a happy child. My friends would have killed off their own parents, to have the freedom I'd had.

John Schaffer could have slept in my room, with no fuss from Grandmother. She was always busy, and unintimidated by convention. She wouldn't have raised an eyebrow if we'd made love on her parlor floor. I remembered the Christmas she stayed home from Florida, and had invited us. John had not been able to get away and he'd needed me, to stay.

At least I knew, now, why we hadn't gone. Ever since the boys on the street had taunted me with their raping words, I'd been trying not to gloss my memories over.

And after ten weeks on Reason's island, I'd finally met myself, had begun teaching this self who she was, what series of ancestors had made her happen. So I did know, now. John hadn't wanted to meet my grandmother, because it would have meant skating too close to commitment.

I sipped at my cold coffee, glanced again, at the trophy.

I was ready. My father had died in the war. My mother had dumped me. My lover had never been a lover. I was ready.

David came in, on cue.

He darted odd, frightened looks at me, his eyes tip-toeing around my face, never connecting solidly with my own. He reached down and picked up the silver cup, carried it carefully to the table, set it down. His hands tapped lightly on the lid, keeping time to the dance of avoidance his eyes were doing.

"David, it's okay. I told you yesterday, remember?"

He unscrewed the lid, reached in and brought out a dirty roll of papers. They were twisted in the middle, as if someone had once wadded them up. He put them in front of me and patted them, gently.

I stared down at his hand, the fingernails pink and tipped with black from grubbing around in the dirt. Damn it, Reason. He's just a boy. Why him, why David? Why not Ben Beanblossom?

David's hand flitted to my shoulder, gave it a tap, too. And then it dropped and he stood there, hangdog and pale.

"Don't David," I said. "Don't worry about me. I'm not used to it and, really, it isn't necessary."

He cleared his throat. "Reason . . ." That came out squeaky, and he started over. "Reason told me to tell you, he wished he'd had you. Said to tell you he would have loved you, that he did love . . . love you."

A little blood came back into his face. I smiled. "He must have," I said. "He got you to deliver this for him. Thank you."

He shrugged. "I don't mind."

"Sure you do, David. Let's you and I face facts here. He was an old reprobate."

David grinned at me. "That's what *she* called him!"

"Who?"

He gestured at the roll of papers. "His wife."

So there was a letter from Grandmother, somewhere in this wad. I nodded at David, tried to smile.

He waved and whirled around, jogged in a trot for the door. He yelled over his shoulder that he'd check on the gardens, work on the weeding, the mulching.

Into the next piece of quiet came the sounds of the pontoon, sliding along its cable, rusted from the rain that had fallen in the night. My mind drifted across the small stretch of lake with David, in tune with that muted, rusty screech.

I poured more coffee, sat down and opened up the roll of papers fast, so I wouldn't be tempted to tuck them away.

Scanned quickly, the two death certificates on top weren't that much of a jolt. They merely documented what I'd always known, always hidden the knowledge of: Mother's, Father's deaths.

A flash of blunt memory darted out of nowhere. Grandmother was screaming at me, with a fury totally out of character for her . . . Shrieking: "You must believe me! It is true! It is!" It had been about Mother. And it had marked the beginning of Grandmother's period of extended travel with that big man from Saint Louis. I'd had even more freedom, then.

Mother's date of death matched that time. She'd been killed in an automobile accident, in Nevada.

It was hard to read. The papers in my hands were fluttering. I put them down, and then they only shivered.

Grandmother's letter had climbed up on top of the wadded stack. There was no salutation at all, it simply began, "You old reprobate . . ."

So David had read it. He'd probably read all the papers here.

My fingers were cold, and I curled them around the coffee cup for warmth, watched another set of shivering words form up:

You old reprobate,

I'll let you have them, but don't bother asking me for anything else.

She's fine. Leave her alone. We both know you're not capable of raising a child. Besides, she's decided that her mother is alive and I'm an evil witch who's lying to her. That should suit you.

That's all you'll get, so long as I live. But you damn well better keep your promise. She can't live her whole life in denial.

I did try to tell her.

Isabelle

Now I remembered. She'd told me Mother was a whore, in Reno. A prostitute. Prostitutes had to register in Nevada, and the investigator Grandmother hired had sent a copy of Mother's registration.

I remembered, now, that I'd been furious, had demanded that Grandmother explain the cruises she took, the rented houses in the south of France, the condo in Florida. And all those addresses I'd been given for emergencies. There was always a man's name heading the column. As the years passed, there'd been so many different names. I told her she was the same as Mother — worse — I'd called her an unregistered whore.

I told her that she was pompous and self-righteous. That Mother was only doing what she herself was doing, on a less acceptable level.

What women often did, just to survive.

And later that year, Grandmother had told me that Mother was found dead, in a smashed-up car, in a compromising situation. For once in her life, Grandmother had been shocked. Not that her daughter-in-law had gotten money for sex, but that she'd been caught dead at it.

I remember yelling that Mother was alive, that she was trying to keep her from me, that she was only dead to her. That someday I'd find her.

Well, here she was. And she was dead.

I felt myself shrug, dropped Grandmother's note, picked up the next piece of paper. A receipt from a landscaping company in Warsaw: Reason's best stationery.

Under the receipt, there was a copy of a hand-written treaty, dated October twenty-third, eighteen twenty-six. I scanned down the page to an ink mark, which pointed out the words: "Thirty six sections at Flat Belly's village."

I picked up the receipt again and saw my name on it.

"Dear Belle," it began. Reason had not directed any of his numerous receipts to me, before now. I put it back down on the table and my hands dropped into my lap, grabbed hold of each other and clenched. I stared at the paper, willed the words to steady themselves, to form up solid in rows, and I read:

Plant seeds of truth, and let them blossom. Fill your life with the grays and the browns of reality, moisten these with your sweat and your tears, and they will bloom with color.

My prayer is simple: that the spirit seeded by our ancestors will prosper and thrive always within you, and within those you bear.

I have missed the joy of you. Keep well.

                                    Reason Able MacKay

~ *FIFTEEN* ~

David turned the knob, pushed open the door slightly, and peeked in at me. The noise of the hinges squealed around the soundless cottage. His gaze changed direction, charted a safer course and landed in an uneasy shift, on his feet.

God, for the honesty of David's age again, before manipulation engaged the gears, the mechanics of survival. I ought to know.

I sighed. "Come on in," I said.

His glance wavered for an instant in the region of my forehead.

"Hey. It's okay." I stared until his eyes connected. "And thanks for the facts."

He shrugged, sauntered over to the table, dragged a chair out and sat. "Sure," he said.

"Facts are better than going around year after year, making things up, fixing everything the way you want it. I should know. I made up half my life."

He stared at the papers on the table between us. "Yeah," he said, finally. "Reason said you didn't believe. Said you needed to see 'em."

I gulped. "But David, he shouldn't have used you, to give them to me."

"Sure he should've."

"David, really. You had to know what was in that damned trophy. He had no business . . . "

"Did too!"

"David . . ."

"Nobody better'n me, he said! Said I was prob'ly the only person in the world could give 'em to you."

I leaned back in my chair, startled. Why? With Reason, there was always a hidden chore, always had been.

"Okay," I said slowly, "and you did a great job for him, David. I'm sure he was right. I just thought, well, everything in that trophy of yours, it's all lost. All negative, you know? All gone."

He'd stopped bristling, and slumped back. "All true, too," he said.

We looked at each other. I felt defeated, more by Reason's manipulation now then by the facts he'd managed to dump on David, to give to me. And I'd just begun to have some respect for the man. David's face was screwed into a hard-thinking, "how can I make her understand" kind of look.

"The trophy," he said, beaming, "that isn't lost. That was something he won. Want it?"

"Of course not. He gave it to you."

"That's okay. I knew you wouldn't like your part of the present."

I pretended to consider, smiled at him while I tried to think clearly. First, David's mother had died, and Reason must have known. Second, my mother had died, and I didn't want to know, and that was another thing Reason already knew. Third, everything he'd given David represented lost people or things — lost land, really, since that treaty was not the final one signed.

"Thanks David. I can't say I'm exactly happy about having the cold facts, but he gave you the trophy, and you earned it. It's yours."

He grinned suddenly, and I realized what a sacrifice he'd been willing to make. Reason, I thought, how could you? David is a gift, all by himself . . .

"David," I said softly. "You read Reason's letter, too?"

He nodded, and took an interest in his fingernails.

"He said, 'Plant seeds of truth. Let them blossom'."

"Yeah."

"Good advice for both of us," I said, with a great solemn weight in my voice.

He picked his nose, looked at the snot on the end of his finger, and wiped it with care on the inside of his jacket pocket.

I choked, spluttered, came up laughing. "David!" I yelled.

He grinned at me.

"Use a tissue!"

"Nah. Waste of trees."

I couldn't help it, I started giggling and gasping, like a drowning man flailing around in an endless sea. "What a nice package you make, David," I choked out, finally. "All wrapped up in snotty gift wrap!"

He frowned, waited till I had myself under control.

"Reason didn't say it that way," he said.

He pushed his chair back, got up and searched the kitchen while I was busy wiping my eyes. Then he came back and stood over me, pointed at the remnants of the loaf of bread on the plate, asked, "Who ate all the bread?"

I looked up at him, and another laugh got out. I shut my mouth on it, waited, stuttered, "W-well, your d-dad had a couple of pieces, I know."

"Geesh."

Either he wasn't nearly as relieved as I was, or his avoidance techniques were more developed than mine, at that age.

Relieved. Yes, I was relieved, to face the truth at last, to stomp on it, master it. I shivered, and let the giggles return to run the rest of their course, and my whole body relaxed. I leaned back in my chair and gulped air.

"I'll uh, make some m-more, David."

"Okay," he said. "Long as there's enough."

He seemed more cheerful now, and let his eyes hang around my face awhile before he helped himself to slabs of bread, slavered on butter, sat there chewing.

"So how's the garden?" I asked.

"Wet. Don't have to water."

"What'll we do, then?"

"You're supposed to tell me," he said, sternly.

"Okay." I thought a minute. "I think I need a vacation, David. How about you making the bread?"

"Really?"

"Sure. You like it so much, you should learn how."

"Yeah."

"Take that jacket off, though. And wash your hands — with soap."

He took to the job with enthusiasm, and I only had to yell at him once, about wiping his floury hands on the seat of his pants. God only knew what else had been wiped there.

While the bread rose, I put us both to work at household chores: taking the garbage up the hill, moping the patch of linoleum that marked off the kitchen floor, getting the ashes out of the fireplace.

By lunch we had the house clean, the bread cooling on racks — minus a hunk drenched in melting butter, consumed by a judging panel of two, pronounced worthy.

David puffed up his chest and patted his stomach. "Yep," he said. "Better than yours."

"Not a chance."

"You don't like it," he said, "don't eat it."

"Equal, then."

"Okay."

So we attacked it again, ate more than half of the loaf.

The sun had dried out the island a bit by then, but the hillside was still muddy, so we weeded just the flower beds around the house, made trips across the water to the mulch pile.

I'd had a mound of wood chips delivered, just for the cottage beds. David had insisted we use Reason's huge lump of decayed grass clippings, old leaves and rotting seaweed to mulch the terraces.

While we were hauling another load of the wood chips across in the middle of the afternoon, Juda turned up with Adam. They'd already made themselves at home, and sat like a couple of slugs watching us work, sipping at beer, offering advice now and then.

"Careful, towngirl," Adam kept saying. And once, "They're fragile, like my photo ops, like my lens," and he patted his vest, jammed with photographic apparatus.

I finally stopped paying attention to him. I could visualize him and Juda meeting in the preserve, talking over the ducks and the geese, and me. People kept dissecting my personality behind my back, it seemed. And so they thought they knew me, which translated into this unholy good cheer, these trespasses upon my hospitality. A far cry from Reason and the target practice, his personal privacy insurance. So I ignored Adam and shoved more chips under the tender stalks of four o'clock seedlings.

"They're babies, Belle. Be careful."

"He's right. Don't push so hard, with that rake," Juda said.

"Tuck it under, like a *bambino* in a blanket."

"You're acting like a bulldozer, with that stuff," Juda complained.

"You're breaking the baby's neck!" Adam shouted.

"Geesh," David said. We looked at each other, and he screwed up his face, wrinkled his forehead.

"I think they could use a little wood chip with their beer," I whispered to him.

He tried to wink, his face went bland, and he started whistling. I leaned on the rake and kept ignoring the stream of advice from the men, watched David work his way around them, deposit shovels full of mulch, like ant hills, at the edges of the flower beds. Then he nodded at me, and eyeballed the back of Adam's neck.

I supposed since he couldn't do in his own dad, I got the job. So I laid the rake down, picked up another shovel, and dug myself a man-sized helping of tree debris. I lugged it casually over to Juda, who sat there sipping at his beer, slugging out tidbits of wisdom.

Adam's eyebrows had lifted, and he was watching me intently. He put a hand on Juda's arm, looked ready to be amused.

He said, "My friend . . . "

David hefted his shovel, upturned it on Adam's head. It cascaded over his eyes, down the back of his shirt, into the many pockets of his camera-clogged vest.

David shrieked, hopped around on one foot, yelling, "Wood chips for dinner — ha-ha! Eat that!"

Juda glanced up and behind, at David. He had his hands on the arms of the old lawn chair, ready to jump out of his seat and grab his son, when I swallowed my last misgiving and let him have it, full face, just as he realized he might be next.

Adam was up, laughing, brushing himself off, getting even more chips into his pockets.

Juda was out of his chair then, shocked, staring at me. His eyes narrowed, and his hands were open, cupping the mulch that still streamed off his shoulders.

I didn't feel like laughing. I felt pinned by Juda's blue eyes. He shook his head and blue sparks flickered through the hail of wood chips.

Then he put his hands on me, brushed a piece of wood off my shoulder, gripped my upper arms, took a step.

His face hung over mine, dark against the afternoon sky, haloed. His eyes pierced down through inches of air, and then slowly they softened, deepened. He let me go, stepped back, and I stood there and let a tremor jolt down through my feet, safely shiver its way into the earth's core.

As if he knew he'd retaliated, his eyes dropped to follow the job in hand, of brushing himself off. A smile was trickling around the corners of his mouth.

"Well, well," Adam said softly.

He was staring at us, assessing, head nodding in tune to some private conversation. He smirked.

I threw a few loose chips at him.

He grinned back and reached for David, began waffling his hair, tickling him, yelling at him.

I fell into Juda's chair, kept my attention safely on Adam's horseplay. I heard Juda raking, and peeked. He was gathering up the mulch we'd thrown, pushing it onto the flower beds. He edged carefully around me to get at the chips, intent on the job.

Adam finally quit deviling David and collapsed into the chair beside me, reached over and took my hand.

He cackled at me. "Life at the lake," he said, "has begun heating up."

I moved my fingers, dug the nails into his palm, glared at him.

He sighed deeply, contentedly, and he held my hand tighter.

Juda flung the rake down and checked his watch. "Time to go, David."

"Don't beat your son," Adam said. "I already have."

And David was up, scrabbling in the wheelbarrow, throwing another handful of mulch at him.

I glanced up at Juda. Adam had let my hand go to brush himself off, and Juda was staring at where our hands had been resting, on the lawn chair's arm.

He lowered his eyelids, jerked his chin up and said, over my head, "See you next weekend, Belle. Adam, remember our date."

"Ah, yes," Adam said, winking at me. "Our date."

"With the dock," Juda said, clarifying matters.

"Date with the dock? Hmmm. Oh well, she'll be easy to romance. She's already drunk."

Juda threw back his head and laughed, and then headed for his rowboat.

David yelled, "Wait, Dad! Almost forgot my trophy," and he rushed into the house. He was back in a minute, shouting, "Belle, can I take the rest of the bread? Please? I made it . . . "

"Go ahead, sure."

"Thanks!" he yelled, and took off for the boat.

He'd already taken it, had it tucked under one arm, had his trophy under the other.

I heard Adam chuckling and watched Juda's arms dip and pull at the oars, dip and pull. Then the boat vanished behind the other island.

He never looked back.

The week seemed long, and unusually quiet. Each day, I tried to forget the papers David had brought.

On Monday, I escaped the island and went in to Uriah's store for flour, argued with him about selling Reason's land.

Tuesday, I rowed out to the raft and dove off into deep water, pulled myself up the ladder, laid in the weak spring sunshine, dove in again. I loved the cold, clear rush it gave me, began to feel that the water was shredding old pieces of me away, flaking off dead skin that once protected my flesh, clearing old ideas out in a sort of spring cleaning frenzy.

On Wednesday, I had a piece of mail from Ben Bean-blossom. I'd been doing so well, he said, that the ten week meeting was unnecessary and therefore canceled. Since I'd found the notebooks already, there were only two things I was to be given, and he'd enclosed them: another check for five thousand dollars, and another of Reason's famous re-

receipts, a large one, folded in thirds.

The sales slip was made out for the purchase of tulip and daffodil bulbs, four dozen of each. "Thanks, Reason," I said aloud. "I enjoyed them."

On the back of the receipt, Reason had a chore for me, naturally. I turned it over, scanned what appeared to be a list of Indian names and meanings.

"The family of *Henziga*," I read. "The Brown Hair."

The woman in my dream — she'd had brown hair. I remembered thinking that she couldn't be Indian if she had brown hair. My knees started shaking, and I thought, this is Polly. Polly, Reason's grandmother. My great-great-grandmother.

I fell into the big green chair, put the receipt down on my thighs, and began tracing the fern-shaped indentations in the ancient upholstery.

Okay, I told myself. Polly, or Henziga, had brown hair. Or her name meant brown hair, for some convoluted reason. It was no reason to think that Polly had actually been in my dream. No reason. And the other dream, of the woman with strawberries, at the water's edge. Had she had brown hair?

It was a dream. I didn't know. It didn't matter.

I concentrated on Reason's receipt again, began reading again. There was a brief statement of the origin of this branch of Miami, or Meearmeear: "As early as seventeen forty-eight," according to Reason, "the tribe had been noted as being called the Twaa Twaa, or Twau Twau, meaning 'crane' and referring to the sound made by that bird. The Meearmeear themselves believe they originated along the Saint Joseph's River, and were found in what is now the location of Fort Wayne, Indiana, by some of the earliest Frenchmen to arrive in the Great Lakes area."

He went on to explain that the tribe became so numerous they were forced to migrate, and that a man called Wuyoakeetonwau went south to the Wabash River, and settled himself twenty miles below the mouth of the Tippecanoe River. His name meant "the children of the child who cries for his mother."

So what, Reason, I thought. What's the point? Other migrations of the Miami included one to the White River, another to a place now known as Piqua, Ohio, another down the Maumee River to what is now known as Waterville, Ohio, and another west to the Mississippi.

Under Henziga's name was Papakeechie's, with other forms of it: Pahedketeha, Papakeecha, Flat Belly, Bedbug. Reason had noted down Papakeechie's brother, Wawasee, had added the variations he'd found: Wawaesse, Wabee, Waubee, Full Moon, and 'the Round One.' And he'd written down their mother's name, Ma-kin-gwa-mi-na: Makingwamina, the 'Blackberry Flower,' an aunt of Little Turtle, and a sister of Sa-con-quan-e-wa, 'Tired Legs.'

Papakeechie and Wawasee, Miami, had married Potawatomi women. Wawasee became husband to the sister of the powerful chief, Metea, who lived near Kekionga, and they had a daughter, Pokataki, and a son, Toposh. Papakeechie married Anougons, Little Star, niece of Topinabe, the chief of 'those who keep the fire.' They had Henziga and a son, Kemoteah.

Reason next listed the cause of death for some of these, my relatives: Wawasee's wife died of snakebite, the day before he and Papakeechie returned from a trip, and his son Toposh left for Michigan. Papakeechie's wife was killed during a tornado, hit by bricks falling from Papakeechie's house. I'd known that. But Reason said it happened while Papakeechie and Wawasee were gone, signing the treaty of Eighteen Thirty-four, in which much of their remaining lands were transferred to the government.

Ke-mo-te-ah's wife, Ganehyaw, was killed by a man she'd spurned, and Kemoteah, whose name meant 'Whispering Winds,' was killed when he avenged her death. They left an orphaned son, Muk-kose, the Little Beaver.

"Then," Reason wrote, "squatters burned down the village, the old medicine man took Muk-kose by the hand, and led him away."

Well, that's grim, I thought. Thanks again, Reason, for this mountain of spiritual and skeletal remains.

One last phrase was scribbled at the bottom of the receipt: "Only his aunt, Henziga, remained."

He'd left me with Polly, the "Brown Hair," who'd married John Hiram MacKay. Why? Why this additional history lesson, and worded with such subtle bluntness? Reason had thought it necessary to smack me with all this trivia: A people who were descended from the child who cried for its mother, perhaps, a small boy orphaned, a woman left behind when her village packed up and left. And woven through all these threads was a greed for the land, pervasive, incessant. Reason kept forcing motivation on me, forcing emotion down my throat, and I was beginning to feel mulish. So what, Reason? So why are you harping on Polly?

Did she come in the night, to see you?

~ *SIXTEEN* ~

My nights had become serene, filled with the songs of insects, the melodic lapping of water on the shore.

Saul and Adam borrowed a speed boat from a friend on Friday, and took me on a tour of Lake Wawasee. Saul had brought a picnic basket that held a vast assortment of Italian delicacies.

"*Prosciutto!* See, towngirl, you're not the only one with connections."

Saul looked smug, and Adam snorted. "He has a good buddy at a store in Warsaw. But I can't figure out what's so fabulous about this stuff." He licked his fingers, pretending to weigh judgement.

"It's best when you eat it with cantaloupe," Saul said. "See, you take a bite of melon, a bite of meat . . ."

"Yuck. He's always bringing home weird food. You ought to try living with him, Belle."

Saul wore bikini swim trunks that swathed his limbs like a loin-cloth. He merely smiled and crossed one elegant, grace-defined leg over the other.

"I'm a great cook, Adam," he said mildly. "You are one lucky *uomo.*"

Adam raised his eyebrows, at me. We were lounging in the boat, anchored out in a beautiful bay under a pacific blue sky, but Adam and calm just couldn't mix.

"It means 'man'," Saul said.

"How appropriate."

"Cretin."

"What? What did I do now, Saul?"

"Those looks you're giving Belle. In other words, what you always do."

"God, Saul, don't be so critical. You're taking the day off, remember?" Adam sighed. "Off duty. Don't dissect me."

We lingered for ages, enjoying the lake breezes, the hot sun on the water, the slow touring of shore-side mansions on a par or nicer than Ben and Maude Beanblossom's. Then Saul guided the boat past sections of the lake where canals leaked in, fringed in a cross-hatch of docks and boats. The fingers of water sprouted neat rows of assorted housing on either side, connecting former marshes in a maze of beehive busyness.

Later, he got wild with the boat, and we flew over the three-thousand-acre lake laughing, shrieking, shouting him down. He found a cove finally, and dropped anchor again.

"Sorry," he said. "Blowing off steam, I guess."

"You've had a hard week, Saul. Looks like the girl from the big town has, too."

"Have you?" Saul asked.

I shook my head, ran fingers through my hair, searched my bag for a brush.

"She's been assaulted on all sides lately, you know," Adam said.

"Well, Belle." Saul stepped into the back of the boat, sat down in the other rear-facing seat. He picked up my hand. "Any more dead animals?"

I tapped his hand and disengaged, yanked a hairbrush through my hair, said, "No, nothing like that, Saul. Don't worry, Adam's just playing."

"No more idiots, banging on your house?"

I shook my head. "Nope."

Adam stood up in the boat, snapped the elastic of his swimming trunks, slapped his hands on his hips. "Hey. I am not playing, here, towngirl. I can see the stress in your face, in the prickling skin of your legs, in the very electric roots of your curly, vibrating hair follicles, in the . . ."

"Shut up, Adam," Saul said. "Got a problem, Belle?"

I grinned up at Adam, smiled at Saul, said, "Not a real one, no. Just fed up with Reason, that's all."

"See!" Adam sat himself cross-legged on the floor of the boat, raised his eyebrows, looked prepared to wait.

Saul looked confused. "But Reason's dead . . ."

"Doesn't seem to stop him," I said. "He's managed to set up all these things. It's like they're invisible, and marching down this road he built, one after the other, then they suddenly appear, roll over the top of you."

Saul was listening with his head cocked, eyes so intent they were pricking at me, demanding.

There seemed no way out from under his focus. "Bet you're a good physical therapist, Saul," I said.

Adam let out a small cackle.

"What things?" Saul prodded.

"Everything things. All things. He's permeated every single moment of my life."

"And you're fed up with it, right?"

"He keeps giving me work, giving me money."

"I wouldn't mind the money," Adam said.

"I do. I can find my own work, make my own money. I always have."

"So he's helping you too much?" Saul said, guessing.

"Well," I said slowly, "yes. And it's hypocritical. This latest data, for instance. Reason sent it, through Ben, with some more money. But it's not the historical trivia so much, as this constant lecturing Reason does. He goes on and on, acting as if I was lost from my tribe, from my village, so to speak. Comparing me with his grandmother, whose village moved away from her, see?"

"Umm."

"But she was fine. She had a husband, and much later, she had a son."

"So how is this like your situation?"

"It isn't! That's what I mean. Reason never left me. He just never had me. Grandmother wouldn't allow it."

"Hmm." Saul raked his bristling cheeks with one hand, scrubbed at his chin. "What about your folks?"

"It has nothing to do with them. They're dead."

"Oh, well then."

"What?"

"Maybe you have been lost from your village, and Reason's just trying to make sure you get home okay."

"Oh for God's sake," I yelled. "I'd like to get away from him, get a vacation from him!" I stood up, registered a quick glimpse of comprehension in Saul's eyes, and dove into the lake.

The clear, green water was warmer than Papakeechie's, and stripped away the frustration more gently. I dove deep enough to feel cold, currenting eddies, before I turned, peered up through a turquoise canyon, and headed for air.

Saul and Adam had jumped in, and were floating around on rubber rings, splashing, playing. They must have made a pact while I was underwater, to let me forget about

Reason for the rest of the day.

We took the boat back and stopped in for a cocktail with Saul's friend, then drove back to Papakeechie for a snack and another round of cheer.

I duly admired the views from their living room, tried to pay equal attention to their eclectic collections; Adam showed photographs and Saul brought out his travel brochures.

"Firenze, Florence. This is where I want to go first."

Adam nodded. "He wants to buy himself a gold bracelet."

"They have a bridge with stores built on it, above the river, great gold jewelry, decent prices. But they have art, too. Great art, great museums."

"Really?" Adam said, and stopped prowling the path around the windows.

"They have Michelangelo's work," Saul said softly.

"Oh." Adam's eyes were glazing over. "Saul, where did you put that Italian tape?"

"Cretin! So this is what it takes? All along, I only needed a carrot of naked torsos to motivate you?"

"Michelangelo did more than naked torsos," Adam said primly.

"Yes, the Sistine Chapel, the entire ceiling, in Rome. And the *Pieta*. He did wonderful work with stone."

"From Carrara," I said.

"You've been?"

I nodded. "I used to travel with, well, with a friend."

Saul leaned forward in the Morris chair. "Another cocktail, Belle?"

"Enough, with the travel talk," Adam said. "No, no more drinks, I'm taking her home now. Tomorrow's a work day, remember Saul? I told you. Juda and I, we have a plan."

"You have a plan? What are you up to?"

"Towngirl, it's a secret."

I frowned. "What?"

Adam ignored me. "You're going to help, aren't you Saul?"

"Sure," Saul said.

A date with a dock, I remembered. My dock? "No way," I said.

"Never," Adam drawled, "turn down a present, before you open it."

"It's about the dock, isn't it? I have plans for it."

Adam flung his hands up. "Hah. What do you think, we're going to go in and take care of everything for you? Wouldn't think of it! You don't *like* help, remember?" He glared at me.

"Reason's help," I said, defensive, embarrassed.

He posed, a slighter, but well-muscled Atlas, flexing one arm and then the other. "Not that we *couldn't* do it, of course. You'd need brute strength, for that job."

"A brute, yes," I said.

"But do you need a real man?" Saul asked.

"We have need of *you*, yes," Adam answered.

I badgered Adam about his plan, all the way back to the island, but he just kept dipping the oars in the water, pulling and grinning. I couldn't get it out of him.

"I'm preparing a way," he finally said, when he'd delivered me to my good, short dock.

"The way to where?"

"*Amore*," he said, and grinned. "One of Saul's words." I stood above his boat and stared at him.

"See, I'll get all us men to take our shirts off, tomorrow. You can serve beer, towngirl, and pretend to be an adoring female, watch the laboring brutes."

"Adam, this *is* about my dock. You said to Juda Kinzie . . ."

"You might recline in a chaise, wear a dress even, if you've got one." He raised an eyebrow, appeared to think this was doubtful, went on, "But your real duty, towngirl, is to observe the drips and the odor of our manly sweat."

"Adam, you are truly warped."

"Nope. I didn't make the match. I merely observed its potential."

"So what are you, in gigolo training?"

"I am shocked, Belle. Don't you know there's a tradition on this lake, to find someone for the poor, lonely soul on Little Turkey Island?"

They dribbled in, in the morning. Juda and David came first, and they huddled up at the table, pouring over a book Juda had brought with him. They wouldn't so much as let me peek over their shoulders. Then Adam came, announced that Saul was fixing a food basket and would be a little late.

I pounded down bread dough on the counter, trying to figure out the diagrams from a distance.

I wasn't sure what to think about Adam and his amorous plans, or about the dock. I'd never accepted a gift of labor. I'd never had need of a gift of labor.

And I'd never had need of interference in my love life.

The bread was getting slapped violently around by the time the men got up and left, taking their book with them.

It's a gift, Belle, I told myself. Just a gift. Be a little gracious, now and then.

I didn't feel gracious.

David came back in and slouched against the counter, watching.

"We could'a done it," he said.

I yanked at the dough again, dumped it in a bowl.

"Uh-huh. You and me could'a done it. They're just showing off."

"Well, it's sort of a present, David," I said primly.

"Right. Adam's got them trying to figure out who's the strongest. Geesh!"

I peeked. I couldn't help it. Sure enough, all three had their shirts off. Adam was preening again. I stiffled a giggle and turned away from the window.

"That's all right," I said. "We know who really gets the work done, around here."

David brightened a bit. "We better take the rowboat over to work on the garden, for today. They'll have the other dock all tore up. Bet they can't get it back together."

I covered the dough, set it to rise in the oven, and washed off my floury hands. Then I jammed my hair into a pony tail and we went around to the good pier, where the rowboat was tied up.

We were both ignoring the men, I realized. So I must have the emotional stability of a disturbed twelve-year-old.

That did it. We rounded the island and I tried for a little dignity, maybe a dash of gratitude, and I waved at the men. Juda and Adam were thigh-deep in the clump of water lilies at the end of the dock, wrestling with the metal pilings. They both had on rubber waders that strapped under the crotch, and both still had their shirts off. Saul was administering advice from the safety of the shore.

"Back in an hour," I called to them. "David and I have a little work over here."

Juda turned toward me for a moment, shouted, "Okay," and Adam just nodded, kept tugging at something underwater. Whatever he'd been pulling on gave way, suddenly, and the entire length of pier shuddered, lurched, smacked down on the water and heaved a mighty belch.

Waves slapped up at them, poured into their boots, drenched their hair, their jeans, sent them reeling backwards into the patch of lilies, arms flailing, hands grabbing wildly at air.

David pointed and began choking with laughter.

Adam struggled up, spluttering, started yelling, "Out, woman, look what you did!"

Juda stood up, with seaweed hooked over his ears and

dangling down his chest like tendrils of cat-clawed curtain. They both glared at me.

"Hey, I didn't do it," I said.

Adam shook his fist, wiped his eyes with the back of his hand. Juda shook his head, and water and weeds sprayed off him. In the center of his chest dark hair gleamed, pasted together, clumped and curling.

Adam started yelling again, and I dragged my eyes away.

"Woman!" he shouted, "This is work for men!"

"*Basta!*" Saul shouted, and I started rowing fast for the hill.

When we were well away, David whispered. "What's *basta* mean?"

"Uh," I said. I was about to ram the shore, and dump us in the water, too. I began backpaddling as hard as I could, finally gave up and let the boat clunk heavily into the muck near the landing.

David rounded his eyes at me, and he gripped the sides of the boat to keep himself from lurching out.

"It's a swear word, isn't it Belle?"

One at a time, I put the oars into the boat, and sat there feeling put upon by all these men. "I think it just means 'enough,' David. It's not a swear word, it's just Italian. Saul seems to like Italian, especially when he's exasperated, with Adam."

"*Basta, basta, basta,*" David said, and jumped out of the boat, headed up the hill.

"Really, *basta,*" I said, and stood on the landing, looked back at the island. The men were out of the lake now, slapping each other on the back, dumping the water out of their boots. I could hear drifts of words, hints of cursing, louder bursts of laughter. It looked like some weird male bonding ritual had occurred. And at my expense. Adam had set them up for his unique brand of machismo, I suppose, and now he was patching up their egos.

I turned my back. I'd had enough of gifts. They never seemed to be gifts, in the long run.

David and I worked silently side-by-side, tending to the never-ending weeding, the constant building of composted mulch around ever-stronger stems.

Then he worked alone, while I rowed back to pound down the bread, put it into loaf pans, cover it up and leave it to proof again.

This time, I barely glanced at the men. They were all huddled over the book, with the dock laid out on the grass.

When I got back to David he'd fallen into a mood as foul as my own. I asked him when school was out, and he just said, "Out," and grunted at me.

"You mean now?"

He grunted again.

"Oh."

I was tempted to ask him what was wrong. He'd pull a weed, throw it onto his pile. Then, when he had a small heap, he'd pulverize the pile with the heel of his grimy gym shoe.

After watching that too many times, I finally asked what he was doing.

"Nothing."

"You told me to save the weeds for the compost."

He grunted, didn't even look up at me.

"David..."

"Can't save these," he said.

"Why not?"

"Bad. Masma's got 'em."

"Masma?"

He formed the word slowly. "Mee-az-mah," he said.

"Miasma?"

"Yeah." He finished grinding the heap with his heel and jumped up and down on top of it, scowling at it.

"Where'd you learn about miasma?"

He shrugged.

"David, they're just weeds. Believe me, they can't hurt us, especially since you've killed them so — so completely."

He looked up at me from under his brows, as if I were one of the weeds.

"Really, David, people haven't been afraid of the effects of fog, rising off swamps, for a hundred years."

"That's cause the knowledge got lost," he said.

I put my hands on my hips. "No, David. It's because it wasn't real knowledge."

"Is too."

I sighed. "Besides, miasma was supposed to effect people, not plants."

"Huh. You think plants don't get sick?"

"Sure they do, but not from moist air. That's what you've got at a lake, David. Moist air."

He considered this, still pawing the weeds into a green slime. Then he shook his head. "Nope," he said. "Masma's different. Not just wet air. It's bad air, evil air. Spirit air."

"David . . . "

He grabbed the slobbery green pile of mush with a potato fork and took off, heaved it into the woods, ran back for another, till all the "contaminated" weeds were gone. Then he made a dash for the lake, and rinsed his hands.

I followed him. "Okay," I said. "Let's have some lunch. You can tell me if our island flower beds are in any danger."

He snickered. "Masma doesn't kill flowers. Just food. And people. Masma kills people."

"Really, David, that's just not true. People were afraid of swamp land, years ago. They blamed all their illnesses on it. They didn't know then how fevers spread, about viruses, or bacteria, or influenza."

"Lot you know," he said.

I got in the boat, and he stood on the landing above me with his fists clenched, his feet planted firm. I smiled. "David," I said softly, "you're always so adamant. You've got to learn how to see both sides of a thing, look around the edges of an issue. The Chinese think of mist as a source of life energy. They believe it brings long life, and virtue."

"They got swamps?" he asked.

"Sure they do."

"Bet they don't," he said, and stepped into the boat. He shivered, and added, "Not like we got in the preserve, right over the hill, there."

I started rowing gently, almost afraid to jolt him. "I saw part of the preserve marsh," I said. "Adam gave me a tour of the lake. There's a low place in the big basin, where the road dips down over a culvert, and connects the preserve with Papakeechie. Adam said the State wanted to claim public easement rights, because the waters are connected."

I went on quietly, talking about the case that the Papakeechie Preservatory had won, but David let the words roll over him. He sat slouched in the rowboat with his head propped in one hand, the other dangling in the water.

I'd forgotten the men. When I pulled up at the good dock, slipped the noose of rope over the piling, Adam was there to meet me.

"Hey towngirl. Time to serve lunch to your men."

"Okay," I said, surprising myself.

I went up the path, caught myself smiling at Juda and Saul. They grinned back.

I asked David to get an old card table out of the shed, and to wipe it off. I turned on the oven to bake the bread, opened up cans of tuna fish, diced onion and pickles, added mayonnaise, and shoved it in the freezer to chill while I boiled water for macaroni. I turned the old radio up loud, so it could be heard outside, took out a tablecloth and napkins, gathered the lawn chairs around, brought glasses and cold beer, a pitcher of water.

Adam smiled approvingly at me, puffed up his chest and patted his bare stomach.

Saul opened his basket, spread odd dishes out, poked serving spoons into them. "Assorted antipasto," he said, and urged Juda to try them.

I brought out plates and silverware. Then I actually walked around behind the men, poured beer into each of their glasses.

They ignored me, and discussed the food, the project.

I went back in and cooked the macaroni, rinsed it under cold water, tossed the tuna in, dumped the bread out on a platter and shoved a knife in the middle of a loaf. Then I carried the bowl and the platter outside and put it on the table, heaped tuna salad on each plate, in turn.

Adam reached for the knife, stood and sliced the bread. "Yes, yes," he muttered.

I smiled sweetly at him, and said nothing. I guess I was letting him have his show, doing penance for having resented their generosity.

David and I filled our plates and went over to the dock. It rolled across the lawn slightly in a warped twist, much as Adam's mind did, I thought, and I sat on it carefully, balanced my glass of water.

Rubber hip boots were scattered about on the grass, with two stout, screw-tipped posts. Another two of the reset pilings were already in the water.

David sat farther down the dock, and eyeballed the grass. "Gotta get this cut, this afternoon."

"Don't worry about it. I'll do it next week."

"No!"

"Why not? I can manage."

"You might cut the wrong stuff," he said.

"What?"

"Geesh. Okay, see those grasses, over there?" He

pointed to the back of the house, where the shed hunched over what had been the back door. "That's sweet grass. Reason was growing it, and he said we're not to fool with it."

"Why not?"

He sighed. "It's Indian grass. You burn it, and it'll give you answers."

"Look, David," I said, and stopped. I looked over at the shed, at the graceful green stems, and wondered what answers Reason had asked for.

"Do you smoke it?"

"It's not marijuana," he said, and flashed his best disgusted look at me.

I shut up, and started eating.

David took a bite too and glared at the dock again, and at the pilings poking up through lily pads. "We could'a done it," he whispered, and he began spearing the air between planks of the dock, with his fork.

"Shh. We've got enough work."

He turned the glare back to his plate.

"David," I said, "the truth is, we would have had trouble. We like to think we can handle things ourselves, but..."

"I can."

"I know. You've handled a lot, on your own."

I stared over the lake at the hillside, then looked back across the water to the little cottage, the new flower beds. "But maybe," I said softly, "letting people give to you, help you, is like, well, another kind of strength. And a gift in its own way."

"Nah. It's pegleg."

"Pegleg?"

"You know, a fake leg."

I stared at him a minute, figuring it out. "Sure," I said. "But that pegleg is helping a person to be stronger, get freedom, take care of himself."

He frowned up at me. There was a hint of glazing about his blue eyes, and it reflected my worries back at me.

I lowered my head, as if to sneak under the blanketing fog in his face and attack direct. "Everybody needs help sometimes," I told us both.

He shook his head wildly, and his plate slid off his lap. Noodles fell like a lump of brain on the dock, disintegrated, dribbled between the boards, were sucked through, gobbled up.

~ SEVENTEEN ~

David was steadily more sullen for the rest of the day. When the men took a break to row out to the raft and swim, he insisted on mowing the island grass, refused to go along.

When he finished, he came inside and told me, "They act like little kids. They're out there pushing and shoving, tripping each other, playing 'king of the mountain'."

I wiped my hands on the dish rag and looked out the window behind my desk.

Adam was the worst offender, of course. He was playing sumo wrestler at the moment, had one arm grappling at Saul's thigh, the other lifting at the waist. He was bent over double, and as I watched he managed to lift, stumble to the edge of the raft, heave Saul in, and topple off on top of him.

"Somebody's going to get hurt," David grumbled.

Saul let out a roar when he came up, and tackled Adam, who was just coming to the surface. Juda rocked wildly on the raft, laughing, sole proprietor of the heaving platform. His belly rippled, gasped through convulsions, his neck arced his chin into the blue horizon. And he still managed to crouch, riding the wild back of a stampeding raft.

A knot somewhere in my abdomen softened, loosened, as I watched Juda balance, tap dance a bit to bring his own jolting body into tune with the rolling raft. By the time it was tamed by a tethering anchor, slowed by subsiding waves, the knot had untied. The hard-cored resistance in my belly had entirely gone.

"Damn it," I said under my breath.

David looked at me, carefully.

I watched my hands wipe themselves on my blue jean-covered thighs. I could feel his stare, feel the beginnings of his understanding grow, feel him study the implications as carefully as he watched the color fade from my face.

"You like my dad," he said.

I laughed, but even to my ears it sounded staccato, and my mouth nipped it off. I moved fast, back to the sink and the safety of the chore in hand.

He followed. "You do. You like my dad."

"What's that, an accusation?"

He stuck his hands in his pockets, and rocked back and forth on his heels.

I grabbed hold of a sudden panic, wishing for the knot back to tie me together again, safe. I plunged my hands into the warm soapy water, let my fingertips caress it, relish heat, soothe away the tingling.

"I'm attracted to your father," I said slowly. "But that doesn't mean I like him."

"Yeah, you do."

He was two feet away, and his eyes were pinning me.

"And if I did, what would you think?"

"Huh." He dropped his eyes, scuffed at the floor. "I don't know," he said. "But it doesn't matter, what I think. He won't like you."

He raised his face, cocked his head and squinted at me.

"David . . ."

"Jennifer. He likes Jennifer. She's pretty, too, kind of fluffy, you know, like a cat — always snuggling up to me, and to Dad.''

"I thought you didn't care for Jennifer.''

"I don't.''

I tried to untangle his feelings and mine, raise myself above the antagonism he was using, to shield himself.

"Okay, you're right.   None of this matters.''   I shrugged.   "Why are we worrying about it?''

He grunted.   "Thought you should know,'' he said, still surly.

"Thanks,'' I said.

"What else you want me to do, today?''

I turned back to the dishes.   "I don't care.   What do you think?''

"Got some paint in the shed.   Dock's out.   Might as well do it.''

"Okay.''

He walked out.

He seemed more grown-up today, more complex and filled up with moods.   Adolescence, I thought, rearing its raw-boned head.   Add all the changes he'd gone through: the ·loss of a mother, his father dating, scoping out replacements for someone irreplaceable.   And Reason died on him too, after dumping a ton of emotional responsibility on him.

That doctor Juda trusted had better be good.

A roar went up outside, when the men were finished playing.   They'd come ashore and found David painting the planks of the dock.

"What are you doing, son?'' Juda was shouting when I ran out to see what was wrong.   "We were working here.''

"Now we can't do it,'' Saul said.

David stuck his brush back in the can, swirled paint, dipped it out and took another swipe at the decking.

"I'm talking to you, David,'' Juda said.

David sniffed, dipped again, swiped again.

"I told him to go ahead,'' I said.   "I thought it was a

good idea to get it painted, since it was out of the water."

"Woman!" Adam yelled. "How can we finish? You have all these men helping you out, and you manage to screw it up." He shook his head sadly.

"David . . . " Juda growled.

"Yo, Judy-boy, leave him alone," Adam said. "Yell at her." He pointed at me, and snickered.

Juda's eyes dragged up, up, all the way up as if he had to find the way, find the words once he got there. But there weren't any words. We simply stared at each other. And then he retraced his route back down my neck, over my breasts, taking a detour as he found his way around them, down again, slipping sideways to sketch out my hips before his eyes slid down over my legs, and across to frown again at David.

I tried to breathe, forgot to open my mouth and sniffed air in quick little puffs through my nose.

His trip around my body had taken years, and I glanced around to see if anyone had noticed. They hadn't. They were watching David, still doggedly swiping paint on the decking. The years had been instants, secret seconds. I hoped.

When he looked at me again I was tempted to take my own little tour, give him a taste of my own carnal curiosity. I remembered watching him ride the raft and, oddly, Reason's words. "Plant seeds of truth," he'd written. So I grabbed reality by the neck, let myself return what I saw there, in his gaze.

And within moments, we'd reached understanding.

"Hey, so what?" Adam was saying. He looked up, then back and forth between Juda and me. He raised an eyebrow. "Yeah, so what?" he said again, and shrugged. "So we finish the job tomorrow. No big deal. Anyone want a beer?"

Juda frowned at him.

"Well, I'm getting a beer." He jogged off to the house,

whistling.

Saul cleared his throat. "It's not really a problem," he said. "Adam is right, for once. We can still set all the I-beams. Then all we have to do tomorrow is heave the pier out, bolt it down . . . Juda?"

Juda was frowning at David now, and didn't answer. Saul bent down to pat David on the shoulder. He ruffled his hair.

David shrugged his hand off.

Saul straightened up, said slowly, "You know, we should have figured out that the dock needed painting. Isn't that funny, grown men needing a small boy to think for them?"

"I'm not small," David said, steadily swiping at the dock.

"I can see that. You're a kid who thinks bigger than men."

Adam sauntered down the path, swinging his bottle. He nodded at Saul, studied Juda's face, took a swig of beer.

Juda was still watching David, still frowning. For once, I couldn't read his mind, and finally the silence and the tension got to me, and I laughed.

Adam shook his fist at me. "Keep it down, towngirl. You're the root of all this, anyway. We're four men, against one woman, you know. This one intelligent specimen," he pointed at David, "and three big, silly fools."

Saul laughed out loud, and Juda cracked a smile.

I shook my fist back at Adam. "You shut up. Or I won't feed you."

I pretended to stomp off in anger, but my knees were still a little mushy, weakened by Reason's seeds, I suppose.

I was grateful for a chance to run.

Adam knew. I could even believe he'd been pumping up Juda all day, priming him for the declaration his eyes had given me. Priming me to receive it, with his ridiculous chauvinistic prattle.

Even David knew.

I needed some answers, because it was time I knew, too.

I stayed indoors the rest of the afternoon, while the men worked on the pilings and beams of the dock, and David finished painting. I should have gone out to thank them, when they left, but I didn't.

I couldn't face Juda, couldn't endure another nonverbal proposition, another slap of that truth. Not yet. I ran from job to job indoors, batting away at my past.

It was coming, and I kept thinking: Go to hell, John Schaffer. Don't screw this up. But I wasn't really angry at John any more. It was me, against me.

I wasn't angry at Reason, either. Wasn't mad at Adam and his idiotic manipulations. I wasn't even hungry, although I'd never finished lunch, and hadn't eaten breakfast.

Answers. I wanted answers. They were all here, somewhere, if I could just see them.

I wanted another chance, wanted Juda's hands to find the path his eyes had taken, find it soon and fondle, caress, warm me inside and out, for as long as I could have the loving. And I wanted more — much more. I wanted to argue with him, agree with him, support him. I wanted to nourish him.

So perhaps I already had my answers. It was only courage I lacked. The courage to see the truth. The faith required to live.

The house turned steadily darker, oppressive, and I'd done every job I could think of, except eating. My stomach felt oddly full though, full of frustration, confusion, denial.

I opened the door and went out.

It was all so stifling, even outdoors the air was quiet and hanging overhead like a purple shroud. I stared at the dock, gleaming white, wet-tacky, on a speckled, paint-splattered bed of grass. And staring at it, I soaked up David's words, all his antagonism, the quagmire of shifting moods and the stark need in him, for caring.

Who better than me, to find a way to answer his devils?

And it looked as if Reason had found him for me, wrapped him up and shoved him, kicking, down my throat.

There were so many people, dead and alive, for me to care for, suddenly. And an odd relief in being alone, for now, with all their needs gnawing away at me, hungry. I had to find a way to feed them all, satiate their needs, fill their hearts and my own.

I couldn't do it; too many of them, too needy. Reason was relentless, David was flipping personalities as if he didn't care if he landed on his head. Juda would drain me, steal back what I'd so recently won: myself. I began pacing circles around the island in the dusk, cornered, caged up, chasing freedom and frightened to death.

I passed Reason's sweet grass for the third time and saw it, heard David's words in my mind: "Indian grass. It'll give you answers," he'd said. Answers.

I gathered a hank, raced for the house and the kitchen matches, ran back out and found a rock to burn them on. I ripped them into shreds, squatted over them and lit, blew puffs of air, lit them again. I breathed in the smoke. "Not marijuana," David had said. So I simply let them burn, admired the scent, watched the blue-gray, delicate strand rising thinly in the calm of evening.

Nothing. What did I expect? He was a little boy, entranced by all things native American, all the fluff and the folderol Reason had stuffed in his head. How could the fluff have form, and meaning, and fact?

And I was probably doing it wrong. This burning of sweet grass was probably a ceremony, and I couldn't concentrate, couldn't fabricate spirituality. I was crazy, sick of the death I worked over day by day, failing to bring it to life. All I could offer the spirits was naked fear, the broken-down barriers I'd built against caring, and nothing, nothing I'd ever really given anyone, of me.

I fell back on the grass, relieved, accepting the failure, feeling satisfaction and the absolute honesty of admission. There was no need for guilt, or shame. I'd simply never been able to love.

Lily pads paved a make-believe path across the water, and my eyes followed them, into the darkening shadows where the hillside draped itself over the lake, under a dimming sky.

There in those shadows, where the trees overhung the water, were eddies and silent currents, a gentle murmuring.

It was peaceful, to sit and watch, to let myself wander in the movement of the water. And I was tired, willing to let go of the constant busyness, all the pressures conducting all their frenzied movements of need. A bird broke the stillness with a sharp call, and swooped over the lake, flashing winks at me with his wings and the white eye of his tail. A yellow shafted flicker, a type of woodpecker, calling through dusk, flitting home again.

I stared, and haze began lifting off the lake, drifting. The hazing became fog and swirled patterns in misty, graceful movement. Watching, I let my thoughts flow too, and they danced over lilies and crisp green petals, now here, now hidden, playing out the music in forever air and water, a lilting, playful, visual tune of life.

Wet, swollen, primeval smells dragged at memory, reminding me of kitchen scent, and a friend's Thanksgiving feast: There was the sudden acrid tang of her father's cigar, a sniff of rich, sage-laden stuffing, burning grass and of cedar boughs deep in the woods. I smiled, thinking that this was only summer, only the usual fog over the lake on summer nights, after a rain.

My eyes were inside the mist now and dreaming a face,

a laughing face, woven of air and water and the deep shadows reaching upward to trees, hung with the night. But the woman was made up of spinning, moving moisture and so her hair swirled, tangled itself like seaweed, tossed flickering white petals in the air like leaves before the wind.

"Artemisia," she told me, and the word was trilling over the water, laughing and moving toward me right along with her. "Not sage, artemisia," she said, "and the other sacred herbs are cedar, tobacco, and sweet grass."

She smiled, and asked, "Will you hear?"

Then a hand, sweeping forward, taking mine.

I stood up without a thought and went with her, felt my feet bare against the crisp green stepping stones of lily pads, felt my body lifting, springing over darkness. There was another whiff of grasses, burning, and a sense of life surging in my body like an angry herd, running intent in a flowing prairie.

But these fields were filled with trees. This was a woodland, and I was running alone, following her through living shapeless sensation; I was running wild inside joy. I knew the way, I'd always known my way. It was an easy downhill sweep, and my arms lifted, my hair flew, lifting too, and my feet knew every step and faultless leap. A singing inside me pushed at fear, sent anger lurching off my tongue. And winds swept them silently away, into the past.

Ahead, a clearing full of people. A fire. Comfort, waiting. The headlong singing slowed into lullaby sounds, and I slowed, and stopped, and hid myself in shadows. Was this comfort for me, this fire to warm me? Would these people welcome me?

And I wanted them, and waited, unsure. She came again. She took me by the hand and smiled, and led me into the yellow, the fire-lit, the nearly full, moonlit clearing.

People gathered. They were staring at me, waiting too.

They wore long skirts of a patterned cloth, with loose-fitting blouses, and long, long ruffled collars. Or leggings with ribboned wings, and frilled shirts, and faces rich with color, creased in cares and blessed by happy years, by years of worry.

The woman drew me down next to her near the fire, and I saw the patterns in her clothes, the cheerful mix of color and fabric, her shawl sewn with shining waves of silver broaches, glowing in firelight. And her brown hair, glowing too.

She held out a delicate china bowl, white, with a European blue, scalloping design on its rim, and offered it to me with the words, "You are hungry."

I reached for the dish and held it, warming my hands, smelling the rich broth and the scent again, of the burning grasses, of the fire, and now the close, the pressing people.

"It is squirrel soup," she said. "You will need the strength it gives." And she smiled.

I tasted, and I thought that this was the dish she'd made for John Hiram, and for Hiram MacKay, her son. And I knew that these people, these were the ones I'd written of. These were my people, too.

As I ate, they settled around the fire, and they waited.

Then a man's voice began speaking, faltering, gathering resonance and fiber as if collecting stray tones on the wind. He had a silver ring in his nose which caught at light, sprayed it sparking into the moist dark air.

The melody of his words seemed at first, to my ear, low, chanting. It grew slowly stronger, or I grew to reach his meaning, and to separate tonality among the various gravels of the syllables. Some of his words were known to me, and I wondered if Polly whispered meanings in my mind.

A drum beat began, softly, reaching around, lifting up the old man's words, strengthening, offering them to the night, to the blackness of branches above.

"They say that," the old man was saying, and I blinked, feeling each of his words inside my head.

"A long time ago, the Turtle listened to her ancestors and did as they directed her."

There was eager agreement from the people, and they pressed a little nearer, urging him with their closeness to continue, stirring the air, adding a warm, human odor of herb-scrubbed hair, and of sweat and of living.

"She placed pieces," my uncle said, "of the mud of her home onto her back, and she asked Grandfather Sun to dry it, so that she might be protected from the cold of the Buck Moon, *Ii-Yau-Peear Keel-Swah.*

"And she asked of Mother Earth, *Neengeeau Kak-kar-mee-kar-kee*, to grow the woodlands and prairies upon her back, and that the Great Spirit make the People of the Turtle to care for these."

A hush grew, and even the drums were silent as the people respectfully considered the words of my uncle.

"But there came a time when the water of Turtle's home was stirred by many feet, searching for food. And in this time Turtle could no longer find food to give her strength. The animals of the forest were no longer willing to give up their spirits to feed the People of the Turtle, for the waters were muddy, and food was scarce for them.

"Then Turtle began to trade pieces of mud from her warm shell for food, to keep her strength. She traded more pieces from her shell, and still more, and it was never enough for the many feet which muddied her waters, which kept the animals from returning to feed the People of the Turtle.

"Turtle grew cold as the pieces of her shell were traded, and the day came when she had only a few pieces left upon her back. In these pieces Mother Earth had caused the Tree of Life to grow, rooted deeply in her back, and these pieces she could not give, not even to feed the People. Turtle knew that she had nothing more to trade."

There were murmurs of "*Ee-yar,*" sounding of a sigh, ee-yah, yes. And whispering "*Kee-to-lee-nu-waa,*" from one or more of the people listening, agreeing; "You tell the truth."

"And in the Bear Moon, *Muk-Wau Keel-Swah,* with the cold and the emptiness gnawing at the strength of her

People, there came a small Squirrel. The Squirrel was very clever, and had lived in the forest above the Turtle's home for many seasons, and had hidden away much food for the winter. Squirrel shared these stores with the People of the Turtle in the old way, in the way of Mother Earth, who gives what is needed to those who take only what they must have.

"And the People of the Turtle became strong again from Squirrel's food, and Turtle was warmed by Squirrel's gift.

"And then in the Crane Moon, *Tshe-Tsha-Kwua Keel-Swah,* the spirit of Squirrel's mate left this life, and Squirrel's spirit wished to follow.

"And the People of the Turtle gave strength to Squirrel, and made him our brother. The People had need of all those they call brother, as there were not now so many of them. Few pieces remained of Turtle's shell now, once so strong and thick with woodland, and with grasses, and with life. Many of the People had left, to find homes where waters were not stirred by many feet, where fishes still clogged weirs and offered their strength to the People.

"And few sons of the People were left, then, and fewer daughters could marry.

"And they say, if a warrior shaves his head, and leaves only a little hair, still what remains bears all of his strength. And so it is among us."

There was a nodding and an agreement around the fire, a chorus of *"Ee-yar,"* and the old man continued. "Turtle then asked of the People, 'Who among us is willing?' And a daughter came forward, and said that she was willing.

"And so," the old man said, "the People of the Turtle give honor to our Brother, Squirrel. We are joined with him, and upon this branch, in another time, a Flower of the Lake gives honor back to us."

In a whispering, varying cadence, the people said, *"Kee-to-lee-nu-waa,"* and turned toward me, and let welcome flood around me.

It was a story told often, I thought, and like a tale told

to a child, rife with nuance, with not-so-subtle meaning.

I turned to the woman who'd drawn me here, the woman who must be Polly. "A beautiful story," I said.

"Yes."

"Who is Turtle?"

"We are the People of the Turtle."

"You are Henziga?" I asked.

She nodded. "I am called Henziga by my People."

"The Brown Hair," I said. "And who is Squirrel?"

The words warmed me, as they came, floating like warmth into my heart. "My husband."

John Hiram MacKay, my mind answered, and she smiled.

"And I," I said. "I am the Flower of the Lake?"

"So I have named you, *Nee-pee-sen-gee Pah-kah-ta-kee.*"

Papakeechie's mother's name was *Ma-kin-gwa-mi-na,* Blackberry Flower. Henziga had named me after her grandmother, my ancestor. What was there to say to a gift as lovely as this? What would be right? I had no gift for her, and felt a sudden, intense shame.

"I have no gift," I whispered. And another word came to mind, was there a moment and then spoken aloud: *"N' oakaumau."* *0-kah-mah,* Grandmother.

She smiled, and said back to me, "You must know that you are loved. That is enough." And she took me by the hand and introduced me to each of the People, said my name over and over, and they hugged me, all of them.

There were no words. And so I stuttered something, "I am honored," perhaps, or "Very kind." What I said mattered little. I closed my eyes and knew what was in my heart.

When I opened my eyes, it was dark, and they were all gone. I was alone, on an island in a lake, and there beside me lay a white lake lily, damp, with teardrops of moonlight.

The air was clear, balmy with the summer's drifting breath, and if there had ever been mist, it was gone, too. I felt bereft, abandoned on an orphanage stoop. Again.

~ *EIGHTEEN* ~

"When's your last day of school, David?"

"School's out, for the summer," David said. He shot me a scowling face, with a pursed-up mouth.

"Oh. That's right, you told me."

I stood and picked up the shovel, leaned on it. I was sick to death of gardening. Mulch, weed, more mulch — all tucked up around the growing plants just so, just as David wanted it.

There was something about it I liked, that tugged at me, made me appreciate orderly rows and the rich color of healthy plants. But only a little something, not enough to make up for a backache and stiff knees, the constant dip and kneel technique that David seemed so good at.

I could see Adam and Juda across the lake on the island, deep in some weighty conversation. Today, Saul and Adam were wearing the hip boots, adjusting the metal piling sleeves for the cross-bars of the pier. From here, they seemed adrift in a sea of water lilies, surrealistic, the way that one lily had looked last night, wilting fast on the grass beside me.

Adam had laid aside his pretense of machismo today, had shown another flash of his serious side.

"But it's Sunday, we should have a little fun again, Adam," Saul had said this morning, complaining. "You like a bit of silliness in life, don't you, Juda?"

I remembered Juda looking up, distracted, saying, "What?"

Adam had snorted, then gave me a look under his eyebrows. "God," he'd said, and had returned to his brooding.

Juda just looked back and forth between us. He'd carried his coffee cup to the sink and stared for a moment at the soap bubbles there. Then he'd walked out the door.

Standing here on the hillside, watching him from a safe distance, I remembered hanging onto my cup of coffee for dear life this morning, stroking it. My emotions were ripped open and raw, seeping. I hadn't felt this vulnerable for a very long time. As if I was exposed, naked, unsure.

My body had changed, too. The tips of my fingers were suddenly delighting in the texture of everything they touched. Even absorbed in some mundane task, every nerve ending would tingle, I'd feel his hands running over my body, and I couldn't breathe, couldn't do anything but feel. The sensation was new, and yet felt so old — as if it had always been there, just under the pores of my skin, ready to ripen.

Hell. I threw the shovel down. It would never work. There was Jennifer. There was the fact that we didn't agree on David's needs. There was David, and there would always be David's mother shining with the poignancy of perfection, the sainthood attached to dead mothers somehow, shrouding the futures of their sons and daughters, their husbands. I ought to know. No. It would never work.

"David!" I yelled.

"Huh?" he said from behind my back, barely two feet away. He gave me a rare smile at the joke; I'd thought he was so far, and here he was, with me. A lot like Polly, I thought, with me, but not really here.

"Quitting time," I said, grim.

"No it isn't."

"I'm the boss, and I say it is."

"Geesh."

"You work too hard," I said, and stomped downhill to the dock. It was true, odd that a twelve-year old would be quite so industrious. And so crazy too, doing that little jig in the canoe, carrying on about miasma, and reincarnation, and those delusions of Reason always having been right. And with a stupid father, unwilling to see the facts, the cries for help from his own son.

David was dragging his feet. He put all the tools carefully away, locked up the shed, had a look around to make sure he hadn't missed anything, and finally came down to the dock. I was ready to strangle him, had been sitting in the boat, waiting, rubbing the rough weave of the jean fabric covering my thighs.

"You need some fun, David," I said, "you shouldn't be so responsible."

He glanced at me, stepped into the rowboat and turned to look with yearning at the hillside, as if he was afraid it would disappear if he took an afternoon off.

I slapped the oars onto the water impatiently, and he sat down.

"This is fun, for me," he said.

"Well, I'm sick of it."

He stared at me, wary. "That's okay, I can do it by myself. Sometimes Reason didn't feel too good, and I'd go over and take care of things on the hill."

If we hadn't been in a boat, I would have shaken him.

"I'm not Reason!" I yelled. "You should be going to ball games, swimming, having fun with your friends. Reason took advantage of you, David."

"He did not!"

I dipped the oars into the water angrily, splashed myself.

"He was my friend!"

I snorted, and swiped at the water on my jeans.

"Thought *you* were my friend, too," he said. His eyes

watered, and he wiped his nose with his sleeve, stared at the water. "You're a mistake, that's what you are. You aren't what I thought, anyway."

"People never are, David." I'd begun rowing with a vengeance, tangled up the oars in seaweed and lilies.

He hiccupped.

It struck me, raced through my own chest: A contagious spasm, like a germ. I gave a little gasp of protest and then gave in, tucked the oars in, let us drift, tried to calm down. "You can have expectations, you know," I finally said. "You just can't let them take over. You have to let me, let everybody, be who they are, not who you want them to be."

He glared at me.

"I'm not Polly," I said softly. "I'm not Reason. I'm me, Belle MacKay, David. Me."

He turned his back, twisting his skinny body around in the boat and staring back at the hillside.

I sighed, hefted the oars again and dipped, pulled, dipped again. What was I doing? Taking my own befuddled expectations out on him? Was I angry at him, or myself?

Then I knew. I wasn't angry at anyone. I was simply scared. It had been just a dream. Vivid, but without reality. And how could I tell him about it? How could I call myself *"Nee-pee-sen-gee Pah-kah-tah-kee,"* how could I believe in a family no one could see, but me?

"I'm sorry, David," I said.

"Huh," he said.

I rowed around to the other side of the island, tied up at the sturdy little dock. David jumped out before I was finished, jogged up the path and into the house.

Saul and Adam had come together today, in the paddle boat, and it was there, tethered off the end of the pier.

I sat still and stared at its yellow bucket seats and thought, maybe Juda was right. I should keep my amateur psychology to myself. I didn't know enough, about my own transitions, to be juggling with anyone else's needs.

I swiveled in my seat and looked out over the lake to where the lone fisherman sat again, in a perpetual hunt for lunch. It's never free, I told him mentally. You have to work for everything you put in your belly, in your mind, in your heart.

There were footsteps on the planking above, and the rowboat wobbled under me.

I turned back to see Juda standing there, backlit by blue sky, looming over my upturned face.

"You and David had a fight," he said.

I swallowed air, for a moment. "Yes."

He simply looked at me.

"I . . . I'm sorry," I said. "You were right. David is none of my business."

He nodded. "Well," he said.

"Hmmm," I said.

"I don't think I should leave him alone with Mrs. Koher anymore."

He shifted his eyes, gazed across to the neck of the lake, and beyond. And stood there quiet, hands in pockets, glasses reflecting the afternoon sunshine.

"Oh." So he'd agree with me now, after I told him I agreed with him, and he didn't need to agree with me. I felt my face heating up, and not from confusion, not this time.

"Whatever you told David — well, it sounded sensible. Perhaps you're right."

His eyes focused on my face, and I gulped, said, "Uh . . . you mean about playing baseball, having fun?"

"Having fun, yes," he said.

My heart was beginning to pound with the effort it took to be serene, to follow this conversation. So he was finally going to listen to me, believe me? Damn.

Juda took his hands out of his pockets and reached down into the boat.

I stared at his hand, and slowly realized he meant to help me out. I wanted to shove the hand away as David might, tell him I was capable of getting out of a boat. But I wasn't paying attention to my own advice, and I slipped a hand into his, grasped, allowed myself to be pulled up and out of the boat.

I stood on the dock in front of him, locked in. A step back and I'd be off the pier and into the water. A step forward would put me in his arms. My hand was damp in his and conducting heat. And he was smiling, aware of everything.

"We need to talk," he said.

"Talk?"

"Yes."

I shook my head back and forth, avoiding his eyes, deciding that we spoke better without words, for now.

"Sure," I lied.

Saul shouted from the island. Juda dropped my hand, and turned to listen.

"We got that crosspiece back out, but I've had a call and I have to go."

"Okay," Juda said. "Did you put it in my boat?"

"Yeah. You sure you can get it back on, alone?"

"No problem," Juda called back.

He draped an arm over my shoulder, began propelling both of us off the dock and up the path, telling me something about damaged I-beams. I could barely hear him.

" . . . See, the stress cracked it," he was saying. "I know an outfit in Warsaw that can fix it. Won't take a day. Use the rowboat for a while, till I can get it back on."

I stared up at him, trying to understand. If he'd just take his hand off my shoulder, I'd be able to translate his gibberish.

Finally he did drop it, and walked over to confer with

his fellow workmen. I felt dizzy with relief, went in the door and fell into a chair.

There was a parade going in and out; Saul and Adam were gathering, shuttling the food Saul had brought over, from the house to the paddle boat. Gradually, I figured out that Saul had been called in to work, and was getting ready to leave.

I jumped up and followed them out the door, watched Adam stow the containers.

"Saul," I said, "I really appreciate you and Adam..."

"*Niente,*" he said. "It was nothing."

"Besides, we didn't get the job done, towngirl."

"Huh?"

"God," Adam said. "You and Jude-boy got to take care of this problem. Neither one of you can pick up on a dime."

Saul smiled. "Didn't Juda tell you, Belle? Don't use the pier yet, he's got to mend a section."

"Oh."

"Hey, I don't have to leave yet," Adam said. "Go on without me, Saul, Belle'll take me home later, if I ask nice. Won't you, doll?"

"Hmm. Sure," I said.

"Least she can do, after all."

"Okay, Adam, but remember what the judge said. We'll have no trouble from you, hear?" Saul grinned and shoved away, set off at a steady pedal.

"Too bad," Adam said to his back.

"What?"

"He got Friday off, in trade for being on call today. Poor old Saul. I wouldn't want to be tied down to the threat of a summons, on a Sunday. From somebody with some damned muscle cramp, for God's sake."

I looked out at Saul, passing the fisherman now, waving at him.

"And poor old Belle. Puzzled, aren't you?"

He put a hand at the small of my back, shoved me around and walked me off the pier, telling me he'd hang around, that he was good at giving advice to besotted fools.

Juda was leaving. Juda and David. David wouldn't look at me, wouldn't say good bye, just climbed into the boat and let his father shove it off the sand bar. Juda turned around and shook Adam's hand, threw a quick wave at me.

I stood there, thinking: Juda wanted to talk. I couldn't think of a thing to talk to him about. I stood and watched his back fade across the lake, his body hiding David's, bending into the paddling, disappearing behind the island. Gone.

Adam helped put away the folding chairs and the table, clear up the dishes. He kept insinuating that I should open up to him, spill my guts, get it all out.

I couldn't figure out a way to tell him everything was already out, and I was working on a way to piece it back together. I could have said I was tired of crazy quilts, wanted a new, exciting design to my life, but I didn't think Adam's artistic talent extended to piecework.

I couldn't talk to him about dreams, and visions, and sweet grasses and Polly. Or about dead relatives, hugging me one by one. He'd say my stability was questionable.

And he'd be right.

He was disappointed at the lost opportunity to become my personal guru, and sank into resentment. He insisted on rowing the boat, when I took him home. I admired his powerful strokes, and he "Harrumphed," at me. I wondered aloud where the fisherman had gone, and he told me the old guy probably thought the entertainment we'd provided stank.

"Okay," I said.

"Cause it does."

"Uh-huh."

He scowled, and rowed harder.

"Did you get a chance to read any of this week's history, Adam?" I asked sweetly.

"Nope. Don't care any more, either."

"How come?"

"Ah hell, towngirl. You'll sell off, anyway. Nothing I can do about it."

"Why do you think that?"

"It's obvious. Even Uriah says so."

"That's not right, Adam. I told him last week that I'd keep the land. He told me to check with him, if I ever wanted to sell, asked me again last week when I went in for flour. I told him no, I didn't."

"He told me yesterday, you'd sell."

He was glaring at me, putting all his energy in it, instead of rowing the boat.

"Said, 'Of course you'd sell — hadn't Reason's father sold off acres and acres, then her grandma, Isabelle, she sold off more. . .' That's what he said, anyway."

"It's not true, Adam." The promontory, and the pilings of his dock were coming up behind us fast, despite the fact that he'd quit rowing. I pointed at them, anxious.

He stared at me for a moment, nodded and said, "Okay, Belle." Then, at the last possible moment, he turned around and reached out to keep the newly painted boat from slamming into the posts.

He jumped up onto the dock and shoved me off, all in a smooth movement, waved goodbye.

My pontoon dock hung oddly flat over the water. I had to remind myself that its sturdy appearance was only illusion, and I was not to walk out on it. Apparently, Juda would put the damaged I-beam under it tomorrow. But I was supposed to use the rowboat for now, if I had to go ashore.

A heron swooped low over the water, seemed ready to

troll, changed course, veered off.

I was alone again, but time seemed odd, waiting. I found myself translating frustration into keyboard corrections.

I punched up my mother's section of the family history, and opened up the hard copy I'd left lying next to the computer. Somebody had riffled through the pages, somebody who'd left a trail of smudges. The wrinkled papers David had given me were poking out odd corners here and there. I leafed through to the history I'd written, withdrew mother's death certificate.

Now it was the truth and me, alone together. I sat clutching it and swiveled the chair, gazed out over the water as the last ray of light left the lake. I sat long enough, staring at nothing, that my window on the world became a mirror, shooting myself back to myself. I started to close the curtains, sat back down, made myself look truth in the eye. And stared it down.

Then I got up, went to the mantel, and reached for the scrap of mask that represented my time with John. Like a figure of justice, I held them out and weighed them; Mother's death certificate on one palm, the arrow-shaped sherd on the other. They were equal in one thing: their time was over.

I tapped Mother's information into the computer. The certificate, the piece of clay, they were each as devoid of life as all the others duly noted, dated, itemized: all the collated corpses in this dun-colored, fact-eating box.

The people had been real, had known love. That was the only difference between their remains and the clay piece of mask.

I'd lived alone with their dead identities for too long, and I felt like rebelling. I'd discovered a capacity for feeling, for passion. A desire to love. All the love they'd had was gone now, long gone, even if some had been for me. Reason's regret at not having known me, I told myself, meant nothing now.

So why were tears dripping down my cheeks, why the sobbing, gasping noises coming out my throat? Why did my body ache to feel the fondling of hands, live hands?

And why did I keep feeling those embraces, those hugs given by long-dead ancestors?

People facing death went first to their lovers, then to the funeral. It happened all the time. Perhaps they wanted to cheat death, and create life. Maybe it gave them a chance at omnipotence, a power over the inevitable.

I'd been bombarded with death for all these weeks, itemizing death, living with death dates, with entombments. The corpses all lay quoted in black and white on the computer, and now my mother lived among them. I was left with only the vague little-girl mix of what Mother really was and what I wished for. My mind must have made Polly, dead Polly, give me my wish.

Now I could finalize Mother, finalize fatality.

I broke open a new box of disks, copied the written history and the genealogical charts onto it, dumped it out of the computer and slipped it solemnly into the breast pocket of my shirt. I'd take it to the bank in the morning, rent a little box in the vault, a suitable crypt for dead dreams. The old notebooks could go, too. I wanted all of it out of the house, behind me, past.

Ben could have the binder full of black and white facts, the charts and the history I'd struggled with. He could read it at his leisure.

Me? I was ready for living. My craving for sex must mean that I had finally accepted the facts.

My chance came quickly.

I hadn't eaten dinner. It seemed odd to sit alone at the table, and all the postponed grieving I'd done seemed to feed on itself, on emptiness. Who was around to care, if I ended up raiding the refrigerator at midnight, anyway?

I lay on the couch staring at nothing, in the dark. I listened to night noises, all the strange sounds I'd forgotten to hear lately, and studied the blackness of the windows.

The swish of water lapping at the island, I remembered. And the wind could gasp and heave at the juniper hedge, sigh its way across the lake. Sometimes, birds made midnight flights to feed, and swooped, tiptoed over the water like skipping children.

It seemed so long ago, when a howler broke the darkness with his shrieking, so long since David played Indian in his father's canoe. But I still listened for those sounds.

What came out of the night seemed exactly what I was waiting for: The sound of a boat drawn up, unmistakable, scraping on the tiny sand bar that Juda had used earlier. I came out of the couch and ran for the door, listening. There was nothing but my own short spurts of breathing, and the rushing of blood.

Footsteps crept toward the house and long moments passed. Then a light tapping, a whispered, "Belle?"

He'd come.

"We need to talk," he'd said, earlier.

Now he was here. Under the cover of night, with the moon full-blown and me, alone. I opened the door, and hoped he hadn't come to talk.

"Belle," he said, and reached hands to my ready flesh.

~ NINETEEN ~

There was no pretense in our loving, no promises, nothing at all to say.

There was movement, sliding warmth and cold, cold dread. It made me shake with a fear that this was only dreaming, a product of need, of longing for life and loving, for fondling touch and for passion.

But the pinch of his hands on my buttocks, the heaving, the thrust, they were real. I lapped up the sweat and the kisses, drank in the surges, the power, the tiding fluid mass of him, and of me. It poured from everywhere: from my eyes, too, draining over my cheeks, dribbling into his mouth, merging, swallowed, shared.

And when it was over, it wasn't.

Sweat and tears lubricated our flesh, fingers wallowed in the finding of hidden places, learned the slopes and the valleys, the landscapes of our twining limbs and the breasts of our bodies, all the different textures, all the secrets.

Talking was a separate reality, a lower form. We took our communion in mumbled endearments, in translated phrases of fondling.

Then, sidling through the darkness and stuporing peace of spent passion, a different sound slipped in.

We lay there, Juda and I, confused. It didn't compute. It was a wailing misery, and therefore foreign.

Juda sat up in the middle of the twisted sheets and his body gleamed, damp in reflected light off the lake. His words were hoarse, unintelligible.

He tried again. "What's that?"

It came again, suddenly unmistakable. "David," I said, and struggled free of the sheet, my legs clawing air, hands grappling with tangled fabric, ripping it away.

I was off the bed and hopping around, pulling on jeans, shoving into my shirt, while Juda sat staring, muttering "What? What?"

"David — it's David!"

I bent over and searched for his lump of sweatshirt, mixed up in underwear, bra, socks, a crazy casserole of cloth. I heaved it at him, and ran for the bedroom door.

My shoulder brushed hard against the wall, and I put my hands out to catch myself from slamming against the door in the darkness. Then it was flung open, and I was out.

I stopped on the path to listen. Juda was hopping behind me, grunting, falling. There was a muffled crash. And then another thread of moaning, and I squinted across the lake to where the little island sat like a wart in a shimmering halo.

Juda's boat was on the sand bar. I sprinted across the grass barefoot, down to the break in the juniper hedge. I could see David now, in a yellow rubber raft, floating like an iridescent doughnut in a steam of black coffee. Then Juda was behind me, his breath drawn in, lurching through the hedge, hands scrabbling at branches.

"No." I turned, pushed my chest into his, forcing him back behind the hedge. The computer disk in my pocket slipped between Juda's rib and my bra-less nipple, pinched. "Shh!" I hissed at the pain, and at him.

We stood crouched, watching David's performance. He didn't do his war dance in that bobbing thing at least, simply held himself braced, raised up on his knees, craned his neck to the sky. One hand tapped wildly at his mouth as the ungodly sound came out, and the other was flung outward in a futile grab for balance.

"I'm going out for him," Juda said softly.

"I'll go with you. But be quiet."

We scraped through the hedge, lifted the canoe together and stepped silent into the water, muffled, with only the protest of scattering lily pads and the squelching damp fabric of jeans. David was busy howling, and he didn't hear the slight bump of our feet in the bottom of the boat, the swish or the rocking as we settled, hunched in under the shadows at the edge of the island.

Juda dipped the paddle, and paused. He let the canoe drift near the ring of moonlit water.

David settled back on his haunches and grabbed the ballooning sides of the boat. He glanced warily around, and I held my breath, heard Juda gasp. But David was staring off east, towards the hillside.

From where we drifted, I couldn't see the dock there, just the back end of the pontoon dangling from its line.

Whatever David heard must have passed back into the woods. A foraging deer, probably. Something had been nibbling, recently, at our green beans.

David rose back up on his knees suddenly, doubled the volume of his howls, defiant, screeching into the dark, pleading for Papakeechie or for himself, for resurrection, for salvation.

"Poor boy," I said softly.

I could feel Juda's mesmerized agony behind me. He held the canoe motionless, with the paddle dug into the muck at the roots of the lilies.

"He's getting wild, Juda. Let's get him now."

Nothing. No movement, only rapt, focused attention.

"Juda," I said, louder. "Come on."

Something garbled came out of his throat. It sounded like, "My God." Juda had never seen this spectacle. I reached behind and grabbed the paddle. He was staring, catatonic. Taking the paddle away was easy.

I made a wide arc, paddled silently, whispering on the water as if I'd been born with a stalking gene.

David lurched up in mid-war-whoop, in a crazy tight-wire act of out-flung arms and a hot-coal hopping of feet.

A few frantic shoves on the paddle later and we were beside him, the canoe ramming, David toppling, falling. Juda flung himself, reaching for David, the boat rocked and quaked, righted itself, rocked back. Juda tipped, grappling with air, and both of them were in the water.

David didn't fight him. He lay still in Juda's grip, allowed his body to float behind. It was strange to watch such a similar scene recreated, my role replaced. Strange enough to be staged.

I pulled for the island, and the aluminum bow scraped rock, shuddered violently when I jumped into the shallows and helped drag David up onto the same weedy clearing I'd pulled him onto weeks ago.

But he was different, this time. He wouldn't cry, didn't speak, yell or kick. He just lay on his back with his eyes open. He looked dead, or doped.

Juda grabbed him off the wet earth and shook, already yelling at him. I stood back and watched David stiffen his head, watched his eyes close and his teeth grip tight, his jaw jut up as his father rattled his body. I peered closer to make sure, then touched Juda's pumping shoulders.

"He's all right," I said softly.

Juda kept shaking him, yelling, "Damn it, David! What the hell do you think you're doing?"

"Stop it, Juda, he's all right!" I said louder, then I had to get behind him, hook my arms through his, drag him off David. There was a muffled clunk against the mashed weeds and hard dirt of the island as David fell back. Juda's arms were shaking in the soaked sweat shirt, and I let go of him long enough to circle his chest, hold on, whisper to him, "It's okay. He's safe. He's okay, sweetheart."

David must have heard the endearment. He forgot his version of living death, rose up off the dirt with a powerful warlord shriek and a bound.

"You went home!" he yelled. "You said you had work to do, and you went home!" He threw himself on his father, kicking, pummeling, smacking sideways at his head.

It took Juda a moment or two to adjust from terror to shock, back to fright again. Then he got hold of the flying limbs, and they rolled together over the dirt and the straggling grass.

"You set this up!" Juda yelled. "You saw us, didn't you? You knew we were there, waiting to save you!"

David went slack on the ground again, and started sobbing. Juda grunted, pushed himself off the ground, stood up, paced at the foot of David's body.

David covered his eyes and wild little squeaks came out of his mouth, his chest heaved and he rolled over, drew his knees up, cuddled into a fetal shape.

I knelt, and smoothed his hair, waiting to see if he would hit out at me, too. When he didn't, I lifted his shoulders and dragged him into my lap. I began stroking, whispering small sounds that came from nowhere. I bent down and hugged his head, poured out words and caring — strange, sweet caring.

Miraculous, this night full of birthing, of mother-tending instinct. Juda dropped down too, and pulled the rest of David's skinny body onto his knees, hunched his own head over ours and wrestled with expressions of loving.

Gradually, David relaxed, and we all rocked gently with clumsy, throbbing motions, together.

Juda cleared his throat. "Son," he whispered, "I thought we'd talked this out. You know I love you. You know we can't ever replace your mother. Is that what this is all about?"

David turned his face, nuzzled deeper into my arms.
I stroked the silky damp of his hair, murmuring.

"David?" Juda prodded. "Is that it?"

"No," David said, muffled.

We all stayed still, for a moment. A bird flew
overhead, squawking.

He came up out of my lap then, pulled himself away
from us both, shoving at our hands, our legs, disentangling
himself from any need for affection. "No," he repeated,
and scuttled crab-like on his hands and bottom till he was
a couple of feet away.

"You said you were going home — to Warsaw. You
said you'd be back tomorrow."

"I changed my mind, David. I've been worried about
. . . well, I've been thinking some things over, and I
decided we needed some time together."

"So why'd you sneak over to her place?"

"I didn't sneak over. I thought you were asleep, and
I wanted to talk to her."

David snorted. "Like you talk to Jennifer?"

I winced.

Juda took it in stride. "You don't even like Jennifer."

"Sure I do. Besides, Belle was *my* friend."

"So. You're not willing to share?" Juda shook his
head in the gloom, and specks of water glistened in the air.
"Is that it, David? You think I'm stealing her from you?"

"Nah." He cast a quick glance at me, and his eyes
threw shards of light. "She's not what I thought, anyway."

"So I'm not your friend?" I asked sweetly.

"I don't know," he snapped back. "You're not what
Reason wanted."

"So you think I'd have disappointed him? Have I disappointed you?"

He turned his back on me. "I saw what you wrote."

"That sounds like an accusation."

"Reason wouldn't like it," he said.

So that's what he'd done, Saturday, when his tuna salad fell through the planks of the dock, after we'd had the "pegleg" argument. He'd run inside the house, angry at me. And he'd stayed there while the men finished lunch.

"I don't remember you asking if you could read it, David."

"You're supposed to be blood!" he yelled. "You're supposed to tell it from their side — Reason's side."

"I'm not taking sides," I said.

"You're Indian!"

"I'm a person!" I hissed. "Remember? I'm a little of everything — Scots, English — hell, even Polish. I'm not Polly. I'm part of all of them, I'm me! And damn it, David, I get to tell the story the way I see it."

"You can't!" he wailed. "You can't see it."

Juda was looking at us, his eyes making the jog back and forth, trying to follow.

David's back was shaking. There was something flickering there, hazy smears of white. I thought of the foggy miasma that worried him, the fogs that clouded his mind.

"What do you mean?" I asked softly.

"You can't see it," he whispered. "But I can."

Water lapped rock at the edge of the island, slid back on itself, lapped again.

"You can't read it in books. Can't write it, either." His shoulders slumped in the moonlight, and his head dropped back, his eyes scanned the sky. "Indians have verbal histories. You have to *listen* to their stories."

My own neck fell back, my eyes searched a dark sky, my mind tried to follow David's lead.

"And have you, David? Have you listened?"

I felt Juda rise up on his knees beside me, felt an expectant hush from both of us, then a shiver as David's voice came, low and prophetic.

"They have verbal histories," he said again. "They keep the spirits of their ancestors within them, keep legends in their hearts. You have to know them, and meet them, and hear them.''

And I understood. He'd met Polly, too.

"Oh," I said, finally.

"I wish you were Polly," David said, whining.

I sighed. "I'm sorry, David. I didn't understand, before."

"See? Maybe you are Polly. Maybe you just don't know."

"I know, David. I know who I am. And I know that Polly's only a part of me, as your ancestors are a part of you. We can be guided by them, if we listen. And we can borrow their strength. But we still have to be us, live and learn to be happy here and now."

David sniffed.

"Then the ancestors will be happy, too," I added.

"Happy, huh? Dancing around the fire?"

"Putting bones in their noses, for an evening at home."

His breath caught. "What kind'a bone was that, anyway?"

We looked at each other in the moonlight, aware.

"Skeleton?" Juda asked.

"Fish bone," I said.

"Rattling bones, Dad. Are you scared?"

"Confused," Juda said.

"Wawasee," I assured him. "Just his way of putting his guests in their place."

"White sheets. Ghosts, Dad. Things that glow in the night." He giggled nervously.

Juda shivered, looked over his shoulder and up into the night sky, as if he expected their arrival. He shook his head at me, completely confused.

I wondered which words might explain the spiritual kinship his son and I shared.

Then David said, "Know what?"

I smiled. "What?"

"It's *us* that glow in the night. We should go for a swim."

"I've been for a swim, thank you," Juda said.

"No, really." David craned his neck back, looked up at the stripped bones of branches overhead. "We're covered in bird poop, you know."

"Oh yuck," I said, and brushed at my sleeves. There was a sticky feel to my fingers, and I looked back up, frowning at the few trees that grew on this bump of an island; they were straggly, leafed-out only in splotches, wherever the woodpeckers and the storms had allowed.

I remembered the flickers of white on David's wet jacket, looked down to see the same patchy glazes on my jeans, swiped at them. I scrubbed my fingers in the grass, frantic.

"That won't help," David said. "Island's covered with poop. You never been here during the day, and seen it?"

"Oh, God, David," Juda said. "You could have told us." He wiped his hands on his sweatshirt, started laughing.

"Shhh!" I whispered, and reached without thinking, put a hand on his gooey shoulder. I let out a muffled shriek, pulled my hand away and swabbed again at the grass.

The sound came again, wafting over the water. A groan, beastly, inhuman.

I thought of David's ghosts.

~ TWENTY ~

It was a sort of moaning sound, rusty and creaking, mechanical.

It came again and was drowned in a rumbling, then a scream, then a series of splashing sounds.

"Somebody's there, on my island," I said.

The three of us stared, tried to see through the bright reflection of moon on water, into the shadows beyond.

"Come on!"

Juda was up, already running for the canoe, and David and I slipped down the muddy slope behind him, climbed into the boat. I was blinded in the open, moonlit water, blinking, and then we were through and into the shadows, closing in on the juniper hedge.

Faint shouts, another flurry of splashing grew louder with each paddle stroke, then the bottom of the canoe hit the sand bar and shuddered to a stop with a muffled, shredding-glass sound.

Juda flung the paddle, leaped out of the boat, barreled through the hedge. David was right behind him when I caught up and grabbed his collar.

I hissed, "No," and pulled him with me into the shadow of the hedge. The full moon brought everything on the small lawn into clear relief, and I saw Juda first. He was hunched behind a stunted tree near the pontoon.

The pontoon. It was supposed to be across the cove, tied up at the hillside dock.

Two men were slogging through tangled lilies in the water, dragging themselves onto the shore. The dock was back to its former drunken slope, sagging even heavier, an exaggerated memory of its pre-repair state. The men were arguing, shoving at each other. They got up on dry land and one of them turned around, poked a fist hard into the other's chest, knocked him backward and reeling.

He regained his balance and whined, "What the hell'd you do that for?" he whined. "Ain't my fault. Damn pier fell in on me."

The bigger man shoved again. "Wimp," he said. "Your dad's right about you. You ain't got the guts of a worm."

"Shut up, Bert. Somebody'll hear."

The man called Bert let out a snort, dragged a hand over his head and flung a hank of seaweed to the ground. "Told you. Saw her go off to the figguts'. Why do ya think I came an' dragged you outta the bar?"

"That kid then. He'll hear you."

"Yeah, well," Bert said. "Like to get my hands on that kid. Thought he quit doin' that shit, howlin' at the moon . . ."

"Just a kid," the other whined.

"And you're a fucking wimpo maggot." Bert leaned forward, stuck his nose into the other man's face, clenched his fists.

The smaller man backed off, arching his long, skinny chest, and I knew him. Brian, Uriah Sopwell's son.

"Can't even get the rents for your dad, can you? Fucking wimp. He's gotta go hire me to get the work done around here."

"Right," Brian said, curving himself forward again, poking his neck out. "Cutting on snakes, stickin' a dead mouse in a mailbox — that's real good work, Bert. Takes brains."

"Scared her real good, I'll bet."

"Pop said to quit scaring her. She ain't goin' to sell. It's why we got to get it this way. No need to go jumpin' on that kid, either."

David stiffened, beside me. I hung on tighter, just in case he got any ideas.

Brian was swiping water off his shirt sleeves, jerking his head toward the pontoon, saying, "Let's go."

"Hang on."

"Come on, Bert. Let's get out of here."

"Hell no. We're here, ain't we? I'm the one been watchin' this place. Ought to look around some."

"We got what we came for." Brian was whining again. "Come on . . ."

"What a wimpo. Fucking thing's in the fucking lake, thanks to you. Could of at least sold it. I'm gettin' something here. Your dad ain't paying me enough." Bert threw his head back and chortled to himself. "And I like to get paid."

"Bert! You're getting some of the land profits. Let's get out of here now, before she comes back."

The land. Always this greed for land.

"Hell, what if he don't get the land? I ain't waitin' around for . . ."

"Stay here," I said to David. "I'll get the gun." I took another look at Juda, glanced to make sure the men were still intent on their argument, and darted for the door.

It creaked open so I didn't dare close it. I ran to the window behind the kitchen table, checked to see if they'd heard anything.

Bert was starting up the path to the house. They weren't arguing any more. They'd heard me.

I looked around, wildly searching for a place to hide, lunged across the open room, dove for the big old davenport. I thought a second, jumped up and made a grab at the mantle, whipped back down behind the couch.

The door opened. I covered my mouth and nose, tried

to muffle my ragged breathing, wished I'd had time to get the gun.

A streak of light beamed around the room. It tickled at the wall behind me, turned the moonlit room into a black hole, strobed over the table that held my computer. I stared blindly along the wall, to the looming small mass of the spotlighted table.

There was something wrong. The light swept on, and I figured it out in the dark. My computer was gone, the neat stack of papers for Ben were gone. The table was empty.

There was a rush across the room toward me. Hands reached behind the couch into my hiding place, grappled, dragged at me under the arms, flung me over the back of the couch and onto the cushions, dragged again till I was sprawled, kicking, half on the floor.

Something sharp bit into my palm, and I remembered grabbing the piece of mask. I clung to it.

"Get the rope," he was saying. One of his forearms smacked across my neck while the other hand slid under my butt and up, skipped over a thigh, cupped my crotch. He drew his breath in, chortled at me, said, "Well now. It ain't the kid, no. Not at all." Then he flung me up onto the couch, dropped to his knees in a landslide of lardy flesh.

"Hey, Bert. What are you doing?"

Bert's belly heaved — I could feel it jiggling on my cheek — and he let out a throaty chuckle.

"I ain't goin' off without gettin' paid, I'll tell ya that. Hey sweetness?"

His voice had a raspy, taunting sound I'd heard before, somewhere. Oh. The kids, with their raping words, their skinny legs pumping away, down that alley. . . . so long ago.

"B . . . Bert, let's get out of here. We got what we came for."

"I did that job, wimpo. And now I got me," Bert drawled, "a bonus."

"Leave her alone," Brian whined.

"Get the rope!"

"Pop said not to hurt anyone . . ."

"Damn it, she scared the shit outta me, with that damned banshee chanting crap. Got me a chance to get her back, now." Bert snorted, his breath souring in my nose, and whispered, "Give her a real good one . . . " He turned his head, hissed over his shoulder, "Get out. I'll show her it's time to sell up, move on."

Brian whimpered something. The door opened, shut, and there was nothing, only the sound of my blood rushing, panic rising and pounding, surging shrieks.

Bert's face hung over mine and his hands were mounding over my breasts, clenching, running over my blouse, ripping. His mouth suddenly slavered a nipple, bit, and I heard a yelp from somewhere close. Mine? But I was overhead, watching, fighting off feeling. Then an odd, hard lump slid over my shoulder. I focused on it, worried at what it was. My hands were working, clenching, pinned under me, and something scraped at my palm, ripped pain through it. He lifted his weight and I pulled my hand out, felt the arrow shape in it. There was a sound of zipping, and a grunt. His head dipped to watch himself gripping. His penis winked like a pink bulb, on and off as he massaged it.

There was a whimper. It came from outside, near the door, skittered at the edge of awareness. David. They'd done something to David.

Fury took over from fear and my body lurched up, flung itself. I was savage with anger, every part of me became revenge, torturing and horrible, a slicing, killing retribution. My teeth bit flesh, there was a wail of pain and it wasn't mine, this time. I gripped my weapon and struck, and struck again and the wailing went on, on, into the sound of the howling I'd heard, frightening me, causing me to rip his skin again, again.

Land. Or any excuse to destroy, to defile, to lay seeds of evil. Not this time, not this man.

The howling was gone and in its place was moaning and pleading. I reached out to rip again, and was stopped. There was a glittering sense of silver disks, flashing, soft hair brushing my face and strong arms around me, hugging, words, whispering; *"Nee-pee-sen-gee Pah-kah-ta-kee,* it is enough, little Flower, enough." And a sighing, and those soft chanting phrases of her song. The anger left me, then. My arm dropped and the piece of mask slipped out of my hand and fell, powerless, to the floor.

Then the light came on above. I ached to see Polly, and couldn't. There was a rush toward me but I couldn't move, and bodies fell out of the brightness on top of me, rolled and pummeled at me. Fluids seemed to grease and slide around on my breast, the skin of my belly. I recorded all the sensations carefully, filing them away for reference later. Later, when I could see, when I could think.

The bodies fell off me, onto the floor. I heard thumps, more moaning, all a part of some strange ritual.

Then nothing. No sense of violence. Just as if I was opening my eyes, I began to see. I focused on a face — two faces, two sets of eyes.

"What happened?" I heard myself say.

"Get a towel, David."

David's face shivered, and I watched it vibrate. I became desperate, trying to understand.

"Blood!" he whimpered. "She's bleeding all over, Dad! She's bleeding!"

I looked down at myself. There was blood smeared across my chest, soaked into wadded fabric, pooled in my navel, war-painted in streaks over my abdomen. But I didn't feel any pain at all. I looked back up at David and felt my forehead wrinkle into a frown.

Juda's eyes speared and pierced my skin, hot, examining. I shivered, and reached for the pieces of my shirt. His eyes dragged up. "A towel, David," he said.

David didn't move. "Don't die, Belle," he said. "Please don't die."

"Why would I die, David?"

His head jerked, and he blinked.

I shifted my gaze to Juda, but his head was swallowed in a mass of cloth, flopping with arms. He appeared again from underneath it and reached for me, pried my hands away from my shirt, pulled it open, damp-dabbed at the sudden chilly wet of my skin.

"David," he said. "Call nine-one-one."

"Dad, she's hurt, isn't she? She's hurt . . ."

"No David. She's not hurt. But the guy on the floor is."

Both of them looked down, and my eyes trailed along behind. A lump, a thatch of brownish hair, a face I blinked past, a shirt smeared over with white goo. And blood. An accident victim.

"Call."

David skittered sideways, out of sight. There was a quick tapping sound, and then his nervous voice talking to someone.

I suppose shock had made me curious, only curious. I looked back down at the man, found myself wondering why I wasn't worried about him, wondering if this was what dying did, made you oblivious. I was grateful not to care. Grateful not to worry about me, or the man bleeding all over Reason's rug. I was grateful to be in shock, delighted to know for certain that's exactly where I was.

The early hours of morning passed in a haze. Juda bathed me, and I lay staring up at him from the womb of warm water. I watched him as his fingers lathered, and stroked, and cleaned my body.

I kept thinking that I'd struck, and scarred the flesh of another living being. And I kept hearing Polly's words, caring words, soothing sounds of loving. She'd stopped the madness, the fury, the rush to kill, I knew.

They say violence begets itself. Perhaps that's exactly what had happened. It could have been worse, had I not heard, had I not listened to the voice of the ancestors.

Rage had been seeded in me long ago, and all of Reason's efforts to supplant that seed with flowers and food, chores and loving, still it had fought, had kept its place among them. The boys in the alley had watered it, had begun its growth cycle. My whole life had waited to start till the day that seed burst forth, brimming with stifled fury, with the rage of being lost, the fear of showing need. Bert had merely fertilized it all with a dead mouse and his mocking howls over the lake, at midnight. With mindless force, with intimidation.

But I could have killed him.

Polly had saved me. She'd pulled the weed of rage, kept me from murder. And now, perhaps, Reason's seeds would grow, would thrive.

Perhaps now I could love, and live, be free of secret rage.

~ *TWENTY-ONE* ~

"A rose," I said. "How prosaic."

"If you're my woman, you'll learn to accept a gift with a bit more grace."

"Why is that, Juda?"

"I've got a lot to give, that's why," he said, and grinned at me.

It had taken a day or two before the drifting sensation, and the complex curiosity about having such a violence in my nature, and the bottomless depth of gratitude to Polly, who hadn't allowed me to kill, left me, and I began to take up my new life, and live it.

Juda and David stayed with me on the island. I began to think they were guarding me from myself.

The police came and went.

The bloody mess I'd left of Bert healed into a scabbing wart of a man in the courtroom at Warsaw.

Uriah had desperately wanted Reason's land. The court case between the Papakeechie landowners and the state, that push for public access, had started him thinking.

He'd explained it all to the judge, in the preliminary hearing; no harm was ever to come to me, he'd said. "The boys was just to borrow the computer, and the papers she'd written."

"Simple theft?" Judge Farwell asked him, peering over his bifocals.

Counsel for the Defense objected.

Ben reached over and squeezed my hand, raised his eyebrows at me.

"Why, sir, I'd have given them back."

"Is that so?"

"Sure, if she'd sell. I'd have paid a fair price for the land, too."

"Oh?"

"Sure. That fool, Reason. All his fault. He was going to sell, I know. Could have held on a couple more months."

"We all die too soon, Mr. Sopwell."

Rain pattered at the windows of the room we were in. Uriah's knuckles rapped at the table. His mouth worked silently over his choice of words, and the judge waited, scratched at his balding pate.

"See," Uriah said, and cleared his throat, spread the long, bony fingers of both hands flat and smiled at all of us. "My boy, and that Bert, they were just to get the papers and the computer, so we could convince her to sell."

"And those items just happened to end up in the water, Mr. Sopwell?"

"That was an accident, Judge. Besides, ended up she had a copy, ain't that right?" He looked around at everyone, blinked his way past me, hopeful. "So she doesn't lose nothing, the Preservatory don't get the land, right?"

"That is correct, Your Honor," Ben said. "Ms. MacKay has fulfilled the terms of her grandfather's will."

"Old Reason won," Uriah mumbled.

Yes, I had a copy. I'd put everything onto a disk, that night, put it in my pocket. When Bert attacked me, it had fallen behind the cushions of Reason's old davenport, safe.

Ben had already printed out a sheaf of hard copy, given me the deeds to the island, the lots on the hillside, and even more of Reason's squeezed-out savings.

Uriah told the judge that the 'boys' were only supposed to scare me with the howling in the night, the dead mouse, a snake slit open that I'd never even seen. He denied ransacking the house before I arrived.

He tucked his chin into his chest and shook it side-to-side, insisted Bert was never to harm me. He, Uriah, had only wanted to buy the land. The mouse, the snake, the howling, even the theft and subsequent drowning of my computer were pranks, only pranks.

"It was the kid, see," he said. "He was out there acting like a banshee, and he give me the idea. She was just to have a fright, see. But Bert, he went too far. That wasn't none of my doing."

The judge nodded at him.

"Just a fright, see? That's all. I would've bought her land, give her a good price too, Judge."

"And what, Mr. Sopwell, did you want with this property?"

Uriah screwed up his mouth. This was the hardest part, I could see. It must have been the one plum in a lifetime, and precious.

"I would've made a good job of it," Uriah said, defiant. "Had the best interest of the lake to heart, I did."

"How is that, Mr. Sopwell?"

"Why, I'd bring in trade with that island and all that shoreline. Would've passed a good fair program for improvements."

"Continue, Mr. Sopwell."

His face flushed, and his eyes glittered as Uriah spoke. "A lodge, Judge, and cabins — plenty of cabins — nice, too. Folks would have paid good for a bit of the fishing. And with a pier out to the island, all those water flowers and such, why it'd be pretty as a picture, Judge, real pretty."

"As I understand it, sir, those particular improvements are disallowed on Lake Papakeechie," the judge said.

"They are now. But, see, with me being in charge, why, I could have swung it."

"And what if you weren't elected?"

Uriah pulled his tall frame straight. "Wouldn't matter. She don't know it," he said, bobbing his head at me, "but she has the only place on the lake with an easement on two ends."

The judge seemed confused.

"Two ends," Uriah repeated. "See, the island's got easement, the hill's got easement. The Preservatory gets the first foot of shoreline, but ain't no law says a person couldn't connect up, between two lots."

"Mr. Sopwell, wouldn't a connecting pier deny access by water craft to a section of lake?"

"Just a cove, there, Your Honor. Could'a made a drawbridge, see, or made it so boats could go under."

The judge's mouth twitched. "A fishing pier of your own, while you waited for public access?" he asked.

"Got to come sometime Judge," he said. "They aren't going to keep that lake private. Could have made good money.'' Uriah Sopwell sighed.

''I see,'' the judge said.

The plan of a lifetime.

Living in an uncomplicated present seems to agree with David. There has been only one discussion of Reason's needs, one more garbled vision, all through the long summer.

What he said was, ''Reason's happy now.''

I asked him what he meant by that and he smiled, said, ''It's a boy, and Polly says he's called 'Dancing Goose'.''

I just looked at him, and thought of the geese tap-dancing over the water in summer, slapping the lake with their wings, making that banging, raucous, vibrant noise. I patted my belly and smiled hopefully into the future. I prayed that this child need never cry for his mother, and go unheard.

David's doctor seems to think he's done his work. Again.

Perhaps David has made a choice, figured out that there is plenty of excitement in life, and no need to dwell in the past. Perhaps Polly, in telling David the baby's name, also told him, ''Farewell to you, my friend.

Tarnarkeear mear neekau.

It doesn't matter how, or why. What matters is his joy in life, his growing confidence.

He doesn't call me ''Mother,'' and I've no desire for it, but he does love me. And he loves the child in my womb, his brother. He's very possessive, and pats my belly morning and night, says ''Hi, Goose,'' to it . . .

So the hillside sprouted tomatoes instead of cement foundations and sweetly-placed paths, that summer. The birds continued to fly over both the islands, dropping what was unnecessary of the nourishment they'd taken, not bothering us, too much. The water lilies bloomed.

And so did I.

Dance on the Water Complete Research List:

Research recommended by the Minnetrista Cultural Center for Great Lakes Native American Studies (Muncie, Indiana):

NATIVE AMERICAN CULTURES IN INDIANA, Proceedings of the First Minnetrista Council for Great Lakes Native American Studies, edited by Ronald Hicks, 1992, The Minnetrista Cultural Center

WOODLAND PEOPLES: AN EDUCATIONAL UNIT, Nicholas L. Clark, Sr., 1993, Minnetrista Cultural Center

SOME MIAMI HISTORY AND LONGHOUSE LANGUAGE, Miami Nation of Indians, Inc., 1993

THE JOURNALS AND INDIAN PAINTINGS OF GEORGE WINTER, Wilbur D. Peat, Gayle Thornbrough, 1948, Indiana Historical Society

MEEARMEEAR TRADITIONS, C.C. Trowbridge, edited by Vernon Kinietz, April, 1938, University of Michigan Press

THE INDIANS OF THE WESTERN GREAT LAKES 1615-1760, W. Vernon Kinietz, 1940, University of Michigan Press

Other Research:

THE MIAMI INDIANS, Bert Anson, 1970, University of Oklahoma Press

TRAVEL ACCOUNTS OF INDIANA 1679-1961, compiled by Shirley S. McCord, 1970, Indiana Historical Bureau

LETTER BOOK OF THE INDIAN AGENCY AT FORT WAYNE 1809-1815, edited by Gayle Thornbrough, 1961, Indiana Historical Society

INDIANA AS SEEN BY EARLY TRAVELORS, selected, edited by Harlow Lindley, 1916, Indiana Historical Commission

STORY OF INDIANA, Robert Judson Aley, Ph.D, Max Aley, A.B, 1912, O.P. Barnes

THE MIGHTY MIAMI, Marvin Baker, Ed. D, 1963, E.C. Seale & Co

Research, Cont'd.

*SHAWNEE STEMS AND THE JACOB P. DUNN MIAMI
DICTIONARY,* C.F. Voegelin, 1940, Indiana Historical Society

*JACOB PIATT DUNN: HIS MIAMI LANGUAGE STUDIES AND
INDIAN MANUSCRIPT COLLECTION,* Caroline Dunn, 1937,
Indiana Historical Society

HISTORY OF KOSCIUSKO COUNTY, IN, Vol. 1, Hon. L. W.
Royse, Supervising Editor, 1919

*BIOGRAPHY AND HISTORICAL RECORD OF KOSCIUSKO
COUNTY IN 1887,* Lewis Publishing Co.

*COMBINATION ATLAS MAP OF KOSCIUSKO COUNTY, INDIANA,
1879,* Kingman Brothers

TERRITORIAL DAYS OF INDIANA 1800-1816

EARLY WAWASEE DAYS, Eli Lilly

*LETTER BOOK OF THE INDIAN AGENCY AT FORT WAYNE
1809-1815,* edited by Gayle Thornbrough, 1961, Indiana Historical
Society

INDIANA AS SEEN BY EARLY TRAVELORS, selected, edited by
Harlow Lindley, 1916, Indiana Historical Commission

STORY OF INDIANA, Robert Judson Aley, Ph.D, Max Aley, A.B,
1912, O.P. Barnes

THE MIGHTY MIAMI, Marvin Baker, Ed. D, 1963, E.C. Seale & Co

*SHAWNEE STEMS AND THE JACOB P. DUNN MIAMI
DICTIONARY,* C.F. Voegelin, 1940, Indiana Historical Society

*JACOB PIATT DUNN: HIS MIAMI LANGUAGE STUDIES AND
INDIAN MANUSCRIPT COLLECTION,* Caroline Dunn, 1937,
Indiana Historical Society

Research, Cont'd.

HISTORY OF KOSCIUSKO COUNTY, IN, Vol. 1, Hon. L. W. Royse, Supervising Editor, 1919

BIOGRAPHY AND HISTORICAL RECORD OF KOSCIUSKO COUNTY IN 1887, Lewis Publishing Co.

COMBINATION ATLAS MAP OF KOSCIUSKO COUNTY, INDIANA, 1879, Kingman Brothers

TERRITORIAL DAYS OF INDIANA 1800-1816

EARLY WAWASEE DAYS, Eli Lilly

SKETCHES OF LAKE WAWASEE, Scott A. Edgell, 1967, Indiana Historical Society

NORTH WEBSTER FROM BOYDSTON'S MILL TO CAMELOT SQUARE, Kip Sullivan, Warsaw Library

TRACES, Indiana Historical Soc. quarterly pub., spring, 1992

INDIAN TRIBES OF NORTH AMERICA, John R. Swanton

HISTORY OF KOSKIUSKO COUNTY, INDIANA, TO 1875, Coplen

INDIANAPOLIS STAR, news article, 8-8-93

HERALD TIMES (BLOOMINGTON, IN) news article, 9-20-93

PAPAKEECHIE PROTECTIVE ASSOCIATION info guide and directory, 1985

MIAMI INDIAN STORIES, told by Chief Clarence Godfroy (Ka-pah-pwah), great-great-grandson of Frances Slocum, comp. by Martha Una McClurg, 1961, Light and Life Press, Winona Lake, IN

AMERICAN INDIAN MYTHOLOGY, Alice Marriott & Carol K. Rachlin, 1968 Thomas Y. Crowell Company

WHAT THE WHITE RACE MAY LEARN FROM THE INDIAN, George Wharton James, 1908, Forbes and Company

Research, Cont'd.

AMERICAN INDIAN SURVIVAL SKILLS, W. Ben Hunt, 1973, Macmillan Publishing Company, 1991, Meredith Press

NATIVE AMERICAN ART AND FOLKLORE, edited by David Campbell, 1993, Crescent Books

LEGENDS OF THE AMERICAN INDIANS, Henry Rowe-Schoolcraft, 1980, Crescent Books

THEY CAME HERE FIRST, The Epic of the American Indian, D'Arcy McNickle, 1949, J. B. Lippincott Company

THE AMERINDIANS, From Acuera to Sitting Bull From Donnacona to Big Bear, Donald M. McNicol, 1937, Frederick A. Stokes Company

THE POTAWATOMIS, Keepers of the Fire, R. David Edmunds, 1939, University of Oklahoma Press, 1978

THE INDIAN HERITAGE OF AMERICA, Alvin M. Josephy, Jr., 1968, Alfred A. Knopf

INDIAN LORE, composed and written by E. Wendell Lamb and Lawrence W. Shultz, 1964, Light and Life Press, Winona Lake, IN

THE HIDDEN COMMUNITY: THE MIAMI INDIANS OF INDIANA, 1846-1940, Stewart J. Rafert, 1982, dissertation, Monroe County, IN, Public Library

ATLAS OF GREAT LAKES INDIAN HISTORY, edited by Helen Hornbeck Tanner, 1987, University of Oklahoma Press

THE SPIRIT WORLD, by the Editors of Time-Life Books, 1992

About the Author

Laura Lynn Leffers is a woman of many talents. After receiving her BS degree in Art Education at Indiana University, she married international waters boat captain, William Bybee. After the birth of their first son, the family moved to Marina di Ravenna, Italy, and from there traveled throughout Europe and the British Isles.

Back home in the USA, son number two was born and mom began restoring a 100 year-old farmhouse, which is home today to the now three sons, husband and dog.

Ms. Leffers's writing career began with newspaper articles covering local artists, and continued developing through her conception and production of a monthly newsletter. Her first novel, *Faith Unfounded*, was followed by a second, *Waylaid by War*. *Dance on the Water* is her first published work. In addition to actively promoting *Dance* and holding workshops, she is hard at work on her fourth novel.